Praise for *Wolf on the Lake*

A great read! *Wolf on the Lake* is an engaging delight to read. Ed Thilenius has a keen eye for local circumstances in the modern South. Cheers for Thilenius and his lively imagination and brisk tales of adventure happening in our very midst.

—*Michael M.*

A wolf at the beginning and the end…. Great read! Enjoyed it very much. It's hard to put down. Maybe someone will make a movie out of it?

—*David C.*

First book I ever ordered on Amazon. This is a fascinating book! I'm on Chapter 11 already. There are so many descriptions in the book to which I can relate [to from] my own childhood, and [it] takes me back there so clearly.

—*Dave M.*

Praise for *The King's Raven*

Great second book! If you liked the first book in the Cotter brothers mystery series, *Wolf on the Lake*, it gets better with *The King's Raven*.

—*John K.*

The King's Raven, indeed! A great follow up on Michael Cotter and… another page turner. Can't wait for the third book. Hoping it will be released soon.

—*David C.*

The Red Monkey

Ed Thilenius

DEDICATION

This book is dedicated to my darling wife Debbie. She is my best friend, my best fan, and will always be the sweetest love of my life.

Thank you to all my family, friends, and fans of my first two novels, *Wolf on the Lake* and *The King's Raven*. Your faith in my books and your unending encouragement have made this third book possible.

Also, many thanks to the great people at Durham Editing and E-books. Your wisdom, advice, and being the best editing company in the world have made my books shine. Thank you for everything.

CONTENTS

Preface i

Chapter 1: Michael's Dream 1

Chapter 2: I Gave at the Office 4

Chapter 3: Is There a Replay Button? 12

Chapter 4: Dimitiry and the Gift That Ate His Lunch 16

Chapter 5: Ship Ahoy! 23

Chapter 6: Does Godzilla Speak Russian? 30

Chapter 7: The Three-Step Dance 35

Chapter 8: The Secret and the Thief 38

Chapter 9: Look What I Found in a Nuclear Waste Dump 43

Chapter 10: Whoops! Did I Do That? 52

Chapter 11: What Did the Petri Dish Say? 56

Chapter 12: Michael, Meet Michael 58

Chapter 13: The Organ Grinder Who Plays the Accordion 65

Chapter 14: When One Flies Too Close to the Sun 68

Chapter 15: False Medals 73

Chapter 16: The Boss Wants to See You 75

Chapter 17: The Pizza and the Bad Penny 79

Chapter 18: I Think This Is a Collect Call 83

Chapter 19: Spying with a Kaleidoscope 85

Chapter 20: Don't Shake a Stranger's Hand 90

Chapter 21: Something Here Just Doesn't Belong 93

Chapter 22: What Does "*Yad*" Mean? 97

Chapter 23: A Bandage Won't Fix This 100

Chapter 24: There Are Always Creepy Things in the Basement 103

Chapter 25: He Touched Me 108

Chapter 26: This Beluga Tastes Fishy 111

Chapter 27: They Even Left the Light on for Me 113

Chapter 28: My Nightmare Is Here, but I'm Still Awake 116

Chapter 29: A Spider Can Set a Nice Table for Her Guests When She Dines 121

Chapter 30: Rental Cars Don't Care What Language You Speak 123

Chapter 31: Excuse Me, but You Have Drool on Your Collar 125

Chapter 32: Crossword Puzzles Can Kill You If You Don't Finish Them 126

Chapter 33: Did You Just Hang up on Me? 129

Chapter 34: You Can't Come inside If I Lock the Door, Right? 130

Chapter 35: Why Didn't You Call? 136

Chapter 36: The Puppet Master's Strings Have Been Cut! 138

Chapter 37: Come into My Parlor Said the Spider 140

Chapter 38: It's Hard to Play Hide & Seek with You When You Aren't Hiding 142

Chapter 39: The Mossad 145

Chapter 40: The Tunnel, But without the Ooh and Aah 148

Chapter 41: The Rain Clouds Above Hide the Shadows Below 150

Chapter 42: The Doorbell Wasn't Working—May We Still Come In? 153

Chapter 43: We Called and Made Reservations 156

Chapter 44: The Auto Rental Doesn't Include Bullet Holes   159
Chapter 45: Okay, Mr. Mole, Where Are You?   162
Chapter 46: Is It a Total If the Airbags Didn't Deploy?   164
Chapter 47: Picking up Strangers Adds Excitement, Right?   166
Chapter 48: I Slept with the Gophers Last Night   169
Chapter 49: If You Knew Kitty Like I Know Kitty   171
Chapter 50: When the Dam Door Won't Open   173
Chapter 51: Does Call Block Work in Russia?   175
Chapter 52: It's Not Whack-a-Mole—It's Better   178
Chapter 53: The Bottom Floor Has Specials   180
Epilogue: A Meeting with a Cardinal   186

PREFACE

"I always wanted to be a writer." This sentence has become so clichéd because there are so many people who want to write. As for me, it was a purpose to get these fantastic ideas, stories, history, and my constant imagination onto paper.

My very first short story was in the eleventh grade in high school. Titled "The Nimbus Diadem," or "The Shining Crown," it was about a small shepherd boy who stopped the devil from stealing a special crown that a local village made for Jesus of Nazareth. It was typed on an aqua blue portable manual typewriter called a Corsair by Smith-Corona. This little beast of a machine was one of the neatest gifts I received from my wonderful and loving mother Nancy. I used that typewriter wherever I traveled, but it was in college that I got the most use out it.

The use of White Out and correction tape was the only way to correct a typo other than retyping the whole page over. The trick I learned in college was using the photocopier in the library. When there were a lot of typos that had been corrected, and the page with the corrections began to look like a relief map of the United States, I would go to the college library and photocopy the corrected page. It produced a semi reasonable page that didn't have the correction ridges and bumps. How funny that today's generation has never experienced a world without spell check or even word processor capabilities!

I travelled the world and witnessed so many things in my life. While traveling all over Europe, I studied history and geography. I witnessed countless moments of inspiration and beauty.

In my journeys throughout Western Europe, I actually got a chance to travel through communist East Germany and into East and West Berlin. I was even detained briefly by East German officials as to why I was going to a place where I was not allowed. Namely, it was an East German security

i

zone, but, truly, I did not even realize that I had walked right into trouble. I lost a roll of film because of my mistake.

Later in my life, while serving as an international flight attendant, I had the wonderful opportunity to repeat some of my earlier explorations. I was totally hooked on the idea of becoming a writer. My chief inspiration was the author Tom Clancy. His quick-reading chapters filled with heart-pounding action shaped my writing style. He told stories. He didn't bog the reader down with filler sentences *ad nauseam*.

Sadly, somewhere in the many travels of my life, I lost my beloved Corsair. I still remember to this day, however, my typewriter's unique smells. The hard, rubberized roller in the center with its pungent rubbery fragrance. That, coupled with the lubrication oils for the typing keys, gave the Corsair its identifiable essence of a well-oiled machine. The additional smells of correction fluid and the aqua blue plastic that made up the body rounded out my Corsair's aroma.

These days I find myself typing away on an Apple MacBook Air, a much different experience than the clicking and clacking of a manual typewriter. But, in the end, the outcome is the same: a way to release the stories and details of history and my travels into a more permanent form.

The Red Monkey is the third book in the Cotter Family trilogy. The Cotter brothers and their cousin Elizabeth, now several years older, find themselves in another deadly situation that only their determination and experience can solve. I hope that you will enjoy joining the trio as they race against the clock in their greatest adventure yet.

The Red Monkey

THE RED MONKEY

CHAPTER 1: MICHAEL'S DREAM

Michael Cotter cannot tell if he's floating or flying. He's weightless, that much he knows, as he glides along the winding mountain road of Interstate 64 through the farming valley of Murphy, North Carolina. Dried corn stalks, all but buried from an earlier snowfall, wave gently as he passes by on the cold winter breeze. Each tattered stalk acts as a grim and decayed reminder of a past fall harvest, a great harvest when they were green and filled with corn and when life was fresh and new. The only sounds he can hear are the dried and lifeless leaves on the stalks as they gently flap and the calm breeze depositing new snowflakes as they fall.

Michael comes to a stop, hovering in the middle of a snowy white cornfield. Hundreds of yards from the road, he is alone and now shivering in the cold gloom of the late winter afternoon. The snow piles loosely upon his shoulders and the back of his navy blue overcoat. He can't feel his feet. It's not because they are bare or because of the bitter mist that surrounds them as he floats above the snow.

In the distance, he sees a figure in a snow-dusted navy blue overcoat like his own. He isn't sure who the figure is, but he is drawn to it as if it shares his very blood. The figure faces away from Michael as if it is looking to the future. He cannot see its face, but it seems so familiar to him. He feels he must know who it is.

Michael calls out, but the figure doesn't hear. He is too far away, and his words dissolve in the wind.

The slow-moving clouds above are heavy with their wintery mix and roll gently to the north. Michael looks up to see the clouds embrace the far hillside and gently roll past its ridge. As he watches, fingers of darkness spread across the sky, reaching from behind him and enveloping the grey clouds above. Michael is frozen, unable to look behind him as the darkness climbs across his back and over his head. He cannot tell if it is an apparition or a shadow. It crawls through the heavens and looms like an evil beast above the figure in the distance.

Michael shouts to warn the figure, but his words are muffled, as if they spiral from his mouth like swirls of snow. He is paralyzed, unable to run, to help, to warn. His eyes widen

1

as he watches in terror as the darkness lurks above the distant figure that stands facing away from him and oblivious to the impending danger.

As he watches, the creature emerges in a dive from the blackened ceiling above. The unholy specter is a pitch-black raven. It is as large as a draft animal and swoops down towards the unsuspecting figure below, its talons ready to seize its prey.

Again, Michael tries to scream, but the words will not come. The wind from the immense wings of the creature buffets his helpless form from side to side as he watches it descend upon the figure. He struggles to move freely, to warn the figure, but he is caught up in the wind and moves farther and farther away.

Michael's deep brown eyes blinked as he tried to acclimate himself to the darkness around him. He could feel his wife's slender hand gently rubbing his left shoulder. The dark bedroom was always a refuge for the two of them. Their brick home had been designed in such a way that the sun set on the opposite end of the house, and their bedroom remained relatively cool throughout the night. That night, however, Michael found himself embarrassed and covered in a cold sweat, something that was becoming more common than he would like. His t-shirt was drenched, as well as his pillow and dark brown hair.

"Michael? Are you awake, darling?" whispered his wife of two years, Debbie, in her soft, gentle voice.

Michael turned to face her, and she quickly turned on the small lamp that sat on the table on her side of the bed. She brushed her shoulder-length brown hair away from her face as she looked down at him, her green eyes filled with concern. "You must've been having a bad dream. You were tossing and turning again."

"I'm okay," Michael said, smiling weakly to reassure her as he sat up and pulled off his wet shirt and tossed it to the floor. He knew that she must be wondering again if he was suffering from PTSD from his two tours in Afghanistan with the United States Army where he assisted the British Army in their drone technology. She wondered that every time he had a bad dream.

"Are you sure you're okay?" Debbie asked, laying her hand softly on Michael's leg.

"It's that stupid nightmare again," Michael began to explain. "You know, the one where there's this giant black raven—"

"The giant raven that swoops up the person, but you don't know who it is? Yes, darling, I know the one. I'm sorry that you have that nightmare again and again. Maybe you need to talk to someone. Someone with some knowledge about PTSD?"

"I told you. I don't have that." Michael wiped his damp brown hair back from his forehead and let out a slow breath to ease his rattled nerves. "It's just that I keep remembering creepy things from my past. King Henry VIII's ancient raven named Caesar that my brother Steve, our cousin Elizabeth, and

I encountered back in England; the old witch named Cassandra that wanted to steal the ancient relics from Canterbury Cathedral."

"Darling, that was more than two years ago."

"This time it was in North Carolina, though," Michael said, shaking his head in confusion. "I wish I could just tell who it is... that figure standing there. I feel like it's someone important to me, like we're connected in a way I can't explain. Maybe it's Steve, or even Elizabeth. Maybe it's you or me. I just don't know, and I wish I could figure out who it is and what it all means!"

"Are you sure that this isn't because of your time as part of the US army that assisted our British allies in fighting the insurgents. You helped the British army on that artillery base with your special drone named *Wolf*, and you saw some heavy fighting."

"I'm sure, darling." Michael could see the concern in Debbie's eyes. He smiled at her reassuringly for a moment, but his mind drifted back to the dream. Worry clouded his eyes and drew down the corners of his mouth as he struggled to figure out who it was in the dream and what it meant.

She smiled meekly. "You're a hero. You saved the day."

Michael smiled again and rolled his eyes jokingly at Debbie's admiration.

"Come on now, snap out of it. You're fine, Elizabeth's fine, and Steve is fine. There is no such thing as a giant raven that grabs people to eat." A mischievous smile tugged at the corners of Debbie's mouth. "Now, there's the Big Chick restaurant in town. They have a big chicken statue in front of the building. Are you going to be scared of the big chicken, as well?"

"Oh, hush up!" Michael said with a smile as he flipped his wet pillow over.

Michael, clearly upset with himself, put his head back down on his pillow and turned away from Debbie. He looked past the nightstand next to his side of the bed to the small desk he used to write checks and answer mail. On the desk was a framed picture of Steve, Elizabeth, and him during an awards ceremony by Her Majesty the Queen of England, the Archbishop of the Church of England, and the attending members of the Royal Court. He still remembered what the Queen had read aloud in Buckingham Palace.

"For his gallant actions as an American combat soldier versus a ruthless enemy in Afghanistan. For your heroic defense of the United Kingdom forward firebase and its soldiers stationed within. For your service above and beyond self and safety, I hereby invest you, Michael Cotter, as KCVO, Knight Commander of the Victorian Order. Rise, Sir Michael Cotter."

Michael rolled back over to see his beautiful wife looking at him. He reached out and took her hand and held it tightly.

"Thank you, darling, for being you. I just worry sometimes about us and Mom since Dad passed last year from cancer."

"It's okay. Let's get you a new shirt and go to the kitchen for some soothing hot tea," Debbie said with a smile as she patted the top of Michael's hand.

CHAPTER 2: I GAVE AT THE OFFICE

Kochubey, Dagestan, Southern Russian Territory, August 2019

The vapor lights in the parking lot flickered to life as the rickety white box truck pulled up to the loading dock at the radioactive material storage facility near Kochubey, Russia. To a tourist, or even a local, the enormous building was nothing more than a gigantic corrugated metal shed that was desperately in need of a makeover to deal with its rust and deterioration, but it had been designed to handle lower grade used nuclear materials no longer needed by scientists or medical facilities.

Once the truck was in place, four workers in faded khaki uniforms began to unload the shipment of dental x-ray machines, hauling the first of many from the truck and dropping it unceremoniously onto a sorting floor. There, another team of workers took over. They broke apart the metal housing of the x-ray machine to extract a very small box located behind the white ceramic cone inside. The small box was then put onto a conveyor belt that whisked it away to an unusual-looking lead-lined glass and metal room in the middle of the warehouse. The room seemed to emit a yellow glow as its fluorescent lights inside reflected off a faint yellowish dust that coated the glass from inside the room. A small door opened automatically, allowing the box to enter the room after it had passed through an airtight decontamination chamber.

A worker, protected by the leaden glass, used mechanical arms to manipulate steel robotic hands like a surgeon. The box from the x-ray machine, which held a small quantity of cobalt-60, was lifted from the conveyor belt and placed in a prefabricated jig. When the box was secure, the worker lowered a large metallic wedge that sliced the box open and exposed a small yellow pill, slightly larger than a baby aspirin. The whole process was

4

reminiscent of a wild sea otter using a rock to crack open a clam or oyster to get at the juicy morsel inside.

Once the cobalt-60 pill, or *tabletka* in Russian, was exposed, the worker used the mechanical arms to remove it and deposit it into a small, padded container about the size of a D-cell battery. The small container was then stacked in a heavy lead-lined box that was about the size of a small locker box. When 300 tabletkas had been deposited into the box, as the most recent container made possible, the mechanical arms were used to seal and lift it onto another conveyor belt. That conveyor belt carried the box through an automatic door in the opposite wall from which the cobalt had entered the room, through another decontamination chamber, and then down through a lead-lined tunnel to its next destination in the far back corner of the facility.

At the end of the conveyor belt, Pytor, a large-bellied Russian in his mid-thirties, and his young Persian coworker Shayan sat reading old copies of *Kommersant*, a business-oriented magazine with articles on everything from commerce to politics. Pytor glanced up when he heard the approaching container coming down the line. "Sounds like we've finally got another bit of work headed our way. What do you think? Should we get up and put this one away, or should we wait?"

Shayan, an exchange technician from Syria, looked up from his reading with a smirk. "You tell me. You're the one in charge."

Pytor laughed heartily, his shaggy brown hair bouncing with each guffaw. He tossed his magazine onto a disheveled stack of random back issues in a box next to Shayan's chair. He grabbed the empty chair beside him, pulled it in front of him, and propped up his legs.

"I guess that means we wait," said Shayan, shaking his head. He reached over and pressed a red button on the wall next to his chair as the lead container approached the end of the conveyor belt, grinding it to a halt. He looked back down at his magazine and continued to read as Pytor settled back in his chair and closed his eyes.

Nearly half an hour later, Pytor stretched and groaned like an old man waking from a long night's sleep. He quietly watched the slim, dark-haired young man across from him before clearing his throat loudly. "What's so interesting in that article you're reading?"

Shayan didn't bother to look up. "It's about our jobs."

"What do you mean? It's about our warehouse?" Pytor stretched his thick neck and moved his head from side to side, trying to catch a glimpse of the article over the top of the magazine.

Shayan quickly hid the magazine against his chest. He couldn't refrain a broad smile at the piqued interest of his coworker. He chuckled. "No. It's about the man who created the Deep Sonic technology that made our jobs possible."

"Oh." Disappointment clouded the Russian's wrinkled and worn face as he settled back into his chair. "Well, at least I've never read that one. Tell me what it says."

Shayan began to read. "*With the advent of the new Deep Sonic imaging device, the need for using an x-ray machine, and its resulting radioactive materials within, instantly waned. Deep Sonic was invented by Dr. Matthias Durnford from the United States, the recipient of the Nobel Peace Prize in 2018 for Science and Medicine. Durnford's opus was created as a safe alternative to cobalt and iridium x-ray machines and their radioactive side effects and hazards. This world-changing wonder is a safe and effective way for both dentists and doctors to view teeth, bones, and internal organs using low frequency ultrasound waves.*"

"It certainly is the wonder that changed the world. At least for us, huh, Shayan?" The jovial Russian laughed. "We got the best job in the world because of it. No one bothers us. We sit around and read and talk. A few minutes of work for a lot of pay. I like this article. Tell me what else it says!"

"*Dr. Durnford's inspiration for this invention was the death of his uncle, Dr. James Durnford. The older Dr. Durnford was a dentist in a small town in Georgia. Being the only practice available in a twenty-mile radius, his little office was always bustling with patients. His x-ray machine was one of the older models that used cobalt-60. Sadly, none of the rooms had lead shielding to protect the doctor from the harmful doses of radiation created by the use of his x-ray machine. While relatively harmless to a patient there for a routine yearly checkup, the constant exposure that James Durnford unwittingly saturated himself in daily led to his demise.*"

"That would kill a man? Just using an x-ray machine? I don't believe it." Pytor shook his head and frowned.

Shayan narrowed his eyes and stroked his slender, bearded chin. "Well, let's think about that. There are 52 weeks in a year, at five and a half days per week…. That's 286 days of exposure a year. If he only did x-rays on two patients a day, that would be 572 x-rays. But since most patients would need, say, five x-ray images to accurately display a set of teeth, the number of radioactive exposures to cobalt-60 per year would be 2,860. Now think about doing that year after year. I'd say that's enough to kill a man."

"I never understand how you can do figures so quickly." Pytor shook his head, his green eyes wide. "I guess the good doctor cooked himself until he glowed at night."

The two laughed heartily.

"What else does it say?"

"*In a short time, Dr. Durnford avenged his uncle's needless death from cobalt radiation and wreaked havoc on x-ray machine companies worldwide. Russia, like so many countries, was caught unprepared for this new phenomenon and is now having to deal with an influx of old dental and medical x-ray machines. Thousands of discarded machines are collected each day from medical offices in Russia, Ukraine, and the Balkans. Across the globe, collection depots have been established.*"

"And that's where we come in, eh? The end of the whole process. The ones with the job that nobody else wants. They're all too scared by all that silly radiation talk!" Pytor laughed as he dropped his feet to the floor and leaned forward to slap Shayan on the shoulder. "But not us. We're real men. Eh, Shayan?"

Pytor settled back in his chair and propped up his feet again. He loved working in the quietest part of the plant, especially since he could get Shayan to do the majority of the work. The two men's only job was to load the packaged nuclear material onto a forklift and drive it down a long lead-lined corridor to a vault with six-foot thick lead walls. They received a new package about every two hours and were supposed to immediately store them, but most nights the men let the packages stack up and only delivered them once or twice a night. A single civilian guard with an AK-47 stood watch over the vault, the only other worker in their part of the building.

Shayan leaned back in his chair casually. He only had a few more weeks at the storage facility before he was to return to his homeland. He was ready to leave. The job dragged on every night with little to do but listen to his coworker's unending supply of stories or read. That night, he hoped that, perhaps, Pytor's love of storytelling might come in handy.

"So, Pytor, you seem to know everything about this place. Tell me: what is in that worn-out dark green box in the vault? It's not like the other containers, and it's obviously old. Do you have any idea?"

"Oh, the box. No doubt you've heard the rumors that it's an American rocket. Well," the Russian said, lowering his voice as he leaned forward with a smile, "I know it is."

Shayan's heart jumped. "How? Did you look in the box?"

Pytor laughed and leaned back. He looked from side to side as if checking to see if anyone was listening, even though there were only the two of them there. "I didn't, but I know exactly what it is. It's a portable rocket launcher known as a Davy Crockett."

Shayan shook his head in disbelief. "How do you know that?"

"My grandfather told me all about it. He was stationed in East Germany back in the 1960s. This young American soldier wanted to impress his West German girlfriend by his access to the top-secret weapon. Supposedly, after a late-night dinner of *Jäegerschnitzel* and beer at a local restaurant, the young GI took his *dirndl*-dressed girlfriend to a secluded spot for a night of *amore* in the backseat. Well, he had the rocket in the trunk. When he opened the box to show it off to his girl, she put a gun to the back of his head and killed him."

"His girlfriend shot him?"

Pytor nodded slowly and smirked. "He didn't know he was dating an East German *Stasi* agent. The Stasi was the brutal secret police agency for the East German Communist party. Their agents were ruthless hunters used to ferret out enemy agents, military secrets, and disloyal citizens. And the soldier's girlfriend was none other than *Leutnantin* Erica Mielke, the Swiss Miss."

"The Swiss Miss?"

"Yeah." The Russian smiled broadly and used his hands to draw the silhouette of a shapely woman in the air. "Like the blonde in the dirndl dress that used to be on the hot chocolate boxes. Only this one supposedly wore her dresses pretty low cut and took no prisoner, if you know what I mean."

Shayan fought back the urge to scowl. As a practicing Muslim, he did not share his coworker's fascination with half-dressed women. It was indecent. "That still doesn't explain why the box is here. What's the rest of the story?"

"Well, the Swiss Miss earned herself the Shield and Sword Honor Badge from the East German government for her good work in securing the rocket. They held this great big gala for her, red carpet and all. But as the East Germans were celebrating, we Russians were taking possession of the Davy Crockett for ourselves. My grandfather was one of the soldiers who transported it into Russia."

Excitement filled Shayan, but he was careful to make his response seem casual. "Well, what's so special about this rocket? You said it was a Davy Crockett. I've never even heard of it. Why would the Russians want it, and why is it being stored in a vault with nuclear materials?"

"You know so little. It's a good thing you have me," the jovial Russian bragged. "It was a nuclear weapon!"

Shayan's eyes widened.

"The Davy Crockett had a low-yield nuclear warhead affixed to the top that was no larger than a large coffee or tomato can. It was only about a quarter of the yield used on the city of Hiroshima, Japan, during World War 2, but it still packed a punch. It was meant to irradiate a large area of a battlefield to deny access to invading infantry or to annihilate a target city's population. But, you know, they never used one of those things, and no one knows how safe it would be to fire one anyway."

Pytor laughed loudly and bent his arms behind his head and leaned back. "Yes, you be glad I'm around to teach you things, Shayan. I know all there is to know about this place. Now I'm going to take another little nap. It won't be long until we'll have to do some work."

Shayan rolled his eyes discreetly and settled back into his chair as Pytor drifted off to sleep. He had much to think about.

Although his paperwork said he was from Syria, Shayan was actually from Chechnya. When the Soviet Union had broken apart after the fall of the Communist regime, several smaller states within the Russian Federation had decided that because they were of different ethnic and religious beliefs, they could focus on their own growth and prosperity by becoming independent countries.

Sadly, the new Russian government, riddled with old guard communist cronies, had not liked the idea of their beloved Mother Russia shrinking. Several brutal and devastating micro wars had erupted. Using the *ruse de guerre* of policing the fringe states for rebellious citizens, the Russians continued to use territorial army divisions to pacify the populations. In Chechnya, the increased influence of radical Islamic fundamentalism fostered the resistance to Russia.

For months, Shayan had been trying to find a way to join the local band of Muslim Chechen rebels that were working in the area. He had read about their acts of revenge throughout Russia, including in Moscow, Tbilisi, and other key areas of interest. Usually, it was done through a car bomb, improvised explosive device, taking a hostage, or performing executions. He knew that if he could bring the Davey Crockett nuclear weapon to them that he would be welcomed with open arms. He just had to find a way to get it to them.

The motor on the conveyor belt sprang to life, and the heavy lead container that had been perched near the end of it lurched forward. Shayan jumped up and slammed his hand on the button on the wall to stop the belt just before the large box fell to the ground. Pytor shook his head at his abrupt awakening. When he saw Shayan exhale deeply and noticed the heavy container teetering on the end of the conveyor belt, he let out a loud laugh and got to his feet. "I guess we need to get this on the forklift."

Shayan nodded, and the two worked together to lift the box of radioactive material from the belt and carry it across the room to the awaiting forklift. Shayan walked over to the wall and pressed the button that restarted the conveyor belt. When the new box of cobalt-60 arrived, he pressed the button to stop the belt, and the two men loaded the second box onto the forklift as well.

"Let's get this stuff put away. I need a drink and a smoke," Pytor said. "You drive the forklift, and I'll hang on to the side. I don't feel like walking."

Shayan started up the forklift, and Pytor stepped on to the side of it and held on. They drove down the long, lead-lined corridor to the vault. As they approached, the small-statured guard stood up and stretched. His clothes were wrinkled, and his hair was disheveled, making it obvious he had been asleep for quite some time. His AK-47 was propped against the outside wall of the vault beside the door.

"Hey, Pavel! Open the door! We've got work to do," Pytor called.

The tired guard walked over to the door and entered the necessary security code. When they got close, Shayan stopped the forklift and went to help the guard open the heavy door. Pytor stepped down from the side of the forklift and stretched before walking into the open vault. As the guard followed him in, Shayan stood at the door of the vault. His eyes quickly found the large dark green box inside. It was on a shelf on the right side of the vault.

"I need a drink," Pytor announced from inside the vault as he pulled a small flask from his back pocket. He took a long drink as he sat down on a stack of containers and then held the flask out to offer it to the others. Shayan, whose Muslim beliefs would not allow him to drink, shook his head, but Pavel accepted the flask readily and took a long drink before handing it back to Pytor.

The guard sat down on a stack of containers next to Pytor and pulled out his cigarettes. He took one and offered one to Pytor, who accepted. Pytor pulled out an old silver lighter from his pocket and lit both cigarettes before inhaling deeply. He blew out the smoke and took another long drink from his flask. "This is the life. What more could we ask for?"

Pavel nodded in agreement and took another drink from the flask as well.

"You don't know what you're missing, Shayan. You need to take some pleasure in life like we do." Pytor laughed loudly and slapped the guard on the shoulder. "Russians know how to live!"

As the two men continued to smoke and drink, Shayan glanced from the men seated on the left side of the vault to the weapon he so desired on the right. It was the opportunity of a lifetime for him, and he knew he had to do something.

"Hey, Pavel," Pytor asked, "how is your cousin doing? The soldier who was injured in that explosion at the missile test site?"

The sound of Pytor and Pavel's conversation seemed to fade away as the adrenaline in Shayan's veins surged. His eyes searched the scene for some way to accomplish his goal, and his eyes came to rest on the gun propped against the wall beside him. His hands started to shake as he looked back and forth between the nuclear weapon on the shelf and the weapon next to him that could help him achieve his goal.

Pytor's deep bass voice rose in song as he wrapped his arm around Pavel's shoulder and swayed from side to side. "Long live our Soviet motherland, built by the people's mighty hand...."

Shayan looked from the two men to the gun beside him, the words of their chorus pushing his religious zeal to its apex. Anger and excitement overcame him, and he found himself grabbing the AK-47 beside him and pointing it at the two men inside the vault. As the last words of the old Soviet national anthem's chorus echoed off the walls of the vault, he opened fire. The sound of gunfire rang down the long, lead-lined corridor, but no one alive was there to hear it except the gunman.

"Thanks be to Allah that this moment has come! Allah be praised!" Shayan cried as strapped the gun across his shoulder and ran into the vault.

He grabbed the old green box that contained the Davey Crockett rocket from the shelf. The box was very heavy, but Shayan managed carrying it just the same. Once he had it secured on top of the two boxes of cobalt-60 tabletkas, he restarted the forklift and drove back down the long corridor. He knew that the rebels could possibly use the tabletkas as a weapon, too.

Shayan maneuvered his way through the various passages until he was able to exit the building and drive down a ramp into the loading area behind the facility. He looked from side to side, scanning the area to be sure that he was alone. Seeing no one, he floored it, driving the forklift as quickly as possible across the darkened lot.

In his rush to escape, he rammed into the rusted chain-link fence that surrounded the storage facility. The fence crumpled under the machine and its heavy load, but the rocket's box and the top box of tabletkas tumbled to the ground. The force of the impact with the fence and the fall to the ground forced open the lid of the container of tabletkas, spilling dozens of the unlined containers from within to the ground.

Shayan, in a panic, grabbed the spilled radioactive containers and put them back into the lead-lined box. He latched the box closed and placed it back onto the forklift. Then he heaved the rocket's box back on top. As he got back on the forklift, he noticed his right hand was beginning to sting like a thousand swarming bees. He powered up the forklift's engine and raced into the darkness on his way to a known hideout for the fighters for a free and Muslim Chechnya.

CHAPTER 3: IS THERE A REPLAY BUTTON?

Virginia, August 2019

Several hundred miles up in a low orbit above Earth, a United States KH-80 Dual Mode reconnaissance satellite looked down on a bunker outside of Misqan, Syria. Digital footage of the events below was being transmitted to a specialized information room filled with technicians, Air Force personnel, Space Force advisors, and other related staff deep inside Langley, the CIA's headquarters in Virginia.

Inside Langley, Steve Cotter, the newest member to the CIA Middle Eastern section and the lead technician for the current mission, adjusted the monitor in front of him. "We are able to see our man, sir. He made it outside."

Steve, son of Mike and Sonya Cotter, was from a small lakeside city north of Atlanta known as Gainesville, Georgia. He, his brother Michael, and their cousin Elizabeth Cotter were affectionately known by all friends and family as "techno geeks." They were passionate about their hobbies of drone flying and computers during their time together back in high school, but they had all grown up and gone their separate paths. Still, the trio stayed in constant touch through social media and their regular trips back to Gainesville and Lake Lanier.

Steve was on his own with his work for the CIA and had to focus since it was his very first mission. He wiped the beads of sweat from his brow, his fingers barely touching his short dark hair. His stomach was in knots, not because of the cafeteria lunch of Mexican food that had been loaded with beans, but he knew that at that moment, someone's life was in his hands.

"Contact our extraction team and get him the hell out of there," commanded Air Force Colonel Christopher "Dunsel" Dunolds as he paced the room.

Dunolds was a career Air Force commander. Always first to volunteer or get into a fight, he had been just barely of age when he had joined the military. He was always in shape, even at 57; he was pure pilot and pit bull rolled into one.

Steve's fingers rapidly entered the correct codes to initiate the pickup. Several kilometers to the west of the lab in Syria, at a secret location in the mountains of Al Hasaka, a stealth helicopter's engine roared to life as the special rescue team proceeded to lock weapons and climb onboard to rescue what was known to them only as The Package, a top Syrian nuclear scientist being held as a political prisoner by the Iranians.

The project the scientist had been forced to work on was to create a hyper-heat protection sleeve for a nuclear material dispensing system. The device, no bigger than a can of hairspray, was the main explosive charge to detonate a large sphere filled with slivers of aluminum radioactive material. The warhead package could then be installed inside an ICBM warhead or even a heavy artillery shell. The controlled explosion would create a shockwave that ejected the nuclear material to create a deadly contaminated blanket of aluminum dust that would cover a small city.

The Package's mission was of extreme importance. It would give the CIA crucial evidence that could expose the Iranian and Russian experiments on nuclear re-entry equipment being created in Syria.

Back at Langley, Steve watched the monitor in front of him carefully. "Wait. Something's wrong."

Dunolds stopped pacing. "What the hell is it?"

"He isn't running. Looks like he is holding his hands up. There are several tangos approaching him from the east. Looks like they have weapons on him." Steve glanced quickly over his shoulder. "Sir, I think they've got him."

Dunolds walked over and stood beside Steve. He rested his hands on the edge of the long table that held Steve's computer and leaned in towards the monitor. There, on the screen, were several silhouettes in an eerily greenish glow from the night lenses of the spy satellite above. The ghostly shapes surrounded the trapped scientist.

On the monitor, The Package held his hands up with a canister in one hand. It was the piece from the nuclear weapon that the CIA needed. Steve's eyes widened as he watched the guards surround The Package.

"They seem to be talking. What is he doing?" Steve clenched his fist in frustration. "He needs to get out of there."

Flashes lit up the monitor as bullets were fired. The man known as The Package—and Steve's charge—fell to the ground hard. The canister left his dead hand and rolled along the ground.

Dunolds pounded the table with his fist. "No, dammit, no! We were so close this time. Notify the rescue team to stand down and return to their base."

The intelligence room at Langley fell silent. Steve rapidly entered the necessary information to command the rescue team to stand down, his hands going through the motions while his mind spun with images of hostiles surrounding his charge and gunning him down. He looked back at the video monitor as it continued to display several greenish men as they surrounded the motionless figure lying flat on the ground in the midst of them.

Steve sat quietly at his station, his mind searching for a way to set right that night's disaster. He thought to himself, "Man, I wish Michael and Elizabeth were with me right now. The three of us have always been able to solve things like this before they get ugly."

He contemplated picking up his cellphone. Steve knew it was time to call in a favor from Tom MacAday, Steve's Class 3 training supervisor and nurturing supporter for two years during his training at The Farm. The Farm was the most rigorous CIA training camp. Intensive physical and mental training techniques were applied to all cadets, including torture, as well as a necessary regimen of verbal and physical abuse to expose any weaknesses in a young CIA officer.

Just before he picked it up, his phone rang. It was the man he was about to call: Tom MacAday. Steve answered the phone. "Hello, sir. I was just about to call you. What can I do for you?"

"Well, things are a little crazy right now. I've been promoted to the seventh floor here at Langley."

"I suppose congratulations are in order, sir." Steve knew that every agent who worked in the field instead of behind a desk dreaded the promotion to Langley's executive level where politics and a choking bureaucracy were the number one enemy instead of the bad guys.

"Not necessary. Look, Steve, I need a man like you for a special operation. Speaking of which, how's that mission you got picked for coming along?"

Steve wondered how to answer him. He knew MacAday was able to see mission status updates on his secured desktop computer, so he couldn't lie over the phone. Instead, he used a coded phrase to let MacAday know that someone had died during the mission. "Sir, we had a bad day."

"I'm sorry to hear that, that being your first assignment and all." There was a brief pause before MacAday continued. "Steve, I'll come to the point. You're from the South, and I need someone from that region to gather intel on a Russian spook named Dimitiry Federov. Everyone here thinks he's retired. They think he's aged out and will be replaced. I want you to pick up this assignment and run with it. We need to know who he is really, and if this Federov fellow has been replaced, we need to know by whom."

Steve was thunderstruck. Even though he knew that he had impressed Tom MacAday with his scores, tech skills, and temperament, he couldn't believe that he would be picked out of the blue for such a mission.

"Steve, did you hear me? I have seen you in action back at The Farm. You are good at information gathering. So, are you with me on this?"

Steve shook his head, regaining his focus. "Yes, sir."

"As we speak, I'm sending you a read-only packet. This packet contains all the details you'll need. Take any equipment you need, plus whatever transport requirements that occur. You have top priority on this. Now is there anything else I can help you with?"

Steve nodded as a smile spread across his face. He knew exactly who he needed to help him with this new mission. "Sir, I need clearance to acquire two special tactical assets in Georgia and bring them into this loop."

"Do you know these assets?"

"Yes, sir, I know them very well. We will have to get them the necessary clearance, though. They are from outside the agency."

"If you feel that they're necessary to complete this mission, I trust your judgment. Send me their information, and I will get them the clearance they'll need. Anything else?"

"No, sir. I appreciate your confidence in my abilities."

"Get the job done, Steve. I'm counting on you. Now get your teammates and get to work."

"Thank you, sir. I'm on my way to get them."

CHAPTER 4: DIMITIRY AND THE GIFT
THAT ATE HIS LUNCH

Outside Asheville, North Carolina

Mishka drove her white convertible sports car into the parking lot of her grandfather's townhouse and parked. The attractive, athletic brunette climbed out of the car wearing a fashionable gray skirt with a billowy white blouse. Her designer pumps added three inches to her average natural height. She closed her driver's door and took off her lab coat. She folded it neatly into a square and placed it in the trunk of her car. As a meticulous scientist, she even made the coat pocket readable as it was placed in the trunk. It read: M. Federov, Asst. Dir. Radiology Studies, St. Gabriel Hospital.

She tossed her ID lanyard into the trunk and almost closed the lid. She stopped when she noticed an old reminder from years before: a piece of light blue cloth about three inches long attached to her very first lab coat from when she had started in radiology. It was old, but it meant so very much to her. She kept the old coat as a reminder of who she was and where she came from. She paused for a moment to reflect on what that simple square-shaped cloth represented and how much her life had changed over the years.

The entire Federov family was of Syrian descent but had lived in the territories belonging to Russia. The original family name had been Krasnaya, but her grandfather Dimitiry had legally changed the surname to Federov in Russian courts to help his family survive after the Iran-Iraq War back in the late 1980s. Some distant relatives had aided the al-Ahini regime in Syria, which supported the war. Such action had prompted reprisals for anyone with the name of Krasnaya.

Dimitiry's wife had died of leukemia when Mishka was young a child. Mishka's father, Ebi, had been drafted by the Russian Army to fight in

Afghanistan not long after her grandmother's death. He had never returned home, and Dimitiry had believed he was killed in the fighting. Farah, Ebi's wife, had not given up hope that Ebi was alive. She had left their two children in Dimitiry's care while she traveled to Syria to search for her husband. She had written to Dimitiry and the children for several months, but then her letters had stopped. Several weeks after Farah's last letter from Syria, Dimitiry had received an official communication that Ebi had been killed at a security checkpoint on the Afghan border.

Alone, Dimitiry had done his best to raise his two beautiful grandchildren, Josuf and Mishka. The two children had been accepted by advanced Russian academic centers near Moscow, where they studied multiple foreign languages, including Arabic and English, both of which would prove an asset to them later in life. Dimitiry had been in the Soviet Union's military services as a bomb technician in the 1980s. His last assignment had been with nuclear armaments for the Soviet Air Force. When the Soviet Union had collapsed and had become the Russian Federation, however, he had been allowed to retire. With his grandchildren to raise, Dimitiry had been forced to seek work where he could find it.

Mishka had excelled at science like her grandfather. She had always been incredibly curious about how the theoretical sciences of subatomic particles worked and were related. There had been many occasions when Mishka had received praise from her science professors, an experience that she always relished. Without her parents in her life, Mishka had become more and more dependent on the academic world for her emotional support.

When she was fifteen, several professors and two government officials had entered Mishka's classroom. Calling her up in front of the entire class, an official from the Russian government had stepped forward and awarded her with a light blue neckerchief. The prized cloth had been rolled up in scout fashion and held together by a metallic slide with an atomic symbol fashioned on it. A framed certificate had then been handed to her. Mishka had cried tears of elation and pride and had worn the neckerchief every day.

Josuf, too, had enjoyed the science of radiology. His grades, however, had never been remarkable, for he had constantly been distracted by some student friends who had recently moved from Syria. He had listened to their tales of their fathers who were Syrian fighters. These fighters had fought against the tyrannical al-Ahini government. Josuf had been sad, for he had no story to tell about his father in the Russian Army. His sadness had changed, however, when Josuf had begun to study on his own the Islamic faith and the history of Syria. Sadly, Josuf had also developed feelings of anti-Semitism towards Israel, a hatred that had grown stronger with each year that had passed while he was in school.

When Mishka had graduated school, she had been immediately recruited by a science laboratory in Moscow. For every project she had been assigned to, she had met or exceeded expectations from her supervisors. Her excellent work and undying thirst for being recognized for her achievements had quickly been discovered by the Russian *Federalnaya Sluzhba Bazopasnosti*, or FSB, the equivalent to the United States' CIA. The FSB had wasted no time in acquiring Mishka and her knowledge of radiology to work for them. Mishka had been delighted. Finally, she had found an organization that was perfect for her.

Josuf, on the other hand, had left his university before graduating. Bitter and disheartened, he had looked for solace with fellow Russians who had admired the Islamic faith. He had been able to find a job in a laboratory working with radioactive materials used for cancer research but had later been released when he had started talking to others about religion and starting a holy *jihad* in Syria. Completely distraught, Josuf had taken a position with the Russian Interior Ministry where his knowledge of Arabic and radiology could be of use.

While his grandchildren had been away at college, Dimitiry had made friends with two American Christian missionaries. When they had returned to the United Stated, they had offered to bring Dimitiry with them to find a new life away from Russia. Alone once again, the old man had come to Western North Carolina where he had lived for the past eight years.

Mishka, who had gone on to receive her doctorate as a nuclear physicist, had received a posting to work in the United States serving as an advisor on radiology studies to St. Gabriel Hospital near Asheville, North Carolina, for the Russian government. Not only had the position been very close to Dimitiry's new home, it had been an offer that she couldn't refuse since it had been an order from her commanders in the FSB.

Mishka took a deep breath and shut the trunk. A broad smile spread across her face as she pulled out two antique hair barrettes to free her long dark hair. With two quick shakes using both her hands, her hair was tossed just the way she wanted it: wild and free. She walked to the other side of her car and picked up a wire cage covered with a blanket. Some two and half feet tall, the cage wobbled in her arms because the occupant inside kept moving back and forth, changing the balance of the cage.

"Shoosh! Grandpa will hear you. You're going to love it here," Mishka whispered to the creature inside.

That day, like every Wednesday, she was visiting her grandfather. A widower, Dimitiry Federov was her last grandparent that she knew of. Dimitiry was a kind and gentle man who spent much of his time writing emails to distant colleagues and friends. He also had a passion for music played on his family's beat-up accordion. He enjoyed entertaining his friends and neighbors in the park nearby on sunny days. He added some fun to his musical performances by dressing in Turkish Middle Eastern attire. He wore a handsome vest that looked like a Persian rug and a traditional red fez that he had bought in an antique store for that unique flair. Sporting an aged but well-groomed handlebar mustache, he was the epitome of some sultan or rug peddler as seen in the movies. Old and young alike were mesmerized by his playing and adored him.

Mishka, too, adored her grandfather very much, and she brought his favorite meal every Wednesday: salmon patties fried in butter. It was the lunch special for Wednesday at the local diner, and she was always careful to get some fresh vegetables and an extra dollop or two of super-hot horseradish sauce to complete his lunch. She had been enjoying their weekly date ever since her grandfather had started showing the early signs of aggressive arthritis. Dimitiry enjoyed the visits with his beautiful granddaughter as well, but he especially enjoyed the diner's forte in cooking the salmon patties.

As always, he was at the front door waiting for his granddaughter before she reached it. That time, however, she carried not a boxed lunch, but a covered cage.

"Hello, my Mishka! Welcome, child. It is so wonderful you think of me each week. I have a wonderful present to give you today. It is something you have wanted for a very long time."

"No, Poppi, my present is more important," Mishka said as she held up the covered cage.

"Oh, have the salmon patties gotten so much bigger this week?" he said with a chuckle as he motioned for her to come inside.

"No, Poppi, this is a very special surprise. I have brought you a new friend."

"Oh, child, I don't want a bird or cat or whatever. Please not today. Besides, you are all that I have and want in my life."

"Poppi, this is different. My surprise is better," Mishka said as she walked through the front door. She quickly kissed her grandfather on the cheek as she passed.

Mishka went straight to the living room and placed the covered cage on the rectangular coffee table. She then turned and went back out the front door to get her grandfather's lunch.

"No peeking!" she called to her grandfather as she twitched her finger back and forth while she walked to her car.

A few minutes later, Mishka had placed her grandfather's lunch on the breakfast table and gone to the refrigerator to pour a glass of chilled herbal tea for him. He gestured to her to sit with him and join him for some tea as well.

"*Da*, Poppi" Mishka answered in the affirmative in Russian.

Once the two sat down at the breakfast table, Dimitiry began to enjoy his meal. The smell of the salmon patties was wonderful. It filled the whole room with an ethereal scent, and the cooked beans and carrots added to the menagerie of epicurean delights in the white Styrofoam container.

In the living room, a small, brown, furry hand slipped past the bars of the cage and pulled up the latch holding the cage door closed. The covering blanket moved back and forth as the occupant freed itself from imprisonment, unnoticed by the humans in the kitchen. One hand, then two hands, appeared from behind the blanket. Then a reddish-brown furry head with beautiful brown eyes popped out from under the cover to survey its new surroundings, still undetected by the two humans.

The Capuchin monkey's nimble hands quietly replaced the disturbed cover back over the cage. Like a stealthy ninja, the monkey moved quickly to the far wall opposite the kitchen. Her nose twitched as she followed the scent of Dimitiry's lunch.

There, just behind the wall, she remained out of sight, using the shadows of the nearby furniture to hide in. She was on a mission, and that mission was to get some of that lunch by whatever means. All she had to do was wait.

"So, what have you brought me, my darling?" Dimitiry asked, pausing between bites to smile at his granddaughter.

"Now that you've tasted your beloved salmon patties, come, let me introduce you to her," replied Mishka, pushing back her chair and walking towards the living room.

"Her?" Dimitiry put down his fork, rose, and followed his granddaughter into the living room.

"Well, we don't have a name for her, but she is yours to keep and name her yourself." Mishka turned as she reached the coffee table, excitement visible on her face. "She is a Capuchin monkey. Think of her as a little buddy to have around. She could even retrieve things for you."

With that remark, Mishka lifted the blanket to expose a metal cage. She was watching her grandfather's face instead of the cage to see what reaction he was going to have. She watched as the gleeful joy of expectation on Dimitiry's face turned into bewilderment.

"Is she invisible?" he asked.

Confused, Mishka looked down to the cage and realized that the pet monkey she had brought was no longer in the cage. Frantically, the two looked around the living room but to no avail.

"Where is she? Come here, little girl! Come here!" Mishka called out while she walked around the room.

Dimitiry also began to search the room until he heard something metallic fall in the breakfast area. That sound was the noise of a fork sliding off the edge of his Styrofoam lunch container and hitting the table. He quickly turned and went to peer around the wall, only to see a reddish-brown furry monkey eating his salmon patties and carrots.

"My lunch! My salmon patties! Thief! Get away from my lunch!" Dimitiry said as he raced to the table with Mishka not far behind.

The monkey took one last bite of a delicious salmon patty and leaped upwards towards the small glass chandelier light that hung over the table. In its paw was the other patty. The monkey's fingers gently clutched the golden prize. Looking down at Dimitiry as he came to a stop at the table below, the monkey slowly extended its furry arm towards him. In a unique gesture, the monkey handed back the remaining patty.

"Poppi, look! She's offering a peace gesture."

Dimitiry held out his hand to receive his lunch back, and at that very moment, the monkey and the grandfather bonded. The monkey let out two quick chirps, sounding in a special way like she was saying "I'm sorry."

Mishka and her grandfather simultaneously let out a happy sigh of relief followed by joyous laughter. Even the monkey grinned at that moment as everyone settled down.

After Dimitiry put his salmon patty back on with his lunch, he reached with both arms and gestured for the monkey to come down from the light. The monkey complied and leapt into his arms then scurried to rest upon his right shoulder.

Mishka was very pleased at the beginnings of a great friendship for her grandfather. "Poppi, I brought some of her food. It's out in the car. I will bring it in before I leave. She should eat fruits and nuts twice a day, and you'll need to leave plenty of water in small bowls throughout the house."

"Okay, my Mishka." Dimitiry reached up and stroked his new friend gently on her head and the top of her chest. He looked up at his little friend, and, at that moment, the monkey bent down and kissed him on his cheek. Mishka started to tear up and held her grandfather's hand.

"What do you want to call her?" she asked.

"Well, I think I will call her *Malinky Vor*, the Little Thief. If memory serves me, my darling, you were a little thief when you were a child. Those cookies my dear wife made—may God rest her soul—you always managed to get about half each time," Dimitiry said while crossing himself in the Orthodox Catholic fashion. "Your hair was a reddish brown when you were much younger. And every time you stole from the kitchen, Mama shouted, '*Krasnaya obez'yana!*' For that you are my red monkey."

Mishka chuckled, the warmth of the memory flooding over her. "Okay, Poppi. Malinky it is."

As if on cue, Malinky let out a quick chirp and a goofy smile flashed on her furry face.

The afternoon was filled with some wonderful moments with Dimitiry's new friend and Mishka. Ultimately, as the day wore on, the two forgot about the special surprise Dimitiry had wanted to share, a surprise in the form of a special email that he had printed off for her to have as soon as she had arrived.

CHAPTER 5: SHIP AHOY!

Gainesville, Georgia

It was a gorgeous windy day for sailing. The 2007 Hunter 33 heeled to port ever so slightly as the wind crossed the boat's right-side bow. Michael Cotter was at the helm and loved to tack his new boat, the *Sea Wolf*, back and forth as he fought his way against the wind to Buford Dam on Lake Lanier. His wife Debbie had taken his mother on a daylong shopping trip to the Mall of Georgia, so it had been the perfect opportunity for him to have a day on the lake. His cousin Elizabeth, who lived with his mother, had decided to join him, preferring the water to crowded stores.

"I'm getting another beer, Michael. Do you want another one?" Elizabeth asked as she began down the staircase that led to the salon below deck. She grabbed the brim of her large sunhat as the wind threatened to whisk it away. "They should finally be ice cold, no thanks to that old refrigerator you've got in the galley."

"I'm good right now, but I will probably get the grill going in a minute so that we can enjoy those beef hotdogs you brought. Did you bring some buns?"

"Yep, tasty whole wheat buns."

"Oh, geez, Elizabeth," Michael said, rolling his eyes. "You're about as bad as Debbie."

Elizabeth laughed as she disappeared below deck. Even though she was really Michael's cousin on his father's side, she was as close to Michael as a younger sister. She had lived with the Cotters since the death of her father back in high school to cancer, the same cancer that had later claimed Michael's father.

With the new tack, the *Sea Wolf* had the wind coming at an angle towards the rear of the boat into the cockpit. Michael absolutely loved that kind of breeze, for it cooled off his 5-foot 11-inch frame. His short dark hair was graying slightly around his temples, which reminded him of his dad when he had been in his late twenties. Michael's medium build was still in very good condition, even after getting out of the Army just a short time before. Debbie challenged Michael every day on their treadmill or their new elliptical to see who could keep going at the top level on the machines.

Michael loved to wear a golf shirt, shorts, and a pair of worn-out boat shoes when he sailed, but he had put on some khaki pants for that day's sail. The shorts had fallen victim to a messy dollop of strawberry preserves from his morning bagel. Michael always respected his cousin Elizabeth and never took off his shirt, regardless of how hot it was on the boat.

Elizabeth emerged from down below with a cold beer and found a spot to sit. She picked up a bottle of sunscreen and added a new layer of cream to her bare shoulders to help her very white skin from getting more freckles. Her red hair was braided in a ponytail that trailed down her back and touched her green halter top. Her bright green eyes were being protected by Steve's old sunglasses that he had left on the boat.

When she finished with the sunscreen, Elizabeth pulled out a wrinkled map and began to look over it. She loved being with her older cousin, and on that particular trip she had the privilege of being both the navigator and crew for Michael's boat. As the navigator, she used the lake map and her knowledge of the lake to point out the usual hazards where known sand bars and tree stumps lurked below. Michael appreciated Elizabeth's input, but he also relied on his boat's depth finder and electronic navigation.

"Look, Michael, over there on the rocky bank just underneath the bridge," Elizabeth said as she stood up and walked over to the cockpit. She was two inches shorter than Michael and had to maneuver to see around him. "There are still pieces of that old houseboat that caught fire years ago. The houseboat that our homemade submarine sank."

"No, Elizabeth, that houseboat caught fire in the engine room, and the captain was forced to beach her to keep the boat from sinking."

"What's the difference?" whispered Elizabeth. Her eyes sparkled as she remembered her summer romance with Jack all those years ago. She sat down on the transom, and Michael sat down beside her. They relaxed in thoughtful silence as they looked out over the water.

Summer had been a time of adventure for Michael, Elizabeth, and Steve. The summer at hand, however, was something very special. Michael was celebrating his new life as a civilian after his military duties had ended. The hard work Michael had put in with the Army on drone technology had paid off handsomely. His achievements had been noticed by prospective employers for his advanced studies on drone surveillance. He had a stack of employment offers waiting on his decision at home, each offer as big and impressive as the last. Michael had even been offered a position in England, most likely because of his honorary knighthood for bravery in combat when his drone, *Wolf*, had assisted the British base he had been attached to in Afghanistan in repelling a well-organized Taliban assault.

Elizabeth, too, was at a time of transition. She had just finished her master's degree in computer studies at Georgia Tech in Atlanta. She hadn't found her own apartment yet and still lived with her aunt Sonya Cotter, Michael and Steve's mother, on Lake Lanier. Unlike Michael, Elizabeth had already accepted a position with the local university as an associate professor. Her new career was to start in five weeks.

"All right, time to tack!" Michael said out loud as he rose from his seat on the transom.

"Ready here," answered Elizabeth, standing as well.

Michael checked his rearview before making the 40-degree turn. Tacking was a zigzag pattern that allowed the sailboat to sail almost upwind. As for Michael, it was one of his favorite things to do when he was on board his beloved sailboat.

"Tacking!" he bellowed as the ship's boom slowly swung across the cockpit and firmly planted the main sail to the other side of the boat.

The *Sea Wolf* took the new tack well and proceeded on its new course. The bow pointed towards a favorite spot of all who sailed on the lake known as Greenland. Greenland was really a lakeside section of a golf course, and the name came from the fourteenth hole where the grass was always green. It was a beautiful view.

Michael settled back onto his perch in the cockpit and relaxed some more. Elizabeth smiled and took the wheel for a while. The new tack wouldn't be changed for another 30 minutes, and by that time, the *Sea Wolf* would sail west to take them to the dam.

The peaceful sounds of the water passing beneath the boat were suddenly overwhelmed by the rotating blades of an approaching military helicopter. A dark green Blackhawk helicopter, part of the Tenth Mountain Division based throughout North Georgia, flew in a low pass to the lee side of Michael's sailboat. The *Sea Wolf's* sails reacted violently to the sudden onslaught of wind from the helicopter. The hull of the boat moaned in protest as the extra stress from the unnatural wind flow overwhelmed the trim of the sailboat. Michael jumped to his feet and grabbed the wheel alongside Elizabeth as her sunhat was whisked away in the wind. The two of them hung on tightly as they struggled against the violent swaying of the boat.

"Ahoy, sailing vessel! Is there a Michael Cotter on your ship?" a stern voice from the loudspeaker underneath the helicopter boomed.

Michael looked at Elizabeth and then up at the massive helicopter as it turned slowly. The pilot of the Blackhawk was attempting not to swamp the sailboat with his helicopter's rotor wash, but it was to no avail. The massive helicopter had a maximum take-off weight of 23,500 pounds. The thrust necessary to lift and maintain flight for such a beast required tremendous energy. Even though the chopper weighed a svelte 20,000 pounds for its current mission, the rotor wash still tossed the sailboat like a toy boat in the bathtub near an open drain, leaving the *Sea Wolf* hopelessly askew.

Michael gave a quick thumbs-up and a wave to the helicopter crew chief who was hanging out of the starboard side of the Blackhawk. Another airman onboard used a special digital camera to take a picture of Michael down below. The photo was electronically sent to some upper echelon command for confirmation that the man they were speaking to was indeed Michael Cotter.

After a few seconds, there was a second command from the hovering helicopter above. "Heave to and prepare to be boarded!"

Michael realized the seriousness of the situation and reacted accordingly. He released the main sail line from the holding cleat and brought the main sail down quickly. Elizabeth gathered all the loose items, like the map she had been using and the snacks they had enjoyed during the day.

"I don't like this, Elizabeth," Michael said discreetly as he tightened the draw strings that held the furled main sail securely. "We better be prepared for anything."

Only the jib sail up front remained to move the boat at a slower pace, yet it, too, protested to the violent rotor wash. Michael started up the diesel engine and steered the boat into the wind to get better control on winching in the jib. The helicopter above yielded some space to allow this to happen. When Michael was confident that the diesel engine had indeed engaged and was powering the *Sea Wolf*, he then motioned for Elizabeth to lower the jib sail.

When satisfied that all the sails were taken down and securely tied off, Michael waved to the pilot above. He then reached into a small duffle bag and pulled out two small neatly folded flags used in signal flag communication. He held them out to his cousin. "Elizabeth, attach these flags to the lanyard beside the mast and hoist them up for all to see."

One flag was a blue open square with a red square in the center denoting the letter *W*. The second flag he raised, a combination of two blue lines, two white lines, and a center red line, was for the letter *C*. These two flags, when flown together, were code for "Wants to Communicate."

The helicopter's pilot observed the flags and then used hand signals to convey the numbers seven and zero to Michael.

Elizabeth quickly retrieved the marine walkie-talkie from inside the cabin and brought it to Michael. Such devices were useful for sailors to monitor traffic, emergencies, and towing needs. Michael tuned the walkie-talkie to Channel 70, which was rarely monitored except by local Coast Guard and military personnel.

"Hello, this is Michael Cotter, captain of the sailing vessel *Sea Wolf*. I have one passenger and have heaved to and am ready to be boarded."

"Stand by."

A crew member then attached himself to a towline on a mechanical pulley aboard the large helicopter and was lowered. The Blackhawk crept forward towards the sailboat. The rotor wash was intense for Michael's boat, but it managed to stay on station with the sails lowered and with the boat's diesel engine struggling to maintain its slow, steady progress.

Michael noticed that the man descending towards them was part of the Tenth Mountain. He also noticed from the man's flight suit that he was a warrant officer, a position held in the Army by pilots and individuals on special operations. As the man touched down on deck, Michael approached. "Welcome aboard. How can we help you?"

The helicopter crewman was dressed in military flight gear, a life vest, and a pilot's helmet. The helmet's black sun visor was pulled down over his face, and the man's head was lowered towards the pitching deck of the *Wolf*. Once the soldier was stable and secure, he detached himself from the safety tow line and signaled for the helicopter's pilot to gain altitude and await further orders. The uniformed man looked at Michael and lifted his visor. "I'm Warrant Officer Timothy Cooper here to assist you."

After the tow line was fully retrieved, the massive Blackhawk helicopter increased its power and climbed to a stationary 400 feet. By that time, other boaters on the lake had begun to speculate as they watched the 33-foot yacht being boarded by a soldier from an Army helicopter. Some of the on-lookers had donned binoculars for a better view, while others had dispersed and moved away from the action fearing terrorists or worse.

"What's going on?" shouted Michael over the helicopter's engines as he sized up the six-foot-tall soldier who had just boarded his boat.

"This is a matter of national security. I have orders to find and retrieve you and an Elizabeth Cotter." WO Cooper paused and then looked at Elizabeth. "I have to ask, ma'am. Are you Elizabeth Cotter?"

Elizabeth nodded in affirmation as she tried to brush away the stray red hairs that the wind had pulled free from her braid. The boat finally stopped pitching up and down as the helicopter hovered higher above. Michael's eyes narrowed as he watched the soldier suspiciously. Had Cooper only been there for him, he would have been less wary, but the fact that he wanted Elizabeth, too, did not sit well with Michael.

"Reverse course and take the *Sea Wolf* due east to Happy Marina," Cooper said as he motioned to the pilot above that he was is in control of the situation. The Blackhawk's pilot proceeded to the flat green fairway of the local golf course and landed.

Michael hesitantly returned to the controls. He motioned discreetly with his head for Elizabeth to go below as he increased the engine power and steered the boat towards their new destination. Elizabeth excused herself and stepped below deck. She emerged several minutes later wearing a buttoned-up shirt over her halter top, and her hair was once again neatly braided. She glanced anxiously at Michael as she sat down near the side of the boat. He nodded to her in encouragement, his face stoic as he adeptly maneuvered the yacht through the water.

Thirty minutes later, the three docked the *Sea Wolf* at Happy Marina. They hurriedly walked up the pier towards the parking lot. As they reached the end of the pier, Michael stopped. "Hey, give me a minute. We've got to pay the office the slip rental, or they'll tow away or sell my boat."

"That's already been taken care of," Cooper replied. He motioned towards the parking lot. "The car's waiting for us."

Michael looked at Elizabeth and then back to Cooper. The man's words did nothing to relieve his uneasiness about the situation. He nodded in assent, but he positioned himself between his cousin and the soldier as they moved up the pier. Every nerve in his body was on alert as they stepped into the parking lot.

A large black SUV with several antennae sat in the corner of the parking lot. It was surrounded by several uniformed men. Michael moved in closer to Elizabeth. She glanced at him nervously but continued to walk towards the car. As they approached, the back door of the heavily tinted SUV opened.

"Hey, what was the hold up?" asked Steve as he climbed out of the vehicle.

Relief swept over Michael and Elizabeth at the same moment.

"Steve! Oh my God, Steve, is it really you? What on Earth are you doing here?" screamed Michael as he hurried to greet his brother. Elizabeth was right behind him with a huge smile.

The three shared a few quick hugs and then were prompted by Steve's security detail to climb into the SUV. Cooper climbed into the front of the SUV with the driver. Once inside the relative privacy of the vehicle, Michael punched his brother in the arm.

"Ow!" Steve yelped as the car moved out of the parking lot and onto the main road.

"Thanks for the scare and the helicopter crewman landing on top of the *Sea Wolf.* What's all this about?" Michael said as he wiped some perspiration off his forehead with the back of his hand.

"Well, you are fixing to get on that Blackhawk with me and travel to western North Carolina," Steve said in a serious tone.

"Well, then I've gotta call Debbie and tell her that Elizabeth and I are with you," Michael said as he pulled his cellphone out of his pocket.

"There's no need. I already talked with Debbie and with Mom for you, Elizabeth," Steve explained.

Michael's brow furrowed. "What on Earth did you tell Debbie and our mother?"

"I told them both that we were all on a secret mission," Steve responded with a goofy smile.

Elizabeth rolled her eyes first, and then Michael followed next. Steve shrugged his shoulders and started to laugh. Michael and Elizabeth both let out a chuckle as the tension that had surrounded them receded.

The SUV reached the golf course and made its way along the service roads to where the helicopter had landed on the flat, open fairway. Steve grabbed a large packet filled with materials and information as they exited the vehicle. Together, they hurried with their heads bent down to the awaiting Blackhawk.

When all were secured, the Blackhawk lifted off and headed to North Carolina. Steve handed the information packet about their new assignment and its scope to Michael and Elizabeth. "Here, you two. Read this on the way."

CHAPTER 6: DOES GODZILLA SPEAK RUSSIAN?

Northwest Russia, Nyonoska Military Weapons Testing Range

The dark grey concrete observation bunker was cold and damp inside. The leaden walls within the concrete structure seemed to attract any and all sources of moisture, which only added to the misery of the seven human occupants inside. The two incandescent lightbulbs inside the bunker offered little, if any, heat to the cold room. Like the dark skies above, the bunker offered very little in way of extraordinary views. Its large solitary window overlooked a warehouse-style launch pad facility before it.

Five nuclear scientists from Moscow sat nervously in their uncomfortable metal chairs side by side facing the observation window. Each man was a graduate from Rosatom, Russia's state nuclear agency. In a sixth chair sat General Sergei Alexey Sokolov, the world's most ruthless military scientist, a man as cunning and brutal as the meaning of his last name—"bird of prey." His personal features were a constant reminder on his evil. His wavy dark black hair and sharp descending eyebrows that formed a V-shape above his narrow eyes accentuated the hawk-like features of his grim face.

Lieutenant General Konstantin Budnikov, Sokolov's number one henchman, stared silently out the observation window with his slender fingers intertwined behind the small of his back. He was a towering, thin man in a perfectly pressed uniform. His ashen, paper-like skin gave his frail face a cold, sickly appearance, despite his good health. Budnikov was a sadistic, haughty man, and everyone who had ever encountered him knew that he was not a man to cross.

The hollow ticking of an old mechanical clock that hung on the concrete wall resounded through the tense silence that surrounded the little group of expectant observers. Sokolov was a distrustful man of few words. He drove his scientists hard with almost impossible demands. Like a sadist using an electric cattle prod to push the group of Einsteins, Sokolov used fear as a convenient rudder.

The group was awaiting a live test for one of the new micro weapons that the scientists had created for smaller tactical battlefield conditions. The test was being performed under the guise of a supply launch for the International Space Station.

The micro bomb the scientists had created was mounted underneath a special nosecone that could withstand the extreme heat of a hypersonic launch and reentry into the earth's atmosphere. The missile carrying the warhead was the newer version of a well-tested launch system for the Russian military known as the Skydancer rocket. The bomb's explosive yield would create a radioactive environment that would render any medium to large city uninhabitable for almost a year and wipe out any electrical operating system for several weeks. It was the perfect weapon to clear out a city's occupants, choking all roads with fleeing refugees and removing any tactical defensive positions. Large cities, such as Berlin, Warsaw, Baghdad, Jerusalem, Seoul, and even Washington, would be defenseless. Perfect for any invading army, it would be priceless to any terrorist group if it fell into the wrong hands.

General Sokolov turned to the scientists next to him, his icy gaze sending chills up the men's spines. "Explain to Lieutenant General Budnikov how we get rid of the radiation after the city has been abandoned."

Budnikov turned slowly from the window to look at the scientists. His emotionless face seemed to absorb the darkness of the room.

The middle-aged man next to Sokolov ran his hand nervously though his thinning brown hair and cleared his throat. "The black fungus we discovered inside the Chernobyl reactor in 2019 actually sought out and ate the radioactive materials at the core. The fungus showed no adverse effects and cleared the area that was exposed to it. We have experimented with the same fungus on test areas that were radioactive, also with positive results. We have now perfected a procedure to extract the spores from the black fungus."

The poor man's voice cracked, and he coughed to clear his throat again. Budnikov's narrow eyes watched the nervous man as he sought for the courage to continue his explanation.

"After the city has been vacated and our armed forces have secured the area, we will then dry seed the entire city with our spores. The accelerated growth of the fungus should clear a city within six months of all harmful radiation. Once cleared, we then spray antifungal agents to kill off the fungus, leaving us a clean city ready to be populated with the correct citizens. Its moniker is Godzilla."

Sokolov scowled. "I still do not like that name! Why are we still using it? I want it called Beluga, like our delicious caviar from the Beluga sturgeon in the Caspian Sea. Why is it still called that? Answer me!"

The middle-aged man shook visibly and looked in panic to the other four scientists, his eyes pleading for one of them to help him but to no avail. He turned to Sokolov, his eyes never meeting those of the vindictive general. "Sir, it was… it was just a little humor. The name Godzilla came about because our spores turn into a type of fungus that eats radiation, like the Japanese lizard that was radiated and grew into a monster."

A deep growl resonated from Sokolov's chest as his face contorted in anger. He glanced over to Budnikov to see if he was in agreement with him. Budnikov nodded to Sokolov in agreement.

The five scientists cowered before them. Budnikov slowly turned back to the window without a word.

Disgusted at their cowardice, Sokolov turned to stare out the window, as well. He would deal with them later. He knew that the only thing greater than the scientists' fear of their wrath was their fear of the horrendous wrath of the Russian president himself, President Vladimir Pelevin.

Sokolov's thoughts wandered as he waited patiently for the test to begin. His dream was that one day his own power would exceed the power that Pelevin wielded over people. Pelevin was the epitome of a product of the old Soviet Union: ruthless, powerful, and deadly. He was only five feet and five inches tall with blonde hair and piercing blue eyes. Teased throughout his childhood about his size, he had endured the taunts for years until he had exploded with deadly raw emotion at a hapless classmate who was near him. From then on, all his fellow students had stood clear of him.

Graduating at the head of his class in all academics, Pelevin had been recruited quickly into the KGB. He had quickly mastered code breaking and espionage. His stern demeanor had accelerated his career in the KGB. From lieutenant, to captain, and finally colonel, Pelevin had progressed like a steamroller in his accomplishments. He was a ruthless, unstoppable hunter, and competitor after competitor fell to him.

An evil smile tugged at the corners of Sokolov's mouth as he thought of Pelevin's nickname: The Pelican. Later in life, Pelevin had developed a genetic oddity under his chin, a swaggering lump of excess flesh that had formed a gullet. Not only had he looked like the grand flying sea master, he had been the perfect spy with his incredible patience and keen skill for swooping in for the kill. Pelevin, however, had hated the deformity and the nickname. As his incredible luck would have it, though, Pelevin had been able to have the growth cosmetically removed, and the government had even paid for it, when he had accepted a secret mission that had involved spying on the French president's wife at a plastic surgeon's office.

Sokolov's touch of a smile vanished as he realized that Pelevin had always been in the right place at the right time, making his rise to power swift. Everyone who had failed him had found themselves "counting trees in Siberia," an old saying from the days of Stalin and the Soviet Union.

Sokolov saw this new weapon as his opportunity to gain the power that he so desired. The terrorists in Chechnya would experience the first real battlefield test of the violent weapon. Embarrassed by the two failed Russian army invasions into the rogue territory, formerly of the Soviet Union, the Russian army needed a chance to redeem itself in the eyes of their president, those same eyes that deemed who was worthy of the rank of general for the Russian army and who was to be dismissed, usually with fatal results.

The Russian countdown from four to launch blared over the loudspeaker in the compound, drawing Sokolov's attention back to the scene in front of the observation bunker. *"Chetyre..., tri..., dva..., odin..., zapusk!"*

Instead of the usual satellites, cosmonauts, or supplies to the International Space Station, the sinister test rocket blasted off from the launch pad perfectly. Sokolov's face remained stern as he watched the rocket climb. It reached the upper atmosphere flawlessly. The multiple rocket boosters broke free from the central part of the main body just as the rocket approached the outer bands of the atmosphere. It entered deep space in a quasi-normal orbit like the typical ISS launch, though the rocket's trajectory would soon have a different path.

Budnikov turned to Sokolov. The faintest smile tugged almost indecipherably at the edges of Budnikov's thin lips. Sokolov rubbed the palms of his hands together in front of his chest. An evil smile spread across his hawk-like face.

***

The United States Space Force, still newly organized and headquartered in Colorado Springs, Colorado, noted the Russian launch as it was happening. It appeared to be a routine supply flight to the International Space Station as the rocket achieved successful orbit. It wasn't until the Russian rocket rotated into a trajectory that took it past the ISS and back towards the Earth's atmosphere that alarm bells began to sound for the Space Force.

The Space Force commander leaned in towards the monitor. "Wait, what?"

"The supply vessel never approached the ISS, sir. It just flew by it," the Space Force colonel who had been monitoring the launch explained.

The commander straightened and crossed his arms in front of his chest. "Get on the phone with the Russians and ask them what the hell just happened."

The Space Force colonel picked up what everyone called the red line, a telephone system that still used the decades-old hardline phone wires of yesteryear to prevent any connection loss or interception. The conversation lasted close to ten minutes, as it appeared that the translation team that worked for both sides of the communication process had slowed to a crawl.

He wrote down the message he had received back from the Russians and handed it to the commander. It read: *We have lost the linkage for automatic docking. The payload will try to retranslate and reacquire the ISS docking portal.*

"Ah, bullshit!" the Space Force commander muttered as he crumpled up the message and threw it at the floor.

"Sir, the Russians are lying about this payload. They've never "lost" the docking linkage, ever!" said the colonel.

The commander watched the missile slowly descend into the southeastern part of Russian territory on the monitor. Then it seemed to simply disappear. "Get me the Pentagon."

After a few seconds, the colonel handed the commander a phone with an awaiting superior on the other end. The commander listened to the voice on the other end and then replied, "Yes, sir, it was a scheduled launch to the ISS, 254 miles up, but the rocket kept going and has crashed in Russian Chechnya territory…. No, sir, not a detonation by our scanners. It just seemed to deteriorate in the lower atmosphere…. Yes, sir, we'll keep you posted."

The commander hung up the phone. He pulled out his handkerchief and wiped his brow and around his collar.

CHAPTER 7: THE THREE-STEP DANCE

North Carolina

The large Blackhawk helicopter carrying the Cotters landed on a local hospital's landing pad. A black unmarked limousine in the service of the CIA was waiting to transport Steve and the others to their next destination. After a short drive from the helicopter pad, the vehicle entered the parking lot of a large rectangular apartment complex that had four buildings facing a grassy park in the center. Michael, Steve, and Elizabeth gathered some equipment and other items from the trunk of the limo and proceeded to the entrance of one of the buildings.

"Where are we, Steve?" asked Elizabeth as she looked up towards the roof of the apartment building that they were about to enter.

"This is our new home for a while."

The group entered the apartment complex and walked up the three flights of stairs to Steve's temporary operational apartment on the third floor. They began to unpack the computers, observation equipment, food, clothing, and even a box of donuts, that had been previously collected by Steve and his fellow CIA operatives.

"So, why do you need us again? Aren't you the Assistant Director of Counterintelligence?" joked Michael as he walked over to the window of the apartment and looked out once they had finished unpacking.

Steve and Elizabeth both laughed out loud. Michael put on a goofy smirk as he turned to face them, trying to act like know-it-all. Steve reached into his shirt pocket and pulled out a new business card. He sauntered over and handed it to his brother, bowing ceremoniously.

Michael read the card aloud. "*Steven Cotter, Assistant. Deputy of Interior Intelligence, Tier 1.*"

He smiled at Steve and winked as he slid the card into his front pocket. Steve winked back and walked over to the table where he had been working.

"What does that mean?" Elizabeth asked as she flopped down on the large couch that separated the dining area from the living room.

Steve chuckled as he gathered a tan wooden tripod and pair of binoculars from the equipment they had unpacked. He walked over to the window where Michael stood and unfolded the tripod. "It means I bring the coffee to the assistant of the lowest level of the Interior Intelligence Department."

They all laughed. Michael slapped Steve on the back and walked to the couch. He sat down beside Elizabeth as Steve worked to attach the binoculars to the tripod.

"Truthfully, Tom MacAday, my supervisor during special training, chose me for the assignment. He chose me for my skills in intelligence gathering, but I think the experience I gained working with scientists inside Syria on my last assignment had something to do with it."

Steve looked over his shoulder at Elizabeth and Michael. "After the fiasco my last assignment turned out to be, I really wanted a team that I knew couldn't fail, so I asked for you guys and MacAday agreed. He read about your skills while getting your clearance and messaged me that I couldn't have picked a better team."

"Works for me," Elizabeth said, smiling brightly.

Steve flashed Elizabeth a big smile and then bent to look through the long-range binoculars that he had just set up. He made the necessary diopter adjustment and then rotated the focus ring as he brought a green wrought iron bench in the middle of the adjacent park into focus. He panned the tripod's mount back and forth as he scanned for his target through the binoculars.

Michael stretched and stood. He walked around the couch to the small dining table and grabbed a chair. He carried it over to where Steve was looking through the binoculars and straddled the chair, his arms resting on top of the high wooden chairback. "So, let's run through this assignment."

Steve turned to face his brother and crossed his arms in front of his chest. "Well, my boss thinks we have a chance to nab a retired Russian nuclear scientist… who may be a retired Soviet Special Operations Force spy for the GRU or the new FSB. If we're lucky, it may even be possible to get him to defect to our side."

"The FSB? Isn't that the KGB?" asked Elizabeth as she stood and walked over to stand beside Michael.

"Yes and no, Elizabeth," Steve answered, tilting his head from side to side slightly. "The GRU is the military branch of the Russian secret service. It stands for some really long Russian words, but that's the gist of it. The FSB is the new CIA for Russia."

Elizabeth nodded. "Got it… I think."

"You guys understand the situation in the Middle East right now." Steve leaned back against the windowsill. "Iran wants to defeat Israel. Syria wants to survive for their government to remain in power. As to the Russians? The Russians need a naval base in the Mediterranean to avoid being bottled up in the Black Sea and the straits of Istanbul."

Michael and Elizabeth glanced at each other and then both nodded.

Steve continued. "We have received intelligence that our target could be working for the Russians, Syrians, or even the Iranians. Possibly, they want him for some jihadist strike. There are thoughts that he has access to a weapon, one of many possibilities we aren't sure about."

Steve stood and stepped over to the binoculars again. He peered through them and then looked back at Michael and Elizabeth, shaking his head. "Our target hasn't done a thing for four months except play his accordion while sitting on this stupid bench in the park from what I'm told."

"What else do we know about this guy?" Michael asked.

"His name is Dimitiry Federov. He is originally Syrian or Iranian, but his loyalty is to Russia. There seem to be no adult children in the picture, but there are two adult grandchildren that pop up on our radar every now and then: a Mishka Federov and a Josuf Federov. All three Federovs have been involved with nuclear programs for civilian and military research."

"That's a whole lot of nuclear information in one family," Michael offered, shaking his head from side to side. "A whole lot."

Steve nodded in agreement. "Now that there's a possibility that the Syrians or Iranians want him to design a small nuclear weapon, it makes Washington very curious and very nervous. Our job is to observe this quirky old fellow, and, if the grandchildren show up, watch them as well."

Michael, Elizabeth, and Steve paused for a moment to let the information to sink in. After a few minutes of silence, Elizabeth turned and walked towards the adjoining open kitchen area. "So, our first step is to watch an elderly grandfather playing the harpsicord—"

"Accordion," Steve interjected.

"Yeah, whatever." Elizabeth rolled her eyes as she grabbed a donut from the cardboard box on the kitchen counter.

"What do you mean 'whatever?'" Steve demanded.

"Go on, Elizabeth," Michael said as he raised his hand to quiet Steve, intervening like a judge in a courtroom trial.

"Our second step is to figure out who this old man really is."

"Yep," replied Steve.

"And our third step is to figure out whether his two grandchildren are part of the old man's intentions."

"Talk about a nasty three-step!" Michael laughed as he looked at Elizabeth, and the other two couldn't help but laugh, too.

CHAPTER 8: THE SECRET AND THE THIEF

Dimitiry closed the front door to his townhouse as Mishka left. He looked over at Malinky and smiled at his new little companion.

"Well, my Little Thief, no more stealing my salmon patties!" He chuckled and waved the little monkey towards him. "I have some work to do in the basement. Come, hop up on my shoulder."

Malinky quickly climbed up Dimitiry's leg and torso and situated herself on the old man's shoulder. The Capuchin monkey let out a series of chirps and a howl as if she were saying she was ready.

Dimitiry walked to the basement door underneath the staircase and flipped up a faux thermostat panel to reveal an electronic keyboard to a security system. He looked up at the monkey and grinned. "An old man can never be too careful, my Little Thief."

Malinky watched carefully as her human master tapped an eleven-digit code on the vinyl keys. The monkey let out a soft howl that sounded like a child saying, "Where?"

The door to the basement opened electronically, and the two proceeded downstairs. Dimitiry flicked a light switch as they passed it, and the two sets of fluorescent lights blinked to life in the room below.

When they reached the bottom of the stairs, Malinky looked around at what appeared to be an ordinary basement, dark and very grim despite the fact that the overhead florescent lights were working properly. There was a tool desk with some odd hammers and screwdrivers laying there haphazardly. A few support posts rose from the concrete floor to the subflooring of the house. Retired furniture and cardboard boxes littered the room.

Dimitiry proceeded to the far side of the basement. That corner was not very well lit. In fact, it was as if it purposefully hid something sinister. In the shadows behind an old armchair stacked with boxes, there was an old, green metal door in the wall about four feet tall and two feet wide that appeared to house a large fuse box panel. Dimitiry slid out the armchair and stepped behind it. He opened the green metal door to reveal another small metal door inside that had an electric keypad above a locked door handle.

Malinky focused on her master's actions as he typed the same password he had used to enter the basement into the keypad. The door's electronic lock tumbler aligned its keys almost instantly, and Dimitiry's hand turned the door handle. Again, a sound emanated from the monkey as if she had discovered something interesting.

"Shush! Don't you tell anybody my code, Malinky," Dimitiry whispered and then laughed. He opened the small door and then held his hand up to the monkey. "You won't be able to sit up there in this room, my little friend. I'll have to carry you."

The monkey obliged, and Dimitiry tucked her under his arm as he bent down and slipped inside the hidden room. The dark secret chamber was deep but only about five feet in height. A dark green canvas bag about the size of a large, heavy military style backpack lay in the shadows on the far side of the small room.

Dimitiry adeptly located an electronic button on the wall behind him next to the door that bypassed the thermal scanner guarding the unusual package. The sensor emitted a steady green light meaning no intrusion. The same safeguard was attached to the package. If an intrusion was sensed, the alarm would deactivate the package from any unauthorized use.

The old man shuffled towards the large, bulky package on the other side of the tiny room. When he reached it, he sat the monkey on top of the green bag. "This, Malinky, is something very special. It looks like an ordinary pack doesn't it?"

The monkey hopped around as if she were examining the pack beneath her.

"It's not, though." He smiled at the little Capuchin's inquisitiveness. "This pack is my life's work. This belonged to the American army, and we stole it from the Americans when they were removing the bombs from active service. They call it the W72. It is a thermal nuclear device that is small enough for a man to carry. Someday, I will have my orders to take a little drive and show the United States just what this little pack can do. Maybe it will be to Atlanta where the Centers for Disease Control and that nice railroad hub for all their strategic supplies and military reinforcements are located. Maybe it will even be to Washington, D.C. I don't know."

Dimitiry shook his head slowly from side to side as he unfastened a side pocket on the backpack and reached inside. He pulled out a large olive drab battery about the size of a small coffee can. A backup charge kept the device active, but it only had a 55-minute lifespan.

"I don't know…," he mumbled to himself, lost in thought as he worked.

Off to the side of the pack, on the floor, was a recharger that held in its cradle another battery. A small green light on the charger indicated that the awaiting battery was fully charged. Dimitiry held the depleted battery with one hand as he used the other to remove the fully charged battery from its cradle.

While Dimitiry was swapping the batteries, Malinky peered inside the bag. She was intrigued by the buttons and flashing lights inside. She was especially drawn to a shiny golden key in the console that was used to pre-arm the device before a series of codes were typed in to activate the countdown timer. She reached inside and pulled the key out of the keyhole. She quickly hopped aside, hiding the key in her hands, as Dimitiry reached down to install the new battery.

Malinky turned her back to Dimitiry and opened her hands before her to reveal the key. She admired its alluring metallic luster for a moment or two. Her small eyes looked at the key lovingly, for she was totally unaware of its deadly purpose. To her, it was the prettiest thing she had ever held in her paw. She let out a small coo of admiration, drawing Dimitiry's attention to the little thief.

"No, no, Malinky! That doesn't belong to you." He held out his hand and motioned for the monkey to give it to him. "Here, give me the key, please."

Malinky shook her head as if she understood Dimitiry. She pulled her arms away as if to protest about her new toy. Dimitiry again motioned with his hand for her to surrender the key. She gave one last look at her treasure and then grudgingly handed it back to him. She then watched him carefully put the arming key back into the console's keyhole and then close the package.

"Now, don't you ever play with that shiny key again, my Little Thief. We must leave that alone."

With the exchange complete, Dimitiry picked up Malinky and left the small room. He placed the monkey back on his shoulder and then closed the door behind them and reset the lock. He closed the green metal door and slid the chair back into its place. Wearily, he lifted the two boxes from the seat of the armchair and placed them on the floor.

The old man lowered himself into the armchair to rest for a moment. He had placed the chair there years before because he always felt drained of energy and had a touch of dizziness after completing his work in the little room. The dizzy spells made him the most uncomfortable since he was well aware that they were probably from his constant exposure to the bomb's lethal radioactive payload inside.

As to Malinky, she was fine. She crawled into her master's lap and held up a small furry hand that touched Dimitiry's face. The old man looked down at his little friend and nodded to her. "It's okay, my Malinky. We are done for today."

Dimitiry closed his eyes and leaned his head against the dusty armchair. In a matter of seconds, he began to daydream of days long ago. In his mind's eye, he pictured a young Lieutenant General Konstantin Gregor Budnikov standing before him. He could hear the General's words just as clear as if it were still the day he had said them. *"Comrade Kapitan Dimitiry Yevgeny Federov, you have excelled at all our tests. You speak English fluently. You passed our survival skills. You passed our stability tests. You passed our loyalty tests to Mother Russia. You have all the knowledge you need to carry out this very dangerous and important mission."*

Budnikov had survived from the days of the Soviet Union to the new Russia of the twenty-first century. Lieutenant General Budnikov had been much younger when he had spoken those words to Dimitiry, but he had still possessed in those earlier days all the vim and vigor of a ruthless commander. His purpose had been to train top KGB spies to infiltrate key strategic targets throughout America and the world with miniaturized nuclear weapons carried in backpacks.

The weapons had been developed in the 1980s as an alternative to counter anti-ballistic missile weapon defenses. The so-called "Star Wars" defense system had rendered most strategic missiles obsolete from accurate acquisitions in Europe and the United States. A human spy with backpack attached, however, could literally walk into a strategic target and detonate the weapon with full effect. Sadly, the carrier of such a strategic weapon died with the attack as well. The Americans had also developed such a weapon to be used by special forces to take out key installations, weapon platforms, and even naval ports, but with the same end results.

It was the Soviets who had perfected the actual use of such a weapon, and Budnikov had been extremely successful obtaining recruits for his program from the many science and military academies throughout Russia. Dimitiry had been one of the most successful recruits of all. He had been successful in acquiring the W72 weapon from the Americans without their knowledge. That, however, had been 33 years before. He had been on standby mode for that long. The times had certainly changed since then.

Dimitiry opened his eyes and blinked several times, trying to get his bearings. He looked down at the little monkey sitting quietly in his lap. He stroked the monkey's head and smiled. "I will tell you a secret, Malinky. I hope I never have to use that package. I'm too old, and the world has changed for the better. Perhaps, the higher-ups have forgotten me, and, in a way, I truly hope they have. Especially for our sake, eh?"

The monkey looked up at him and flashed a quick smile. Dimitiry chuckled. "I am glad my precious Mishka brought you to me. Oh, my! I just remembered that I forgot to tell Mishka about her special surprise."

Dimitiry held out his hand to the little monkey, and she quickly climbed to his shoulder. He stood and carefully placed the boxes back in the chair.

He hurried across the room and started back up the stairs. He had to tell Mishka the great news.

CHAPTER 9: LOOK WHAT I FOUND IN A NUCLEAR WASTE DUMP

Russia

Shayan wiped beads of sweat from his forehead with one hand as he gripped the steering wheel of a small white Toyota pickup truck with the other. It was late at night, and the roads were hard to follow in the darkness. After breaking out of the nuclear depot in a forklift, Shayan had stolen the truck a mile down the road at a local filling station. With the two boxes of tabletkas and the green footlocker in the flatbed area, he raced down the older state-built highway to get across the border to a known Chechen rebel area.

Inside the truck, the cab reeked of spilled alcohol and stale cigarette smoke. In the dimly lit cabin, he found an empty vodka bottle and two packs of cigarettes hidden in the sun visor on the passenger's side. Shayan, being a devote Muslim, immediately grabbed the taboo materials and threw them out the window lest his comrades think he was an apostate.

As he looked into the rearview mirror to watch the bottle smash into a million pieces and the packs of cigarettes bounce end over end to finally stop by the side of the road, he saw the flutter of two blue flashing lights on top of a vehicle.

"You stupid Russian cop, don't you have other people to chase?" he mumbled to himself.

The blue lights increased in brightness as the white and green police car sped closer to Shayan. Shayan could hear the siren blaring as he turned on his signal light to pull over. With no weapon to defend himself, he would be easy prey for the officer to arrest him for stealing the truck or throwing trash onto the highway.

The truck eased to a stop on the side of the road, and the police car pulled in behind him. Shayan watched nervously in the rearview mirror as the police officer got out of the car and approached the truck on the driver's side. Shayan rolled down the window, trying to act casual.

The trooper stopped beside the driver's door and peered in the truck's window. "License and registration papers, please."

"Yes, of course," Shayan answered as he reached into the glovebox and produced a whole handful of paperwork.

The officer stood quietly for a moment as he examined the haphazard collection of registration papers and even a bill from the electric company that was marked past due. Shayan gripped the steering wheel tightly as he stared out the truck's front window, trying to avoid eye contact with the officer.

"This paper says you are 72 years old," the officer noted as he held up one of the papers. He replaced it in the messy stack and held up another. "This electric bill says you live about 215 kilometers from here. Who the hell are you, and who owns this truck? Is it stolen?"

"No, no, no. This is my truck," Shayan told the officer, shaking his head adamantly as he looked at the officer. "My brother who lives far away from here trashed it with forbidden Western vices. I do not partake of such sins. I had to throw them out."

The officer, a local state police recruit just out of training, nodded to Shayan. "I understand your dilemma, but littering is a violation and a ticket must be written."

Shayan threw his hands up in the air in the cab of the truck to make a mock protest but let out a sigh of relief as the officer left to go write the ticket.

As the officer walked to the rear of the truck to get the registration plate's numbers, he noticed the two metal locker boxes and the large green footlocker with English words written in a military fashion on it. The officer paused for a second, realizing that the man, the truck, and its cargo were way beyond a simple traffic violation. He slowly put his ticket book on the truck's tailgate and grabbed his flashlight. He casually shined the light onto the boxes and then looked towards the cab. He could see Shayan staring back at him in the rearview mirror.

Shayan started to sweat profusely and became queasy. He cradled his stomach and leaned forward as a wave of nausea swept over him. He wasn't sure if it was the situation or the beginning stages of radiation poisoning. He didn't care. He just felt really sick to his stomach. He watched the officer through the driver's side mirror of the truck. The officer slowly popped the strap to his service pistol and began to walk towards the driver's side door. Shayan leaned his head against the steering wheel and watched the officer's approach through the side mirror, knowing that his dream of becoming a soldier for the Chechen rebellion was about to end.

Suddenly, with a powerful smack into the officer's bulletproof vest, an armor-piercing sniper round from a Drogunov rifle laid flat the policeman. He died even before he hit the ground. The loud crack off in the distance gave the direction of the shot. It had come from the southwest, the same direction Shayan had been traveling with his deadly cargo. Shayan nervously scanned the area illuminated by his headlights and the darkness beyond from his sheltered position behind the truck's steering wheel. Straining his eyes against the darkness, he made out a tiny dust cloud above the shrubs that lined the highway on the hill ahead.

Shayan smiled and whispered, "Oh, thank you, Allah. His will be done."

Shayan regained his composure, cranked the truck back to life, and proceeded in crossing the unmarked boundary of the Chechens. He waved to the shrubbery as a show of appreciation, but he never saw the hidden sniper who had saved him.

Within a few miles, Shayan approached a makeshift roadblock. Several fully armed rebels with AK-47 rifles and RPGs signaled for Shayan to stop. As he pulled over, he noticed his watch. The time was 22:20 PM.

A tall guard approached the truck as the other two moved into position behind the barricade before the truck.

"We knew you were coming," the tall guard announced as he reached the driver's side window. He stepped towards the truck bed and used his gun to poke at the three metal boxes. "Ah, you brought presents I see."

"These are for your leader," Shayan called to the guard as the guard circled the truck to fully investigate it. "Take me to him. I want to be a part of this great cause."

The guard came around the front of the truck and stood beside the driver's window. He watched Shayan closely. "Yes, brother, yes, but you do not appear well. Are you sick?"

"How long have you all been sheep herders? I was nearly killed by that Russian GRU soldier. He was calling in an airstrike to finish me off!"

The guard busted into roaring laughter at the lies and exaggerations. "Our scout who did you a favor said it was just a foolish territorial state trooper."

"Well, it was dark. Your man could have been wrong," Shayan defended, not wanting to lose face. "At least that Russian scum is dead, praise Allah."

"Yes, praise Allah," the tall guard replied with a laugh as he nodded his head. "I am Ibrahim. I will take to you to the base camp."

With that, Ibrahim waved to the two guards to remove the barricades. He went around the truck and got in the passenger side. He directed Shayan as they drove a short way down a side road into a small clearing sheltered by one of the large craggy hilltops that dotted the landscape.

"What is in the boxes?" asked Ibrahim.

"Something that will make me important."

Ibrahim nodded. "Stop up here."

Shayan parked the truck on the edge of the clearing. He surveyed the surroundings as Ibrahim got out and shouted some instructions to the two men visible in the camp, who disappeared inside a tent. There were a few pickup trucks that have been altered into combat vehicles with heavy machine guns mounted on tripods commonly known as technicals. One of the technicals even had a heavy rocket launcher that could knock out a tank.

The camp had no hard structures like a house or building, only tan-colored 10-man tents. A cache of supplies and weapons could be seen in one of the tents. In the background, Shayan could hear a combat radio. The two men who had gone into a tent came out accompanied by three others. The five men came over and pulled Shayan from the vehicle and frisked him.

"I am here to fight with you men. Why are you looking for hidden weapons?"

"Be quiet, fool," responded one of the men searching him. "You are about to meet Brother Josuf."

Within a few minutes, a bearded figure of average height and weight emerged from the largest tent and approached the group. Chewing on a piece of bread, Josuf sized up the new guest. He stopped eating and stood in silence for a moment before he moved closer.

Josuf wore a *perahan tunban*, a traditional robe worn loosely. The mustard-colored outfit was very comfortable in the extreme heat of the day while adhering to Islamic customs for men. He also wore a dark red Mazari hat, which looked very similar to a flattened red and black fez. Colorful and handmade, the Mazari had made a fashionable comeback due to the protest rallies throughout the region against Russian incursions. Tourists who flocked to that region, however, were discouraged from calling the hat a Mazari. It was to be known as a Pashtun, named after a rebel leader in the area.

The quiet man approached the group slowly. A strange calm came over the group. All the fighters ceased their activities and bowed or held their hands over their hearts in reverence as the quiet man stepped up to Shayan.

"You have brought us gifts, I understand."

"Yes, my sheik," Shayan responded, using the words of a faithful servant to his master.

"No, I am not your sheik. My name is Josuf Federov. I am simply the man that will help your people become free from Russian imperialism. Call me Josuf or Brother, for I am here for you."

With those kind words from Josuf, one of the guards next to Ibrahim shouted in Arabic to praise Allah.

"*Allahu akbar! Allahu akbar! Allahu akbar!*" rose the cries of praise.

Josuf raised his right hand to motion for all to quiet down. He pointed to the sky with his pointer finger to remind his brethren that Allah was watching them. The soldiers knew not to fire their weapons in the air for fear of disclosing their hideout. He then looked deep into Shayan's eyes and assessed he was sick from radiation poisoning.

"You are not well. Come. Come into my tent, and I will give you medicine for your illness." Josuf motioned towards his tent and then looked at the tall guard. "Ibrahim, bring two of your men and yourself and join me for some chai tea."

Ibrahim looked around and picked two rebel fighters to join him. He motioned for the other three to go about their business and then grabbed Shayan's arm and proceeded towards the tent. The men reverently took off their dirty shoes and left their rifles outside.

Inside the tent, Shayan looked around to see a very nice array of pillows, rugs, food, tea, a small table in the middle, and an army radio off to the side. The radio was on a different frequency than the combat radio he had heard outside. It squealed with a different type of sound.

"Sheik, uh, I mean, Brother," Shayan sputtered. "The boxes in the truck are for you. The two heavy lead boxes are pellets of radioactive cobalt-60. I am not a smart man, but, perhaps, you could use them for some dirty bombs against the Russians. The larger box, I have never seen inside before. I think it is some kind of bomb."

Josuf motioned for Shayan and the others to be seated, and some tea glasses were passed around followed by a tea carafe. A small clock on the army radio displayed 22:45.

"My brothers in Allah, enjoy my hospitality," Josuf said as he reached into a medical bag and produced some pills. He handed the pills to Shayan. "Here, take these thyroid tablets. I studied radiology and know that these pills will ease your suffering."

Shayan took the pills and swallowed them with a swig of some chai tea.

Josuf passed a plate of some *khubz*, a kind of local pita bread. "Here, eat some bread. Everyone take a very large piece of this fabulous khubz. It was made fresh earlier today. I know you must be hungry."

Shayan helped himself to a healthy piece of bread, as did the others. Everyone inside the tent was enjoying themselves. It was a time to relax and revel in a little luxury. The plate came around a second time, and the men each took another piece.

In the back of the tent, the strange radio let out a sound like the keying of a microphone by someone on the other end. Then there were two clicks. That was it: just two clicks that sounded very much like when someone had picked up an old rotary phone on the other end and then hung it up. The men looked at each other in puzzlement. Then they simultaneously looked toward Josuf.

"Oh, I forgot to tell you men that I received my radiology education from science universities in Moscow. I am very well paid by Russia to study the effects of radiation on an unknowing population. The GRU thinks of me as a valuable asset in defeating Chechen scum such as yourselves."

The men in the tent were stunned. Their eyes were wide, and their mouths were too full of pita bread to say anything, even as Josuf quickly pulled out a pistol with a suppressor attached from underneath a pillow. They couldn't react, they couldn't cry for help, nor could they shoot with their weapons which were outside the tent. Three rapid shots were fired in silence, and Ibrahim and the two other men fell dead.

Shayan froze in absolute terror. His mouth was full of bread. His forehead was sweating from the radiation poisoning. He dropped his tea glass onto the wooden table before him.

"Don't worry, my friend," Josuf said calmly. "Those pills I gave you were not precious thyroid pills, just baby aspirin. I was right when I said that they would ease your pain and suffering. That part was true. However, I don't think baby aspirin will help you with this new pain."

With that, Josuf pulled the trigger. Shayan could only scream in an agonizing silence as the bread in his mouth muffled the sound.

Once all the men were dead inside the tent, Josuf quickly got up and ran out of the tent shouting to the three other men in camp. "The visitor shot and killed Ibrahim and the others! He's in there! Shoot him! Hurry!"

The three rebels readied themselves and approached the entrance to Josuf's tent. As they entered, they made a gruesome discovery.

"*Dasvidanya, duraki,*" Josuf said in Russian as he fired three shots into the backs of the three foolish men.

Josuf looked around the camp to see if there were any others who were not accounted for. He knew of the sniper who had taken out the police officer earlier, but he was several miles away on foot. It would be some time before he suspected anything had happened. The two guards at the roadblock would be easy enough to take care of later since they knew better than to leave their posts without permission.

Josuf slid the gun in the waist of his pants and entered the tent. The radio at the back of the tent clicked two more times. It was 22:55 when Josuf picked up the transmitter.

"The sheep has had a lamb. The sheep has had a lamb," he said in Russian into the highly encrypted transmitting device.

The satellite transmitter was part of the latest technology in the Russian arsenal of espionage. It was virtually impossible to decode, much less to locate its transmissions. Josuf sent the coded phrase in a millisecond to an awaiting staff on the other end of the transmission.

"This is General Sokolov, Josuf. The missile's reentry is just about to begin. Are you in position? Over."

Josuf picked up the radio and some binoculars and left the tent. He carried them to a clear view of the Chechen city four miles below in a valley. The rocky terrain flanked both sides of his view as he held up the powerful set of binoculars. These heavy spy glasses had been acquired from a well-known ex-East German company that manufactured optical equipment for the Russian armaments ministry.

Josuf spoke into the transmitter. "In position. The city looks like it is asleep. There are a few streetlights on, but that's all. Over."

"Observe. Over."

From high above the city, Josuf watched a bright object in the starry sky above. Brighter than any of the stars, the object appeared to be a meteor descending. It was the Russian Skydancer rocket's payload reentering the atmosphere. Then, at a preregistered altitude just above the city, the bright light exploded. It was neither a large explosion nor sound, almost like a large holiday firework exploding once in the night sky.

Below the explosion, a fine mass of sparkly silver particles rained down upon the quiet city. Like glitter at a party, these fine particulates expanded as they flittered down to Earth. The city's lights flickered off one by one as the city grew darker by the second. The immense power grid began to fail as electric generators throughout the city sputtered to a halt. It was like someone watching helplessly as an unconscious patient slowly died on the surgery table and there was nothing anyone could do to stop it. In just over one minute, the city was dead.

"Detonation good. Dispersal good. Solid hit. Over," Josuf said into the transmitter in awe.

He watched as the glittering dust seemed to dissolve into the darkness of the city. The damage was completely silent and very lethal. He had only recently been informed of the Russian's experiments to develop some sort of dirty bomb. That night marked the first large-scale dispersal of such a weapon. The radioactive dust on each piece of the tinsel chaff was not visible to the naked eye. The glittering effect in the sky was the only telltale evidence that such a weapon had been deployed.

The radioactive material was not instantly lethal to the occupants inside the dark buildings of the city, yet anyone who had ventured out during the dispersal would die within hours. It rendered the entire area uninhabitable. Leukemia, birth defects, and other illnesses associated with radioactive exposure would cause the population to leave en masse. Maybe not immediately, but permanently just the same. The victims had but three choices when targeted by such a silent weapon: remain inside their homes indefinitely, go outside for bread or water if available and risk being contaminated, or leave the city all together.

Russia's decontamination crews had the spores to clean the city, but for a group of people without such technology, it would be a death sentence. Such a weapon would strike fear and chaos throughout the region and someday the world. Since it was not a thermal detonation, other countries could not counterattack using their nuclear forces without world damnations. It was a terrible yet effective weapon that could be used when dealing with future rebellions or even exterminating an entire race.

After a few minutes of observation, Josuf spoke into the transmitter. "Mission complete. Awaiting further instructions. Over."

"Well done, Josuf. Lieutenant General Budnikov is with me, and he would like to talk to you about something. Over." Sokolov nodded as he handed the phone over to Budnikov then walked away.

"Josuf?"

"Yes, General. It has been a while since you trained me back in Moscow. It is good to talk to you again. Over," replied Josuf.

"You see now how my hard training has paid off for you. You are working for General Sokolov now, and that is quite an accomplishment in itself." Budnikov's voice took on an ominous tone. "Josuf, you know that we do not encourage religion, but your faith has been very handy in your past assignments. It allowed you to infiltrate the very group that put you in the position to complete this mission."

Josuf's eyes widened.

"Your training from me—and your faith—have made you the perfect person for a new mission. Are you ready to accept your orders? Over."

"Yes, sir! Over." Josuf responded gleefully.

"Listen to me carefully, Josuf. *The shadows in the corner are not entirely our own*," said Budnikov very distinctly. "Over."

Instantly, Josuf felt somewhat dazed and confused. His eyes blinked hard, and he brought his right hand up to rub his temples. His cheerful attitude in satisfying Sokolov's operational plans quickly changed into an evil determination that overwhelmed him.

"Yes, sir. I understand, sir. Over," Josuf solemnly replied.

Budnikov smiled at the change in Josuf's tone. "You've always been so easy to command, Josuf. I'm glad to have you back on my special team. I will send the details shortly in the usual manner. We have much to accomplish. Over."

"I'm ready, sir. I look forward to receiving the details of my assignment. Over."

Josuf hung up the transmitter. He walked back to the camp and retrieved a Geiger counter from his tent. He went to Shayan's truck and waved it over the cargo. He confirmed his suspicions with the device that the two smaller boxes were highly dangerous due to radioactivity. The larger footlocker, however, showed hardly any activity, which intrigued him even more. Josuf grabbed the large box and pulled it out of the truck bed.

Away from the truck and the two radioactive boxes, Josuf rescanned the footlocker with the Geiger counter. He opened the green container. Inside, he found some very old manuals and a plywood cover. He removed the plywood and discovered an old tripod and a small missile inside.

He opened the instruction manual and began to read. After reading a few pages, Josuf knew he had discovered a weapon that should have been destroyed a long time ago, a weapon that no one dared to use back then or even now. Better yet, it was a weapon that no one even knew still existed.

"You are coming with me. I have the feeling that you will come in very handy."

CHAPTER 10: WHOOPS! DID I DO THAT?

North Carolina

Mishka had been driving for nearly an hour since she'd left her grandfather's house after dropping off Malinky. She was delighting in her drive, especially with the convertible top down. The wind tossed her hair about on her shoulders and neck in a sensual way that she personally enjoyed.

A passing truck driver with a trailer full of sheet rock panels destined for a nearby home supply place noticed Mishka as he approached from behind. The driver maneuvered his truck as to slowly ease up on her right-hand side, a tactic that had paid off for him in the past to get a peek at a pretty woman. It was especially rewarding if her blouse was loose and the wind was flowing through the inside of the car. He hoped that afternoon would be no exception.

Mishka was very much aware of the truck driver's intentions, but she continued her way down the highway. The sun was deliciously warm across her face, and the radio was playing another one her favorite songs. Her right arm reached back behind her head, and she grabbed a full lock of her hair to bring it forward across her chest. After that, she tapped lightly on her brakes to slow her car down.

The truck driver, not realizing that he was being played, didn't notice that she had changed her speed. His truck inched forward ever so slightly as more of his view of the beautiful woman unfolded. She knew exactly what she was doing, and the driver fell for her trap all too easily. It would all be over for the trucker soon, and Mishka knew she had time on her side.

Mishka let her mind wander as the noise from the radio and wind drowned out the world around her. Her thoughts drifted to back to when she was 15 years old and attending an advanced boarding school for gifted students in the sciences. It was then that she had received her sky-blue

52

neckerchief and white hairbow in the Young Pioneers. A scene from those days flashed in her mind as if it were happening.

"All right, Mishka, everyone here thinks you're so smart, but I know you are not as smart as me. Give me that neckerchief!" her aggressive classmate Aella Sturmovicha orders as she reaches for the metal slide holding the blue neckerchief around Mishka's slender neck together.

"No, I earned this! This was my reward, not yours!" Mishka retorts as she grabs one of Aella's arms.

The two girls struggle in the school hallway. They clash, their bodies hitting hard against the hallway lockers and causing almost cymbal-like eruptions of sound. The noises of the fight draw the attention of other classmates who come out of their classrooms to watch.

Aella manages to grab the back of Mishka's hair and starts to pull hard on her ponytail. Mishka is losing the fight, and she knows it. As the girls continue to struggle, Aella manages to rip the large white bow from the two firmly emplaced hair barrettes. A few of the onlookers start to chant for Aella.

Mishka, realizing she is fighting on Aella's terms, changes her tactics. She stares at Aella intently until Aella notices the stare. Once Aella is looking at her, Mishka quickly shifts her gaze over Aella's shoulder and makes a large gasp as if they have been caught by a professor.

Instinctively, Aella turns her head to see which professor has caught them in the fight. The moment Aella's attention is focused on the phantom professor, Mishka strikes as fast and as hard as a viper. She quickly stomps on Aella's right foot with her heel. As the pain receptors in Aella's foot start screaming signals to her brain, Aella lets go of Mishka's hair.

Immediately, Mishka makes her second and final blow. She grabs Aella behind her head and throws Aella's off-balance body into the nearby lockers. Aella's head smacks against the metal locker, causing her to pass out. Her body falls to the floor like a heavy sack of flour. Suddenly, the chants stop and silence falls over all the students in the hallway.

Mishka reaches down and picks up her hairbow and does the best she can to reattach it with one barrette for the time being. She readjusts her neckerchief and pulls back a loose strand of hair that is in her eyes. Her composure regained and knowing she has once again earned her reward, she looks around and gazes into the eyes of the other students. Each student, in turn, slowly walks away in silence.

A quick smile flashed on Mishka's face. No one in school ever challenged her again after that fight. It was very gratifying, even all those years later.

The trucker got closer and closer with his semi. Mishka savored the moment as she sensed his careless resolve in trying to get a better look at the pretty lady. She let a faint smirk develop on her lips as she watched her dangerous game play out. Mishka, being on the left side of the road, allowed the trucker to advance enough for him to focus on her and her blouse. Sadly, the trucker, too busy looking at Mishka and her beautiful skin, didn't notice the slowing traffic ahead. Traffic was down to a crawl on the right-hand side.

The trucker glanced ahead and finally noticed the quickly approaching standstill. The spell Mishka had on her victim broke. The truck's brakes screeched as the driver desperately tried to avoid hitting the rear end of the closest car in front of him and cussed loudly about his predicament. The weight of the trailer full of heavy cargo ruled the encounter. As the truck driver slammed on his brakes, the trailer's kinetic energy slid the rear end forward and to the side, causing what was known to highway patrol officers as a "jackknife."

The next sound Mishka heard was that of multiple impacts as the trucker's vehicle smashed into several cars. Her car was never involved as she continued along the left-hand side and past the standstill on the right side of the road.

"*Durachit,*" she said in Russian. "Fool!"

Mishka then pulled out her red lipstick and applied a fresh application to her lips as she gazed into her rearview mirror and smiled.

Her cellphone began to ring inside her purse. Mishka put down her lipstick and reached into her bag. Retrieving the cellphone, she pressed the button to accept the call.

"Ah, Poppi," she said as the phone call connected, her voice warm with affection.

"My darling Mishka, I forgot to give you my surprise when you were here. I love my little Malinky, but my news is very important to give to you in person."

"Not over the phone?"

"No, darling, listen to me. Today the blue sky is filled with pretty birds who sing and play." Dimitiry used a special coded phrase that many in the service of the Russian spy agencies knew meant only one thing: other people were listening to their conversation.

"I'm sorry. I am due at work really soon, Poppi. I'm actually on-call all day tomorrow, too. Can I come over and see you day after tomorrow just after lunch?"

"That would be fine."

"Great! I will see you in a couple days. Love you!"

"Until then. I love you, too."

Mishka hung up her cellphone and then retrieved a red scrunchy hair band from the handle of the hairbrush in her purse. Methodically, she pulled her hair back despite the breeze from the top being down on the car. With her hair in a ponytail, it reminded her of when she had been filled with the mission and determination of a Young Pioneer.

It wasn't long before she pulled into the employee parking lot at Saint Gabriel Hospital. The earlier shift was beginning to leave the building and go home. She had five minutes to spare to get inside and clock herself in. She parked the car and headed inside.

She enjoyed her undercover work as a radiologist. It was very rewarding. She had even participated in several advanced discoveries with the hospital staff. One of those discoveries had included using a radioactive medical probe to pass through a patient's tumor, which had eliminated the persistent tumor within a day. With that breakthrough, the patient, who had recovered quicker than scheduled, had thanked Mishka for her help. It had indeed been a very proud moment for Mishka, which she reflected on while she put her time card into the wall clock. Sadly, the digital readout on the card read 17:01 PM.

"Damn. This stupid clock hates me," she muttered under her breath. Mishka prided herself on being reliable and punctual, but she was always seconds away from being on time for work.

Mishka looked up to see if anyone had noticed, and, to her disappointment, she saw that a shift supervisor was watching her with a heavy scowl on his face. A similar scowl from years before flashed in her mind. It had been a look that had instilled terror in a young 19-year-old FSB recruit who had to go through GRU training as part of her specialized FSB training. That fear-inducing scowl had belonged to her old instructor, Budnikov, the same instructor who, years earlier during the days of the Soviet Union, had trained Dimitiry Federov.

CHAPTER 11: WHAT DID THE PETRI DISH SAY?

Northwest Russia, Nyonoska Military Weapons Testing Range

Sokolov smiled as he watched Budnikov put down the telephone he had used to communicate with Josuf. After having watched the weapon's launch and entry into space from the concrete bunker, Sokolov and Budnikov had quickly gone to the launch pad facility to follow the weapon's progress on the computer monitors there, leaving the five nuclear scientists in the cold, damp concrete room to wait nervously to hear of the weapon's success or failure.

Sokolov turned to study a large video screen that was playing a computer animation of the rocket's reentry. Pleased in what he saw, he ordered to be connected to speak to President Pelevin on the secure line to make his report on Operation Beluga.

Budnikov walked to a table in the corner of the room and sat down. He slowly ran a finger around the rim of an empty tea cup that sat on the table as he watched the general's men scurry around the room.

Sokolov watched as the animation of the rocket's reentry played again on the computer screen and whispered to himself, "Each city we conquer and acquire will be just like collecting delicious caviar from a Beluga sturgeon."

"President Pelevin's office, sir," said one of Sokolov's lieutenants as he handed the phone to his commander. "He's on the line."

Sokolov turned his back to the rest of the room as he placed the phone to his ear. The officers in the room made every effort to avoid looking at the general. They knew enough not to make the appearance of listening too closely to what was being said, but they could not help but hear the general's side of the conversation in the crowded room.

"*Da*, the mission was a success, sir." Sokolov's booming voice filled the room. "We have targeted two more cities to attack once we have analyzed the data on this first target.... Yes.... Thank you, sir. Thank you. It is a great honor to serve you."

Sokolov finished his conversation and hung up the telephone. He quietly pulled out a handkerchief from his green military coat pocket. Secretly, before any of his subordinates could notice, he wiped away a tear of joy that he had actually spoken to President Pelevin personally. He regained his composure quickly and stuffed the handkerchief back in his pocket. From the corner of his eye, he saw Budnikov sitting silently at the table watching him, still running his finger around the rim of the empty tea cup.

"Where is our tea?" Sokolov yelled, whirling around to face the crowded room.

Quickly, the men around him tried to look busy. A junior officer near the general caught the brunt of his wrath.

"Get us some tea or you will be next on the assignment list to work in the Siberian research facility of waste management!"

CHAPTER 12: MICHAEL, MEET MICHAEL

North Carolina

In the apartment overlooking the park, Michael yawned as he inserted another pod into the coffee maker to make himself a third cup of coffee. It had been another long, restless night haunted by fragments of that same recurring nightmare. He pulled a slightly stale doughnut from the box and took a large bite as the coffee brewed. He couldn't help but smile knowing that Debbie would definitely disapprove of his breakfast.

At the small dinette table, Elizabeth took a sip of her hot chocolate. She was still sleepy but remained focused on the laptop in front of her as it began to warm up. She laughed to herself that as the laptop was warming up, so was she. When everything was ready, she began her research on jihadist weapons and possible nuclear ambitions in the jihadist regimes throughout the world that Steve had requested the night before.

Steve was using his powerful binoculars through the open blinds of the window. His assignment for the CIA was observing the target, and they knew the target's primary location was on the park bench directly across from their apartment window. He wasn't there yet, but Steve didn't want to miss any possible action when the old man arrived.

The old man's file that lay on the end table next to Steve had somewhat valuable information about his past. Two photographs were attached to the manila envelope. One was a copy of a passport photo used when the old man had entered the United States. The other photo was a current one taken by an agent who had been observing the old man prior to Steve's arrival as he had deliberately passed by the old man one day in the park. The camera had been hidden in a soccer ball that the agent had carried.

Michael walked over to end table and picked up the file. As he drank his coffee, he scanned the information one more time to be sure that he hadn't missed anything the day before. "So, Dimitiry Federov was formerly in the Russian military intelligence agency known as the GRU and was earlier recruited as a KGB agent in internal espionage. The file also says he has extensive knowledge of nuclear physics from the 80s and is possibly around 75 to 78 years of age. Due to his age and physical condition, he is on a low to medium profile observation level."

"He probably got fired from the KGB a long time ago for doing a lousy job keeping the Chechen rebels at bay," Steve remarked as he looked over at Michael and Elizabeth. "You guys remember the hostages being slaughtered by the rebels at the Moscow Ballet tragedy? That was this guy's fault for not following through on rumors about some radical religious zealots for the Freedom of the Muslim Brotherhood in Chechnya."

"Didn't the Russian president Pelevin get his start in the KGB?" Elizabeth asked.

"Yes." Steve smiled. He was always amused at how Elizabeth's mind could leap from one idea to another. It's what made her a good researcher.

Elizabeth took another sip of hot chocolate. "Was he really in that photo with a small boy shaking President Reagan's hand in Moscow's Red Square?"

"Yeah," Steve replied, "it was in 1988. He was a junior officer in the KGB. He used a small boy to act as his son to get close to the president. In that famous picture, you see Pelevin with his thumb clenched by his fingers. That was a secret sign that he was a spook."

"A spook?" asked Elizabeth incredulously and raised her eyebrows.

"It's the truth. Go online and look it up," Steve said emphatically as Elizabeth rolled her eyes and Michael laughed. "Go ahead, Elizabeth! Type in Pelevin and Reagan. You'll see it in the picture."

Steve walked over to the table and stood behind Elizabeth as she began to search for the photo online. Michael followed him over to see the infamous photo, too, drinking the last sip of his coffee. He set the empty mug on the table beside Elizabeth's computer.

"There! See!" Steve pointed to the part of the image on the screen that he was talking about. "He was giving the sign that he was a spook secretly, yet he portrayed openly that he was the boy's father."

"Wait. What?" Michael leaned forward to look at the screen more closely. He straightened and shook his head. "That's crap, Steve."

"No, I'm serious." Steve's face was stern. "The KGB used that covert tactic. The hiding of the thumb into one's hand means you are being watched or tortured or you are behaving as someone else. It is now internationally known by most intelligence agencies throughout the world. Pelevin was doing this secretly so he could legally get close to Reagan and bypass the Secret Service protecting the president."

"Why, though?" asked Elizabeth.

Steve walked back over to the binoculars at the window and looked through them. "I guess back then it was to see if the KGB could get really close to a high-profile leader."

"So, what about Pelevin's son in that picture? Where is he now?" asked Michael sarcastically.

"Pelevin only has two daughters: Annika and Galina," Steve said curtly without even looking up from the binoculars.

Steve's cold and quick response shocked Elizabeth and Michael into silence. The mood in the room was icy and subdued. The silence was very awkward and painful, so Michael had to break the ice by changing the subject.

"So, little brother, Elizabeth and I were wondering if you've found a girlfriend yet?"

Steve straightened from looking through the binoculars. He rubbed the bridge of his nose to ease the eye strain he had created by peering through binoculars too long.

"So, you've been in the CIA for a while. Are you allowed to date people?" asked Elizabeth. "Have you met anybody? Anybody cute?"

"Well...," replied Steve as he blushed slightly.

"Anybody that you can introduce to Mom?" added Michael.

"Yeah, I met someone. Well, at least I think I met someone." Steve walked over to the large couch and sat down. "While I was in Washington, I wasn't allowed to go to bars or any social activities. All because the agency had that major screw-up with one of our agents. The guy was caught dating a Chinese spy."

"Yeah, that may be cause for concern," Michael said, chuckling. He walked to the dinette table and grabbed his empty mug before going to the kitchen to make another cup of coffee.

"So," Steve said, ignoring Michael's comment, "I stayed in my apartment for most of the time after work. A buddy of mine told me about this dating site. He said it was awesome, and he was right. They pair you up with people who have similar interests. You know, just like all the other dating websites. I was matched with four women in the United States."

"Dude, no. Really?" asked Elizabeth incredulously.

"Yeah, it wasn't that I wrote down that 'I like long walks on the beach' crap. I just typed into the app that I loved to fly drones with cameras as a hobby."

"Wait," Michael interrupted as he started the machine to make another cup of coffee, "you actually met someone?"

"Well, I made friends with four women. I video-chatted with all of them. Susan is in New York. Clara lives in South Dakota. Hope is out in L.A., and Micah lives here in this part of North Carolina. Susan, Clara, and Hope were really nice, but I really hit it off with Micah. Then, when Tom MacAday needed me to work this assignment, I immediately thought it was fate to be with Micah."

"And Micah's last name is…?" asked Elizabeth.

"Redberry."

Elizabeth began typing into her laptop looking for a "Micah Redberry." She clicked her mouse several times. Each click produced a huff from Elizabeth in silent protest.

"Don't bother looking her up," Steve said.

"She uses a fake name?" asked Michael as he picked up and refilled his coffee cup.

"Yeah, we all do," answered Steve.

"So, what's your fake name?" asked Elizabeth as she was watching Michael take a sip of his coffee.

"Michael Cotter."

Michael spit out his coffee onto the floor below in shock. He coughed and sputtered as he wiped his mouth and Elizabeth howled with laughter. After he regained his composure, he threw a kitchen towel to the floor to clean up the mess. He turned to Steve.

"What the hell! What if Debbie found out about this? You know she'll kill you for this."

"I'm not proud of it," Steve said, coming over to help with the cleanup, "but I had never done anything like this before."

"Have you met her in person? Do you even know what she does for a living?" Michael tossed the soiled towel onto the counter. He looked at Steve sternly. "What if she looks me up online and finds me instead of the real you?"

"I haven't met her in person, but I've talked to her a lot online, so you're safe from the possibility of her mistaking you for me. She works for a local hospital. She does research for them, I think. Plus, she drives a really cute sports convertible. She texted me a picture of the car." Steve flashed a smile at his brother and pulled out his cell phone. He quickly pulled up a picture on the phone's screen and held the phone out to show Michael. "Here, look. That's the front of her car, and here is the back."

Michael looked at the car for a moment and then leaned back against the kitchen counter and crossed his arms in front of his chest. "Nice car. But what does she look like? She can't be all that if you're just showing me a picture of her car."

A big smile spread across Steve's face. "Actually, she is strikingly gorgeous. She has long dark hair and gorgeous brown skin and big, beautiful eyes. Impeccably dressed. I think she's from the Balkans, but her features tend to be on the Middle Eastern side. Want to see her?"

"I do!" Elizabeth jumped up and ran over and snatched the phone from Steve's extended hand as he held the phone towards Michael. She looked down at the screen. "Oh! She is pretty! Does she really look like this?"

Michael stretched his neck to see as he tried to wrestle the phone from Elizabeth's grasp.

"Yes, she does," Steve said proudly. "We've had a few video chats, and that's really what she looks like."

Elizabeth finally relinquished the phone to Michael and patted Steve on the back. "You did good!"

As Elizabeth made her way back to her computer, Michael looked down at the photo of the beautiful woman on his brother's phone. He stared at it for a moment and then glanced up at his brother. Steve looked sincerely happy, and Michael realized for the first time that his brother was no longer the little kid that he always thought of him as, but a full-grown man. He smiled with pride and glanced down at the image of the woman on the phone once more before handing the phone back to Steve.

"She's very pretty, Steve," Michael admitted. "I'm happy for you. So, how serious is this?"

"Well, we haven't actually met yet. Like I said earlier, just messaging a lot and a few video chats. But, maybe…." Steve put the phone in his pocket. A sheepish grin gave away his embarrassment, and he quickly changed the subject. "She really is into my hobby. I can't believe a beautiful woman like Micah is into drones. Michael, she even asked me how we built our drone when we were over in England."

"Does she know you're in town?" asked Elizabeth.

"Yep," Steve replied. "Unfortunately, I had to make up a story about some movie director needing some drone footage for a movie using the North Carolina mountains near Ashville. I'm hoping I can tell her the truth about all this once we meet. I want to."

Michael nodded his head in understanding. "So, when are you going to see her?"

"Well, it's complicated."

"She's not married, is she?" asked Michael, his eyes widening.

Steve shook his head adamantly and waved his hands in front of him. "No, nothing like that."

"She was once a man?" Elizabeth asked, stifling a laugh.

"No, stop it! I guess I'm nervous," Steve said sheepishly. "This will be my first time meeting her."

"I'd be nervous, too. Maybe she's a spy, and she's stealing research project secrets from the hospital via her brown bag lunches," Michael teased his little brother, trying to lighten the mood.

"Guys, seriously. Stop it. It was easy doing video chats with Micah while I was in Washington. Now I'm near her, and it will be exciting to meet her in person. But it's a big step, and I'm just a bit nervous about it. I really like this girl, and I hope that she'll be okay with everything after she finds out who I really am."

"If she really likes you, she will be," Michael reassured his brother. "Just be careful.... We can't have you bringing a spy to our Thanksgiving dinner this year."

The three let out a chuckle, and Michael walked over to Steve and patted him on the shoulder. Elizabeth followed suit and came over as well. Steve had always borne the brunt of so many pranks and teases, and he wore them like badges of honor. The three formed a circle of hugs.

"You know, Mom should be here for this family hug," Steve said.

"Yep, and if Dad were alive, he would probably tell us to...."

"Get back to work," they said in unison.

Steve went back to his binoculars for more surveillance. Elizabeth went back to her laptop. She printed out the information she had already found on commonly used jihadist weapons and jihadist nuclear ambitions. Michael walked over to the printer and picked up the printouts of Elizabeth's discoveries. He read over the pages as he walked back to the couch and sat down.

After several minutes of reading, Michael laid the pages on his lap. "Guys, I just thought of something. I don't know if it connects to all this, but it may. Elizabeth, find everything you can on cobalt-60."

Elizabeth adeptly searched the Internet and came up with multiple sources on the topic within a few minutes. She printed them out for Michael, and he began to quickly read through them as she scanned the information on the computer.

After a few minutes, Michael nodded his head and slapped the papers on his hand, drawing everyone's attention. "When I was reading through the information Elizabeth found, something in my mind made me think about cobalt-60. It was used in all medical imaging devices for a long time, but it is now a thing of the past thanks to Deep Sonic imaging. Deep Sonic is that advanced ultrasound technology that is now used to examine teeth, bones, skulls, you name it."

"Medical cobalt-60 is radioactive, yes," Elizabeth said, "but only when a tiny electrical charge is applied. To use it as a weapon, it would have to be involved in a fissionable environment."

"Tiny electrical charge? Like how tiny?" asked Steve.

"We all have atoms in our bodies," Elizabeth explained. "All of the things around us have atoms. Like this coffee mug that had my hot chocolate in it. It has atoms, as well. Every atom has an equal number of protons—that's the positive energy—and electrons—well, that's the negative energy. Last, but not the least, we have neutrons; they are neither, just neutral."

Steve nodded in understanding.

Elizabeth continued. "An electric current, even static electricity, is when there is an imbalance of protons, electron, and neutrons. These particles race at lightning speed to rebalance themselves. That's the spark, or shock, you get. That's how tiny."

"So, every time I shocked Michael at home during Christmas, it was because of an imbalance of protons and electrons?"

"Exactly. But don't forget the neutrons. The neutrons are very important!" chided Elizabeth with a smile.

Michael shook his head and rolled his eyes. "Seriously, we may need to consider this. This cobalt stuff is everywhere, and there isn't some sort of standardized disposal process worldwide. If this stuff fell into the wrong hands—hands that knew how use it—there could be a whole lot of bad guys making dirty bombs."

There was an intolerable moment of silence between the three. It was so much so that when the coffee pod machine's hissing sound as it reheated its reserve water in the tank broke the silence, everyone laughed.

CHAPTER 13: THE ORGAN GRINDER
WHO PLAYS THE ACCORDION

Dimitiry gathered his jacket, his mini accordion, and an old fez hat. "Come, Malinky, let's go to the park nearby. I want to show you off."

Malinky climbed up onto his shoulders and then they headed to the park. Sadly, when they reached the stairs that led to the park, Dimitiry noticed his favorite bench in the center of the park was occupied by a couple. He continued down the concrete stairs from his townhouse to the grassy park below and approached the couple.

"Hello, young couple. My friend Malinky and I want to play you a song," Dimitiry said as he began to pull and squeeze on the accordion, causing it to come to life with a squeaky tune.

"No, that's okay. We're not interested," answered the young man as he wrapped his arm around the young woman next to him. He suspected the older man was looking for a free handout.

The young woman looked at the young man nervously as Dimitiry continued to play. The couple stood up and proceeded to another bench.

Dimitiry tipped his fez hat to the couple as they passed by him. He stopped his accordion and placed it on the bench. Malinky jumped off his shoulder and wandered around a short distance. The little monkey moved close to an outdoor trash bin.

"Hey! Get away from there, little lady. There might be a stinging wasp or something that might get you," Dimitiry warned.

Malinky acknowledged with a quick chirp. The small monkey hurried back then climbed up onto Dimitiry's shoulder, only to steal the old man's fez hat and jump off again. With the hat in her little furry hand, Malinky hopped along the bench.

"Hey! My hat, you little thief!" Dimitiry protested, reaching for his hat.

The little monkey managed to stay just out of reach as it scampered back and forth along the bench. Dimitiry finally gave up protesting about his hat being stolen. He reached into a side pocket and pulled out his stomach medicine. His queasiness seemed to be much stronger than it ever had been before. He hoped it could be the excitement and drama of his new little friend, but deep down inside, he knew that it was the extended duty of overseeing a nuclear device and the constant maintenance it required.

The only thing that made him feel better was a bottle of the over-the-counter pink bismuth liquid. The current bottle he had was cherry flavored and had a small red cap on top used for taking measured doses. Dimitiry pulled the cap off and held it out towards Malinky. The small monkey came over and took the cap from her owner's hand in one hand and placed it on her head like a miniature version of the red fez hat in her other hand.

Smiling in approval, Dimitiry then picked up his accordion with his hands on either side and began to pump the organ outwards and then inwards. Soon music began to flow as Dimitiry played an old Russian melody known as *Kalinka,* perfectly created for any accordion player. The tune was spunky and lively and started to draw the attention of passersby in the park.

As if on cue, Malinky, with her faux red fez on, walked around with Dimitiry's hat upside down as if she were asking for a handout. Indeed, many people tossed in a coin or two for the cute little musical duo.

After a few quick tunes, Malinky put the hat down in front of Dimitiry's feet. The monkey changed her tactics, and she looked for anyone close by to say hello.

A local woman passed by the bench and tossed in a coin. "Who is your little friend?"

Dimitiry stopped playing his accordion as a gesture of politeness and softly answered her question. "This is Malinky."

Malinky walked over to the lady. She was wearing a dress, and the little monkey gave a small tug at her skirt. When she looked down, Malinky gave a large smile and held up her little hands like a baby asking to be picked up by her mommy. Complying, the lady picked up Malinky and held her on her hip. The monkey then proceeded to hug the lady.

"Oh, my goodness! You are an affectionate little one, aren't you?" The woman smiled and hugged the monkey closer to her, leaning her head down as she did so.

Unbeknownst to her, Malinky gently stole her gold earrings by wrapping her hands around the earrings when the woman leaned down and pulling gently on the loops that passed through her lobes. The furry little thief then put the earrings into her vest pocket and jumped to the ground. Malinky tipped her red plastic "fez" to the lady and made two chirps that sounded like "Thank you."

Dimitiry looked on in shock at the smoothness of his new friend's skill as the monkey made off with the loot. He quickly started to play *Katyusha* on the accordion. It was the perfect song since it was about a girl saying farewell and to remember her. He then smiled while he looked up at the sky as if he had not seen anything happen.

The kind lady smiled and proceeded on her way, and Dimitiry continued to play the accordion until she was far enough away. He paused his playing to scold his accomplice. "I saw what you did, my little thief."

Malinky made a laughing sound that was very uncanny to Dimitiry. Within minutes, the furry little thief found new victims to steal from. Everyone who passed by the old man and his accordion was visited by Malinky. By the end of the afternoon, Dimitiry had several dollars' worth of coins in his hat, and his little friend showed off two pairs of gold earrings, a shiny broach, and an old watch.

"Hey, you! That's my watch!" Dimitiry said.

CHAPTER 14: WHEN ONE FLIES
TOO CLOSE TO THE SUN

Russia

A nuclear, biological, and chemical team, or NBC team, of three scientists in rubberized green suits was sent on a Russian-built M-24 Hind helicopter into the area that had been hit during the Beluga mission. They were accompanied by a small detachment of seven soldiers in similar suits commanded by a ruthless *Desantniki* officer named Captain Pavel "Nezdorova" Morozov. Nezdorova, which meant "unhealthy," had been trained to fight in the same style and tactics of guerilla warfare as his brother who had fought against the rebels in Afghanistan. Nezdorova's brother used to tell him of the horrors when fighting the Mujahedeen colloquially called the *Dushmans*. The name was Persian for "the enemy." The Dushmans were ruthlessly brutal to the Soviet soldiers. The nickname slowly changed into *Dushki*, meaning "phantoms" or "spirits that vanish."

Nezdorova's security force of *Afgansty* soldiers were well trained to fight the Mujahedeen forces in the mountains of Chechnya. The training for such an elite unit had been improved since the days of horrific fighting in Afghanistan back in the late 1980s. Tough and elite, the team's mission was to function as a security detail. The scientists' mission was to take measurements of the radioactive chaff.

The very large, heavily armed helicopter looked exactly like a large flying insect. Similar to a massive tan and green painted dragonfly, it had two connected bulbous cockpits that resembled large bug-like eyes that were placed front to back instead of side by side. It was crewed by two army pilots who were ordered to make a landing on the outskirts of the town.

Within a few feet of the nearest structure, the pilot eased the large beast of a machine in for the landing. A veteran of two wars in Chechnya, the pilot knew not to land out in the open for fear of being too exposed to anti-aircraft fire. Also, the advantage of being close to the ground and below the buildings made it difficult for anti-aircraft rockets to lock on due to the proximity of the ground. The combat team, once dismounted, focused their weapons on any window or door of the buildings close by.

The Geiger counters used by the NBC team showed a radioactive environment was indeed there, but to their surprise, the Geiger counters exploded with activity when the helicopter's wash from the rotors blew the invisible tinsel chaff aflutter like glitter inside a snow globe. They concluded that when the wind blew, it caused the flakes to create a static charge which in turn powered the radioactive cobalt to react. Even the large helicopter had difficulty with its electronics as the chaff began to interfere with the motors on the machine.

Some of the town's people started to stir and come out of their homes. Many appeared to look very ill. Two people were seen vomiting in the streets from radiation poisoning.

The NBC team waved Geiger counters over each citizen and recorded their findings. They also were able to track radioactive trails on the ground that led off from the city towards the rocky cliff nearby. By the footprints revealed, there seemed to have been a sizable exodus of about twenty people.

"What happened to us?" asked a Chechen in Russian as he grabbed the nearest security team member by his green rubber suit.

The heartless Nezdorova shrugged off the older man and made a motion with his hand for the security team to follow the trail found by the scientists. It was very easy to follow and lead straight to a cave in the cliff nearby. Sensing a trap or even an ambush, the security team split into two groups. They used their training in stealth tactics to good effect as they approached from opposite ends of the cave entrance. There they found military equipment and rifles just inside the cave entrance.

Nezdorova looked around and noticed a very large boulder above the cave entrance. This natural outcropping hid the cave's entrance from the air. The officer also noticed something to his utter satisfaction: there was a series of three smaller rocks holding back the massive boulder from rolling down.

"You two, place a grenade next to each of those smaller rocks and secure them so that they are underneath the larger rock." Nezdorova looked at the man next to him and motioned towards the entrance. "Sergeant, I need you to rig the grenades with some of our DET cord we use for breaching holes in concrete. Wrap each grenade one or two times and then move on to the next one. We will detonate in five minutes. Move! We can't go in there, but we can entomb the Dushki there forever."

In a matter of minutes, the team had set up the demolition charges and signaled they were ready. The ruthless Russian commander pressed the firing button on the detonator and watched as his plan worked perfectly. Like clockwork, the three grenades shattered the smaller rocks. Then, without the support of the smaller rocks, the large boulder rolled slowly forward and fell into the gaping hole of the cave. Whoever the 20 or so individuals who had fled to the cave were, they would never be recovered.

The cruel captain stood up and surveyed that their operation was a success. He made a circular motion with one arm to get everyone's attention and then motioned for the detail to head back and load into the helicopter.

Within a few minutes, they had reached the awaiting M-24 hind and boarded. The great machine increased its rotors to achieve lift off. The helicopter soared high into the air and headed towards the mountain ridge that served as a border to Russia.

"Watch this! I've wanted to do this for a long time." Lt. Cmdr. Anatoli Kazmerov, the Russian helicopter pilot, chuckled into his mask attached to his helmet.

The pilot fired off a very long string of heat flares to discourage any Chechen rebel from launching a dreaded heat-seeking missile at their gunship. One after another made a *chink* and *whoosh* sound as each of the flare's tiny rocket engines ignited and launched from the tubes underneath the helicopter. Ten rocket flares to each side of the gunship fired off in succession. The pilot continued to pull the flare trigger on his yoke controller but finally stopped when he realized he had shot them all.

The massive helicopter soared into the night sky like a large yet graceful seagull headed towards the mountains. Once across the ridges, Kazmerov knew they would be safe and soon be home enjoying another day of rest and relaxation.

"Did you have to shoot off every defensive flare we had?" the co-pilot, who was sitting in the front of the tandem cockpit, asked laughingly.

"*Da*, my *Babushka*. The rebels, perhaps, they want to see a firework show before they all die." He laughed into his pilot's neoprene mask.

Nezdorova and his men were inside the cargo area of the great helicopter with the scientists. He pulled off his rubberized gas mask to finish keying in the data that his team had collected. He knew the cargo area was pressurized and that everyone could breathe a little easier. He then sent the collected information via a hyperlink transmission to Sokolov's headquarters. He, too, would be glad to be out of his rubber suit and enjoying some alone time with his new wife.

The pilots were glad to be leaving the dead city. Although they could not see it, they knew that whatever had radiated the city had wreaked havoc on the gunship. The rotor blades created a heavy static charge as the blades churned through the night air. A hazy red and blue plasma charge formed around the forward windows on the pilot's cockpit. Ghostly and ethereal in nature, the plasma danced along the metallic frame around the bulletproof glass. This phenomenon was referred to as "Lenin's Ghost" by Russian aviators. It was an unwelcomed sight, for it was the byproduct of too much static electricity.

Three red master alarms suddenly flashed on the pilot's control panel. The red lights blinked in a continued matter, indicating a major malfunction in the engines. A very loud klaxon sounded in the cargo area that alerted the soldiers and scientists that the helicopter was in trouble.

The pilot tried desperately to get the nineteen-thousand-pound helicopter to climb a bit higher to clear the ridge before them. That same beautiful ridge that was a boundary between life and death of the two countries became their greatest enemy as the heavy M-24 helicopter struggled with its two engines failing.

"Kazmerov, get higher! Get higher! We're not going to make it!" screamed the co-pilot into the intercom.

The front part of the massive gunship cleared the ridge, but the massive wheel carriage below caught the rocky peak, rocking the copter forward. The rubber wheels rolled along the mountain rocks and then became free as the helicopter rounded the top.

Like a cheap roller coaster ride at the local fair, the soldiers and scientists inside the cargo area were tossed about as they peered out the windows on each side of the ship.

One of the soldiers crossed himself in the backwards fashion of the Eastern Orthodox Church.

"Stop being such a baby, Vitali," barked Nezdorova. "The pilots know what they're doing!"

In the cockpit, both pilots let out a sigh of relief as they cleared the ridgeline. It also seemed that whatever had been affecting the copter in the radiation zone was clearing, allowing the motor to operate again at full capacity. The caution lights stopped flashing, and the loud horn in the cargo area ceased its alert. The helicopter finally trimmed itself correctly, and the pilots began the process of descending down the mountain slope.

Nezdorova glared at the young man who had crossed himself. "You see, Vitali. They have this under control."

Vitali, a Russian rifleman from a modest family in Volgograd, smiled at everyone that he was okay and no longer scared of crashing into the mountainside. He quietly turned around to look out of the small window behind his seat.

Through the round-shaped bulletproof glass window, Vitali saw a family of mountain goats moving along some ancient path near the peak. He was amazed at their grace and skill at such a high altitude. Vitali even let out a small giddy chuckle to himself that he had been so scared earlier.

Suddenly, he saw a rebel Chechen fighter shouldering an anti-aircraft Stinger missile launcher pop up from behind the rocks near the mountain goats. Stunned by what he saw, he spun around to scream that an enemy that was about to shoot them. "Enemy in the rocks! He's got us in his sight!"

The other soldiers knew that Private Vitali was new and very jittery, and they brushed off his screams of alarm as to seeing bad guys in the rocks.

The rebel waited long enough for the acquisition sensor on the missile launcher to focus on the target. When the dial tone squealed, he pulled the trigger and launched the heat-seeking missile towards the Russian helicopter.

A new set of alarms went off in the cockpit as the pilots were just getting the helicopter back under control. One single alarm informed them that they were being targeted, and another alarm indicated a missile launch towards them.

"Kazmerov, we have a missile locked on us!" cried the co-pilot.

"I know! I know! Trying to evade!" the pilot screamed back as he hopelessly clicked repeatedly on the chaff dispenser button on his control yoke to shoot out defensive flares, the very same flares he had wasted over the dead city as they left. All he needed was just one superhot flare to draw off that missile's sensor from the heat signature of their helicopter, but they were all gone.

Again, the alarms filled the cockpit with flashing lights and whining noises of annunciators.

"You stupid shit, you got us all killed because of your idea of fireworks for the people!" cried the co-pilot through the intercom.

"Control, tell my mother I died a hero!" the pilot cried in his last radio transmission.

The missile went straight for the huge heat blooms coming out of the exhaust ports of the helicopter's two engines. It exploded with lethal effect and destroyed the M-24 Hind helicopter completely in a billowing cloud of flame and debris. The flaming hulk came crashing down on top of the mountain. There were no survivors.

CHAPTER 15: FALSE MEDALS

Moscow, Russia

General Sokolov sat behind the cold metal desk in the spare office he had taken over at the Ministry of Defense. He and General Budnikov had left the testing range shortly after his phone call with President Pelevin. Budnikov had returned to the training facility he worked at in Moscow, and Sokolov had received a special order from Pelevin to come to the Ministry of Defense to await the results from the Beluga mission and his future assignments.

Sokolov knew that his opportunity had finally come to make a real name for himself. He drummed his fingers impatiently on the desk as he waited for the files that held the key to his future. His thoughts were interrupted by a soft knock on the door.

"Yes?" he called out, his voice full of frustration.

The general's aide peeked inside the door. "Here are the important files you had requested, General."

"Bring them here at once!"

The aide hurried over and laid the files on the desk. He stood there for a moment as the general began to scour the files then nervously spoke. "I was told to tell you that this information was acquired at a high cost in life and material."

"Send out the usual commendations and medals to the deceased. Notify their families that they died for Mother Russia's greater glory," Sokolov replied in a cold monotone voice without even looking up from the files.

The aide nodded and then hurried from the room, closing the door behind him. General Sokolov poured over the damage assessment of the radioactive strike from the Beluga weapon. The chaff dispersal had been almost perfect. Wind conditions had blown some of the silver tinsel chaff off the mark. The satellite images from an overhead flyby had confirmed both visually and scientifically that the town had been radiated.

Sokolov, knowing the devastation he had caused, had still decided to send in a survey team to assess the real damage. He had known the chances of survival for the team were extremely low. If the Chechen rebels didn't blow them out of the sky with their anti-aircraft guns or missiles, the radiation poisoning would surely claim their lives. In either case, he had wanted definitive results, no matter the cost. All that mattered was knowing how successful the Beluga mission had been.

Sokolov smiled as he folded his arms behind his head and leaned back against the chair. His plans were all working out. He began to dream about receiving an award from President Pelevin.

In Sokolov's daydream, cameras flashed incessantly as to the moment Pelevin pinned the Hero of the Russian Federation medal on his chest for his scientific breakthrough in weaponry. Completely bedecked with medals, Sokolov raised his hand in the air to the admiring crowd in the great assembly hall. Pelevin then leaned over and whispered into his ear that Sokolov should come over and relax at one of his favorite *dachas*, or second homes.

His daydream was completely lovely, but then it turned to a sinister side. He began to imagine what had really happen to the survey team.

Sokolov shook his head, pulling himself out of his daydream. He puckered his lips in an awkward smirk and then cleared his throat. He pressed the button on the intercom. "Get me General Konstantin Budnikov of the GRU Training Facility in Moscow on the phone at once."

Within minutes, his aide buzzed him that he had Budnikov's office on the line. Sokolov picked up the receiver and placed it to his ear.

"Budnikov," spoke the voice on the other end of the line.

Sokolov, satisfied that he was not being overheard since he was on a private line, began to speak. "We need to have another meeting. It's time to move forward with our plan. Report to my office with your data within the hour."

CHAPTER 16: THE BOSS WANTS TO SEE YOU

The three black Mercedes-Benz S 600 limos raced at a breakneck speed to travel the three miles across the streets of Moscow. The upper status of Budnikov allowed him and his entourage of subordinates and security to use the private, seldomly used state-built streets from the 1970s that permitted only party officials to travel rapidly through the capital without the normal traffic jams and dangers associated with dealing with the public. Some of the streets went underground through a series of tunnels which branched off in different directions to other buildings. The underground passages were also helpful in dodging American spy satellites and unwanted onlookers like foreign agents.

Within minutes of arrival at their destination, Budnikov and his team were taking the elevator to the twelfth floor of the main building of the Ministry of Defense. One of Budnikov's assistants pulled out his cellphone to text his wife that he would be very late coming home. He quickly realized that there was no signal and let out a miserable sigh.

"It's no use, Prostakov. The elevator shafts are lead lined," chastised Budnikov as he looked down his nose at his assistant.

"I wanted to let my wife know I was going to be late. She suspects that I am having an affair, General Budnikov," Prostakov said, quickly stuffing the phone back in his pocket.

Budnikov grunted in response as the elevator door opened at General Sokolov's floor. He stepped out first from the elevator, followed by his staff like obedient ducks in a queue. General Sokolov's assistant met them in the corridor and escorted them to the conference chamber where Sokolov and several others were waiting for them. The assistant tapped briskly on the door and opened it, stepping aside to make way for Budnikov and the others.

As Budnikov and his staff entered the conference chamber, Sokolov, standing behind a podium at the front of the room, quickly held up a hand in protest. "Budnikov's staff will remain outside the conference room doors. Only senior members permitted in here."

Budnikov quickly waved away his people, keeping the files that were needed for the meeting. He walked over to the long table where several important looking men sat. He took off his dark overcoat and draped it over a chair as he sat down in the one beside it. He opened a file and gave the impression he was prepared. The other men at the table nodded in greeting but did not speak.

Assured that everyone who needed to be in the meeting was present, Sokolov cleared his throat and gestured with his hands for everyone to stand. Behind the podium where he stood, a tremendous LCD screen came to life. Within seconds, a young aide-de-camp appeared on the screen. His tremendous golden braid draped over one shoulder with his dark green uniform accented with red piping indicated he was from the Army branch of the Russian military.

The officer on the screen could see through the video camera that all were standing in the conference room and were ready to receive a very important attendee. He made one nod to the audience and stepped aside.

The large screen blinked only once, and, in a flash, President Vladimir Pelevin's face appeared on the screen. The entire conference room tensed up instantly as if a switch had been turned on that petrified the people in the room. No one dared to breath, sniff, or even blink. It was well known by the elite that whenever the president was involved and a mistake was made, the culprit usually disappeared within an hour. Punishment was always severe and most assuredly swift.

"General Sokolov has my full confidence in carrying out this special operation. You are to obey his every command. If Sokolov fails, you all fail," declared Pelevin as his unblinking eyes seemed to be aimed at everyone in the room.

The LCD screen went dark as quickly as it had sprung to life as the transmission ended. The room remained deathly silent, for each man stood perfectly still. Sokolov switched on the microphone at the podium, causing it to create a feedback squeal in the overhead speakers of the room. He turned to face the room, staring intently at each member in the conference room as he motioned for all to be seated.

"Operation Beluga's trials have been completed," Sokolov announced as a wicked grin tugged at the corners of his sharp mouth, "and the first stages have been a complete success. You men are here to carry out phases two and three. We will be using our old Soviet tactics of *perestroika* and deception."

The men remained motionless as they listened intently.

Sokolov cleared his throat as he turned the page in the plan book on the podium. "We already have key assets in place who are awaiting their orders to proceed with their missions. Our objective: to seize control of Iran and its oil fields. We already have Syria and the strategic ports in the Mediterranean, and now we will own the Persian Gulf. With the United States out of Iraq and pulling out of Afghanistan, they will no longer be a threat to us."

The audience let out a faint murmur of whispers and throat clearings.

"As to the Iranians," Sokolov continued loudly, drawing everyone's attention back to him, "we will initiate a *ruse de guerre* where Iran will be blamed for the nuclear and biological attacks on rebellious cities north of them occupied by infidel tribes to their theocracy. Beluga is designed to look like the Iranians did the horrific attacks."

Sokolov paused for a brief second as he looked around the room for any hint of objection. Satisfied that there were none, he continued. "The United States and Israel will counterattack and destroy the Iranian forces in either conventional or nuclear responses. Russian forces will come in as the liberator and free the Iranian people from the mullahs and theocrats in Tehran. Before the West realizes it, we will have complete control of the country, their oil fields, and their ports. And, there is nothing that NATO, China, or anybody else will be able do about it. The world still uses over 50 percent of all oil produced by Iran and Iraq. Besides, we are all friends at the G-8 Summit, yes?"

No one responded to Sokolov's plan. Even seated, they remained frozen in fear by the mad plan. Everyone, that is, except for Budnikov, who smiled and nodded his head to Sokolov.

"Comrade General Sokolov?" asked an older member of the planning committee. His seniority gave him leeway for the very *faux pas* use of the word "comrade" in a time after the fall of communism.

Sokolov locked eyes with the bold old man. "Yes?"

The old man squirmed uneasily in his chair and cleared his throat. "We have made countless battle plans focused on conquering Iraq, Iran, and Afghanistan—and even a naval assault against Syria—for decades. The capitalists in the United States still believe in making books and movies about this assault. Why do we think this plan will work for us?"

Sokolov cleared his throat again as he backed away from the microphone. His chest grew tight with stress, and he began to sweat profusely. Even his left hand was tingling as his blood pressure soared. The years of eating caviar and drinking vodka all day had taken a very harsh toll on Sokolov's health, and he knew it.

He had acknowledged the old man's question with a simple nod then waved for Budnikov to follow him into another room.

When Sokolov and Budnikov were alone in the other room, Sokolov grabbed Budnikov by the arm and shook him.

"This is our one and only chance to change things in Moscow, Iran, and Syria. Pelevin is watching us. Our beloved president doesn't know about your two very special soldiers and their assignments, and he cannot be seen as the one who started this whole thing."

"Yes, General."

"Have them strike at the most convenient targets in America and Israel. And whatever you do, make it look like Iran did this! Do I make myself clear? America and her number one ally have to be drawn into this conflict!" growled Sokolov.

"Yes, sir. I will make sure everything goes as planned. The first one is easy enough to control, but the second is harder. I will go to America myself and ensure our success," responded Budnikov.

CHAPTER 17: THE PIZZA AND THE BAD PENNY

North Carolina

It was late at night when Michael, Steve, and Elizabeth said goodnight to one another after a long day of surveillance from their apartment near Asheville. Elizabeth retired first, followed by Michael. Steve mentioned that he was soon to follow after he completed his report of the day's observations.

Michael entered the third bedroom on the right just down the dark hallway. The room had only one queen sized bed on a steel frame, a nightstand with a lamp on top, and fresh new autumn-wheat-colored carpet. The room was lit with the lamp already on. Michael flipped the ceiling fan on when he walked in and closed the bedroom door behind him.

He sat down on the side of the bed and pulled his cellphone from his pocket. He pressed his wife's number on speed dial. Debbie answered the phone on the seventh ring. She was out of breath and struggling with something on the other end.

"Hello?" she barely managed to squeak out over the phone.

"Honey, it's me. Are you okay? Why did it take you so long to answer?"

Debbie screamed into the cellphone with a panic that Michael had only heard two times from his wife. Michael could tell by the shout that Debbie was yelling at someone inside the house, for the echo in the phone came from the walls of the kitchen where the backdoor was located. Then the phone must have been dropped by Debbie for it hit the hardwood floor in their house with a crash.

"No! Stop! Stop!" Debbie pleaded in the background.

"Debbie!" Michael shouted into the phone as he jumped to his feet. "Debbie!"

The phone was silent for a long time, which filled Michael's head with pure fear for he wasn't there to save her.

"Debbie!" Michael cried into the phone, but no answer came.

Michael's door burst open, and Steve rushed in, followed closely by Elizabeth. Steve looked at his brother with worry on his face. "What is it? What's wrong with Debbie?"

"I don't know! It sounds like someone's there!"

Steve and Elizabeth looked back and forth at each other. Elizabeth pulled her robe tightly around her with one hand and reached out and took Steve's hand with the other.

The next sounds that Michael heard over the phone were chairs being tossed about, followed by a glass shattering on the floor, and finally a plate which fell and was spinning like a child's top until it slowly wobbled to a stop.

"Debbie!" Michael shouted once again into the phone.

Another moment of what seemed like an eternity passed by as Michael frantically paced through the bedroom, filled with fear for his wife and the overwhelming helplessness of the situation. Steve and Elizabeth stood in the doorway of the room, watching anxiously.

Finally, Michael heard footsteps on the floor on the other end of the line as someone approached the phone. Michael heard the cellphone being picked up, and he then heard the phone coming up to an ear. He stopped pacing.

"Debbie?" he asked, the fear evident in his voice.

"Sorry, Honey, I know that this sounded crazy over the phone, but I had an emergency."

"What happened?" Michael turned to face his brother and Elizabeth, who looked at him with fear in their eyes.

"Well, I ordered a pizza. When it arrived a few minutes ago, I uncorked a bottle of pinot noir and poured myself a big glass and placed it on the breakfast table."

"And then?" He nodded to Steve and Elizabeth and mouthed the words, "I think she's okay."

Steve and Elizabeth relaxed. Steve waved to Michael as he pushed Elizabeth out the door and shut it behind him.

"Well," Debbie continued, "your dog Ginger was scheming the entire time and watched me go through the back door onto the patio to turn off the water sprinkler in the backyard. Ginger waited until I was out the back door, and then she jumped on the table and started eating my pizza!"

"Oh!" Michael said as he let out a huge sigh of relief.

"When the phone rang, I ran back inside to answer it, and that is when Ginger had started on the second slice. Michael, her face was covered in marinara sauce! I screamed at her, and she got scared and jumped off the table with the half-eaten slice, knocking over my wine glass in the process. There is broken glass and red wine everywhere, and my dinner is half gone."

Michael collapsed on the bed and started to laugh as the complete alleviation of his fears washed over him.

"Baby, I'm so sorry Ginger ruined everything," he said between bouts of laughter. "You scared me when it took you forever to answer the phone and then you screamed, and well, I was—"

"Scared? Well, you should be. Now you know how I felt yesterday when your brother showed up at the house to tell me and your mother that you and Elizabeth were going with him on an assignment."

"Yes, I know it must have been scary." Michael quickly tried to change the subject. "How's Mom?"

"She's good. We're just worried about the secrecy of this whole escapade with your brother."

"Debbie, all of us are here in Asheville. We're in a regular old apartment doing a routine job. Oh, how about this? I have a queen-sized bed all to myself," Michael gloated.

"You bum! You need to be here with your wife. I miss being next to you…."

Michael could hear the melancholy in Debbie's voice. "I miss you, too, but I'll be home before you know it."

"Are there any female CIA agents in the apartment?" The lightness had returned to Debbie's voice. "There better not be."

Michael let out another laugh. "I promise. It's just us Cotters here in the apartment. Now, at the corner restaurant…."

"Michael Cotter!"

Michael burst out laughing, and Debbie could not help but join in the joke. The two finished their conversation and said their goodnights. Michael hung up the phone and changed into a t-shirt and gym shorts and climbed into bed. He was certainly glad that Debbie had been able to help Steve gather him some clothes before Steve had picked them up. He surely wouldn't have wanted to wear the same clothes the whole time they were there.

He made one more glance at his cellphone on the nightstand for any messages and noticed the time before he turned off the phone. It was around 2300 hours in military time.

The apartment was quiet with everyone in bed. The ceiling fan was relaxing to Michael. The cool breeze from the rotating blades gently lulled him to sleep.

During Michael's sleep, he began to toss and turn. Being a left-sided sleeper, he unconsciously rolled to his right side. After a few minutes, he rolled back to his left, and he repeated this process many times. His legs swished quickly in jerk-like motions, as if he were running in his sleep. One of his arms was moving up and down the top of the mattress as if he were trying to warn someone. He let out a few muffled moans while he slept.

Michael's temperature and heartbeat increased rapidly. His eyes rolled back and forth under his eyelids as he was in an extremely deep REM sleep. He began to grind his teeth as he was experiencing that very same recurring nightmarish dream that he had been having since coming back from England a few years before.

Only his wife Debbie knew of Michael's dream. She always worried that he was suffering from PTSD from his service in Afghanistan. Michael's answer was always the same: no, it was the same black raven over and over.

Suddenly, Michael awoke and sat straight up in the bed. He knew he had experienced that nightmare again. He found himself breathing heavily, and his t-shirt was again soaked in perspiration.

"Why?" he whispered to himself as he pulled off the shirt and threw it to the floor.

He then reached over to the nightstand and picked up his phone. It read 0215.

Michael sat quietly for a minute. He needed his wife to reassure him that it was just a bad dream. He started to cry to himself. Not out of fear of the bad dream, but, to Michael, it was the culmination of his wife's scary disaster that night with the dog and pizza and him not being there with her.

Michael's tears turned to a smile as he reminded himself that his wife always told him a simple phrase after one of his recurring episodes. *"Darling, your nightmare is just like a bad penny."*

CHAPTER 18: I THINK THIS IS A COLLECT CALL

It had been a long, hard shift at the hospital, and Mishka was ready to get home to shower and rest a little before heading over to her grandfather's house. She pressed the accelerator firmly, trying to make the trip home as brief as possible. Suddenly, her cellphone sprang to life in her purse. North Carolina's road laws prohibited her from answering it right away, so she slowed her convertible and turned into the parking lot of a local gas station to answer it. She retrieved the phone from her purse as she put the car in park.

"Federov," she said curtly over the cellphone, for the number on the LCD screen showed an unlisted number.

"Hello?" came a voice on the other end.

"Josuf? My sweet brother!" she screamed into the phone as she turned off the car.

"*Privet, moya krasnaya obez'yana*," Josuf greeted her, using the Russian for "*little red monkey,*" their family's pet name for Mishka.

"Josuf, how are you? Where are you?"

"I'm on my way to someplace special, and I have a rendezvous with my own destiny. Jealous?"

"So," Mishka settled back against the seat and smiled, "did you call just to brag?"

"Nope, I just wanted to know if you've seen Poppi lately."

"A couple of days ago. I brought him his lunch and a little friend, a monkey he named Malinky." She laughed as she referenced the monkey.

"Mishka, listen to me. Things are clear for me now. I know what I am supposed to do with my life."

Mishka thought quietly before responding. "Josuf, I have been over this with you before. You do not need to become radicalized just to believe in Allah."

"It's not just about my religion! It's about my next mission! I feel alive with something I have never felt before!" His voice intensified with raw feelings.

Mishka could hear over the cell phone that Josuf was becoming emotional. She even heard a faint sniff from Josuf as if possibly he was crying silently. "Josuf?"

"All I want from you, Mishka, is to tell Poppi that I am going to make him proud!" Josuf shouted with rage.

"Why can't you tell him yourself, Josuf?" She leaned forward and grasped the steering wheel with her free hand. She gripped it so tightly that her knuckles turned white. "This newly found devotion has changed you. Poppi doesn't care if you are religious or not. All he wants is for us to be happy with our lives."

Josuf was silent over the phone as he listened to his big sister. A few moments passed, and then Josuf said, "When do you see Poppi again?"

"Well, he did say he had something special to tell me the other day, but his new little friend distracted us. I had to work a long shift at the hospital after that, but I'm going to see him later today."

"Mishka, just tell him that I love him and I want to make him proud." His voice cracked with emotion. "I know my next mission will make him proud."

Mishka's face was puzzled as she looked at herself in the rearview mirror of her car.

"Okay, brother, I'll tell you what I'm going to do. I'm going to Poppi's house in just a little bit. He'll probably be at the park. While I am there, I will find out what his special news is. Then we will all talk on the phone, just like old times. It will be good for all of us, okay? We love you, little brother."

"I know," whispered Josuf in a monotone voice as he hung up the cellphone.

CHAPTER 19: SPYING WITH A KALEIDOSCOPE

Steve rubbed his tired eyes as he tried to focus on his target through his binoculars. The old man sat playing the accordion while his little monkey friend scampered around and got hugs from passersby. It was the same scene that it had been all morning and the entire day before. The mind-numbing boredom of it had been wearing on Steve's nerves, and he finally threw up his hands and stepped away from the binoculars. He placed his hands on his head and gently pulled on his hair in frustration.

Elizabeth looked up from her computer and smiled. "Are you going to make it, Steve?"

Michael, who was sitting next to Elizabeth at the table, paused working on the new drone the CIA had provided for him and chuckled at his brother's exasperation. He nudged Elizabeth with his elbow. "Well, we better be glad you're the brains behind this operation, Elizabeth. We'd be up a creek if Steve had to research for us. He looks like his brain's about to blow."

"Yeah, yeah," Steve said, nodding his head. "I need you to get the drone going. I feel like my brain really may explode if I have to spend the rest of the day watching that old man and his monkey sit there."

They all laughed.

"It's almost ready," Michael said as he got back to work linking the drone to his computer.

The Beta Nine Heavy stealth drone was a new observation tool from the CIA. One of the newest heavy-lift drones, it was a twelve-bladed electric motor drive drone and was completely silent. Designed to carry different heavy surveillance camera suites, the Beta Nine Heavy fit the bill very nicely in high priority missions. Because of Michael's impressive history working with drones, including his use of one to save the base he had been posted at in Afghanistan, it had been relatively easy for Steve to convince his supervisor MacAday to authorize the paperwork for Michael to obtain the necessary security clearance to use the drone.

Michael was very excited that he was in command of the new drone. Like so many electronic toys before, Michael enjoyed the freedom that a drone could offer him. He could fly, crawl, or even swim with a drone. Michael and any kind of drone were one and the same. A driver and a robot, symbiont beings in a unique symphony to achieve one purpose, one mission.

Steve returned to his binoculars while Michael continued to work on readying the drone. Steve swung the binoculars to the northeast from the park bench and viewed his subject's front door. The heavy door was of an older pattern used by the townhouses when they were built in the 1970s. Each townhouse had multiple stories and also included a basement. He panned back to the old man and his monkey, still sitting on the bench entertaining passersby.

Michael finished linking the drone to the computer. "Success!"

Steve let out a shout of joy. "Hurry and get that thing up in the air! I'm going to have to go to the optometrist after all these hours staring through those binoculars!"

"I'm going. I'm going. We can't have you having to get eye glasses made, now can we? It might spoil your looks, and you'll lose that pretty online girlfriend of yours."

Elizabeth and Michael laughed as Steve's face turned red.

Michael gathered the drone and its remote control and headed out the door. He chuckled to himself about Steve needing to visit the optometrist as he made his way out of the apartment, down the hall, and to the roof. Every time Michael thought about optometrists, he thought about his time as an exchange student in Nuremburg, Germany, during college. He had stayed at a beautiful home in the rural part of the city with the Goldhammer family.

One night, Frau Goldhammer had made a German delicacy of cow tongue and potatoes for a special guest coming over from the university. The guest had been a doctor and a specialist in optometry. The lovely formal dinner had been held on the back patio of the home. The backyard had been immaculate with lovely rose bushes that had highlighted a gorgeous green lawn.

"So, Herr Doktor…," Michael had begun in German as he had placed his cloth napkin in his lap.

The doctor had turned his attention away from the delicacy in the middle of the table and had focused his attention on Michael. The optometrist's demeanor had been a touch perturbed due to the fact that Michael had interrupted Frau Goldhammer's magnificent presentation.

"I see that you make eye… work… tools," Michael had tried to say in his broken German, using words he had known instead of the unknown translation for "eyeglasses" since he had not had his trusty English/German dictionary handy.

The German optometrist had cried out in atypical laughter and happiness. He had reached out a hand and had given a friendly slap on Michael's shoulder, congratulating him on a unique way to describe his medical profession.

"*Augen Werkzuege!*" Dr. Hugo Wittman had repeated the German words that Michael had used. He had then added its translation in perfect English, "Eye working tools. I must use this on a sign outside my office!"

Michael shook his head and chuckled to himself as he reached the roof. Quickly, he set the drone down and used the remote control to start it running. Despite the speed of the blades, the little drone was all but silent as Michael maneuvered it seamlessly into the open air above the roof. He set the controls to keep the drone hovering in place as he hurried back to the apartment below, eager to test out the computer controls.

When he entered the apartment, Elizabeth was walking into the living room with a cold soda in her hand, and Steve was in the kitchen making sandwiches.

"Did you get it airborne?" Steve asked from the kitchen, glancing over his shoulder as Michael closed the door behind him and locked it.

"It's up right now. I set it to hover in place till I got back down here. I want to try using the computer to control it before I send it out." Michael walked through the living room and past the table where his computer sat, headed for the kitchen. "I'm going to get a drink first, though."

Michael opened the refrigerator and grabbed a bottle of water from the shelf. He took a long drink and then looked at the sandwiches Steve was making. "Why are you making lunch? Afraid Elizabeth's cooking will kill us?"

Steve laughed. "I'd rather not find out."

"Me, either!" Michael reached into the upper kitchen cabinet for three plates. "I want a long happy life with my beautiful wife. No need to take unnecessary risks like Elizabeth's cooking."

The two brothers laughed loudly.

"Guys," Elizabeth said from the living room where she was peering between the blinds, "have either of you bright bulbs thought about the old man on the bench?"

"I've got it. You finish the sandwiches." Michael walked over to the table and sat down.

Elizabeth walked over and stood beside Michael as he worked. She watched as he used the computer to access the camera on the drone. He then practiced maneuvering the drone and accessing the different features it had before flying the drone out over the park.

Michael quickly found the old man using the drone's camera. He watched with intense scrutiny as a woman approached the old man from behind as he sat on the bench. Unlike the usual passersby their target interacted with, the stranger sat down on the bench with the old man and seemed to engage him in a conversation.

"Hey, there's a woman talking to Federov," Michael said as he set the controls on the drone to make it hover in place high above the park. "You might want to see this, Steve."

"I'll be there in just a minute," Steve called over his shoulder. "I'm almost finished here."

Michael zoomed the immense camera in on the two people sitting on the park bench. The computer screen displayed the vivid image as the drone's camera seamlessly refocused. Elizabeth leaned in slightly over Michael's left shoulder to get a better view of the display.

"That's weird." Michael stared at the screen for a moment in disbelief. "Steve, the woman looks like your girl on your cellphone. I... I think its Micah."

Elizabeth straightened as Steve walked over and stood beside Michael's right shoulder. Steve looked down at the image on the computer screen. To his horror, he recognized Micah as well. His voice stern, he said, "Turn on the audio, Michael."

Michael adeptly activated the audio feed on the drone. The drone was equipped with a microphone boom that could pick up distant conversations. Very similar to NFL games with a technician on the sidelines holding a large acoustic dish listening to all of the communications of the other team, the CIA drone would provide everyone in the room with what was being said between Micah and Federov.

The computer-enhanced audio was quickly overwhelmed by the immense incoming sound data it picked up, making it impossible to decipher correctly what was being said. The output audio was filled with birds chirping, cars driving down the street, and even the leaves on the trees rustling. Michael adjusted the sensor to mask most of the background sounds to a very limited level. He swiftly found the right setting, and the conversation on the park bench became clearer.

"Please stop talking in Russian out here," Federov said. "There are many people in the park, and they get somewhat nervous when people are using a foreign language."

"Sorry," Micah replied, "but I am stunned that Moscow wants you to retire. I am happy for you—truly I am. I wondered why I had such unusual training, and now I know. Are you sure that I am to take your place?"

"Yes, I'm certain," Federov said, nodding. "This is really a great honor for you. It works out perfectly. Now, walk back to the house, and I will be there shortly after Malinky goes to the bathroom."

"Let's walk together," Micah protested. "You know how long it takes you to get back up there."

"I'll be along in a few minutes," Federov said. "This is Malinky's only exercise for the day. We'll be fine. Now go."

Micah stood up. "Oh! I forgot! Josuf called me, and he wanted you to know—"

"Run along," Federov interrupted, motioning with his hand for her to go. "We will talk about Josuf later. You need to read the papers I left on my desk. Those are your new instructions. Now scoot."

Steve, Michael, and Elizabeth were stunned. Steve's hand gripped the back of Michael's chair tightly as he tried to process the revelation that the woman he knew as Micah was not who she seemed to be. He silently watched the woman slowly walk away from the old man on the bench and start up the very long hill back to Dimitiry's townhouse.

"Wow. This is some crazy kinda shit, Steve." Elizabeth placed her hand on Steve's shoulder. "Are you okay with all of this?"

"Quit cussing. You're not good at it," Steve retorted as he shrugged off his cousin's hand from his shoulder. He stepped away from the table and held up his hands in frustration. "And, no, Elizabeth, I'm not okay!"

Michael turned to face his brother. "She didn't mean anything by it, Steve. She's just trying to alleviate some of the tension."

"Just shut up. Both of you. You don't know what I'm feeling right now," Steve said coldly. He took a deep breath, steadying himself as tears brimmed in his eyes. "My mission is to observe this old man. That's it. Nothing more."

Steve turned away and walked over to the binoculars at the window. He placed his hand on them but did not bend down to look through them. He closed his eyes as he shook his head slightly before allowing it to bow under the emotional weight.

Michael looked at Elizabeth and motioned for her to leave the room as he stood up. She nodded and went to her room as Michael walked over to his little brother. Michael placed his hand on top of Steve's hand that still lay on the binoculars.

"It's okay. I got this," whispered Michael.

CHAPTER 20: DON'T SHAKE
A STRANGER'S HAND

After taking a few minutes alone, Steve came back in and went to the kitchen. Steve carried two of the sandwiches he had made earlier to Elizabeth and Michael, who were working at the table. Elizabeth smiled as she took the sandwich and began to eat as she worked on her laptop. Michael nodded as Steve handed him a sandwich. He took a bite of sandwich as he continued his shift observing Federov on the park bench using the drone.

"Hey, the monkey finished pooping, and the old man is pulling up her little pants," Michael said out loud.

The report made everybody in the room laugh a bit as the intense stress began to wane. Steve walked back to the kitchen and leaned against the counter as he picked up his own sandwich and took a bite. The three ate in silence, but it was a relatively comfortable silence.

Michael was relieved a bit that Steve was regaining his composure. Michael realized that Steve was hurt finding out that the woman he liked was somehow involved with his CIA assignment, and he hated it when his brother was hurting.

"Looks like Micah is taking her sweet time getting up the hill. Wait. She stopped." Michael turned the drone slightly to get a better view. "It looks like a couple stopped to ask her for directions… or maybe the time. Sorry. I don't have the drone's audio on, Steve. Should I follow her or stay on the old man?"

"Just keep the drone on Federov," replied Steve and took another bite of his lunch.

Michael rotated the drone to orient it towards the park bench and the old man. His interest was piqued as he watched a man approach Federov and the monkey from the sidewalk to the left of the bench, coming from the nearby street to the park.

The new man was about as old as Federov, or possibly a little older, and was dressed in an impeccable black overcoat and hat. His very presence seemed to overshadow everything else in the scene. Even the monkey looked upon the stranger in awe as Michael watched through the drone's feed on the monitor. The two men spoke briefly and then shook hands, and the darkly dressed stranger walked away.

Even though Michael was intrigued by the bizarre encounter, he didn't mention it to Steve because he wanted his brother to have some down time before getting back to the case at hand. As Michael watched, however, a horrible scene unfolded on the monitor as the hovering black drone's camera feed stayed focused on the old man on the bench. Their target had obviously become ill.

"Hey, hey, Steve!" Michael called out, sitting up straight in his chair and motioning with his hand for Steve to hurry over. "Come quick!"

Steve shoved the last bite of his sandwich in his mouth and rushed to the table.

Michael pointed to the screen. "Look here! Your guy... whatever... the old man is sick!"

"Oh, shit! Oh, shit!" Steve cried out as he leaned down to watch the scene unfolding on the screen. "What the hell just happened? Michael, what happened?"

"I don't know! Some strange guy walked up, they talked for a minute, he shook Federov's hand, and then the old man started into convulsions after the strange guy left the area."

"Find the guy!" Steve ordered. "Elizabeth, get to the binoculars and keep your eyes on the old man!"

Elizabeth jumped up and ran to the living room where she quickly found their target through the binoculars. "Got him!"

Michael immediately scanned the area in the direction that the strange man had headed towards when he had left. His keen eyes scoured the landscape for the black overcoat and hat. He pointed to the screen. "There he is!"

The stranger was in an awful hurry back towards the street. As Michael and Steve watched, the stranger reached a dark European sedan. He got inside and tore away out of sight from the drone's current position.

Michael and Steve looked at each other in shock and came to the same conclusion: someone had just tried to kill their target in plain daylight during Steve's watch.

"Get the drone back on Federov. I've got to call MacAday!" Steve said as he pulled out his phone and dialed MacAday's number. He went into the kitchen with the phone to his ear.

After a brief discussion, Steve hung up and ran to the far wall of the apartment. He placed his right thumb on a black sensor strip to a bio safe door and it unlocked. He retrieved a service pistol, extra ammunition, and a special first aid kit that included a defibrillator. He hurried over to the table where Michael was monitoring the situation in the park through the drone's feed. Michael glanced over as Steve strapped on his weapon.

"Do you really need a gun for this?" Michael asked with an angry look on his face. "We watched the guy drive away."

"I think it's exciting to tell you the truth," Elizabeth said, looking up from the binoculars. "Just don't shoot me, cousin."

"Well, I've had enough guns and shooting at people in Afghanistan to last a lifetime. I hate guns." Michael looked into his younger brother's eyes. "A gun can change your life forever, Steve. Be careful."

Michael's mind wandered off for a few seconds as he reflected back to the horrible combat he had witnessed in Afghanistan.

"Michael? Hey, brother, are you daydreaming?" Steve asked, bringing Michael back to the present. "Listen. The CIA trained me on this pistol extensively, so stop whining. We gotta go! Come on!"

CHAPTER 21: SOMETHING HERE JUST DOESN'T BELONG

Mishka finally made it to the top of the hill and started up the stairs to the townhouse. She quickly glanced to the far end of an adjacent parking lot where her convertible was parked. She always parked in the extra parking spots that were available in a neighboring lot when she could and not in front of her grandfather's house. The very first time she had parked in front of his townhouse, a neighbor had hit her car with his car door by accident. It had taken a month to get a repair appointment for the dent. When she spotted her car, there was a large sedan parked very close to her convertible.

"Stupid idiot!" Mishka hissed, stopping in her tracks. She started towards the two cars. "There are a dozen other spots in the parking lot, and you just had to park next to mine."

By the time she reached the other side of the parking lot, Mishka was fuming. There was barely enough room between the cars to even fit in between, much less open her car door. Mishka smirked. "I guess you won't mind if I accidently scratch your European paint job!"

With her large purse strapped over her shoulder, Mishka turned sideways and squeezed herself between the two cars. Once she was wedged in between them, she turned sharply, allowing the large decorative buckle on the bag to produce a long gash along the car's passenger side door. She edged slowly to freedom, dragging the buckle along the side of the large sedan as she went. She then walked briskly across the two parking lots back to the townhouse.

As she approached the front door, she noticed a secret trick that Dimitiry had shown her. Her grandfather's apartment was not quite the ordinary, run-of-the-mill townhouse. Dimitiry had made very subtle changes to enhance his protection as an agent for the Russian Federation. He had created a special tell for his front door, like a sailor in the days of old who tied a square knot on his sea bag that an intruder would be unlikely to reproduce, letting the sailor know if his bag had been opened. Dimitiry had installed a tiny hinge no bigger than a square soda cracker at the top of the door frame. Super thin and painted exactly as the door, to the unknowing, it would seem like a flake of paint had peeled off from the top of the door. If the door had been opened by an intruder, the flap would be in the down position, indicating an unauthorized entry.

"Somebody is in here," Mishka said to herself.

Mishka opened her pocketbook quickly and retrieved her PSM pistol from inside her bag. She kept the gun hidden within the bag. The pistol felt comfortable in her right hand. It gave her unquestionable strength that she knew she would need in the next few seconds.

Her gun of choice was the government-issued pistol known as the PSM. Contrary to a popular myth about the small weapon, the abbreviation PSM did not mean "pistol, small," but was derived from where the weapon was manufactured. *Pistolet Mologabaritny* was the clever design by the Tula Design Factory in Russia. A favorite for all older KGB and current FSB officers and security forces, it was also a favorite for Mishka because the weapon didn't have a distracting recoil and stayed on target about 82 percent of the time.

Mishka turned the doorknob very slowly. She knew the knob squeaked if quickly let go, so she entered totally undetected. Inside the foyer, she quietly drew her pistol from her purse and looked left and then right before she moved to the next room. Remembering her tactics, she quietly propped herself against the hall doorway and did a quick peek inside the next room.

Mishka moved quietly to the kitchen, and, again, she found no one there. She moved back into the living room.

As Dimitiry had told her where to look, she found the orders for him to retire. There was another page that instructed him to pass on all the codes, instructions for the weapon, viable targets in the United States, and all pertinent information to his successor, Lt. Mishka Krasnaya of the FSB, whose call sign was "Red Monkey."

Mishka shook her head and smiled. The FSB upper echelon had failed in one important aspect: they had always known her as "Mishka Krasnaya." No one knew she was a Federov, for Dimitiry had been very careful when the Russians had come for her and Josuf due to their bright academic scores. Dimitiry had forged their papers and had told the authorities that he was just a family friend who was caring for the orphans.

When Mishka had been secretly assigned by the FSB to the radiology department in North Carolina, part of her mission had actually been to use her association with Dimitiry to keep track of him and the weapon in his possession. The Russians liked to use people's backgrounds to their advantage, but it had also worked out wonderfully for Mishka, allowing her to come and go at Dimitiry's without arousing any suspicion from her supervisors.

Mishka glanced over the orders again. She had always wondered if her orders might one day be to take over for Dimitiry. She was more than qualified. She not only had the regular three-year FSB training and a degree in nuclear science, but she had also had specialized GRU training, unlike the other people in her class.

From behind her, Mishka heard heavy footsteps coming down from the upstairs floor. In a few short seconds, an elderly gentleman with a dark overcoat and a hat in his hands in front of his chest emerged at the bottom of the stairs.

"Stop!" Mishka ordered the stranger in a very stern and authoritative voice. "I have my pistol aimed right at your head. Do not turn to look and do not move!"

"You know who I am, Lt. Mishka Krasnaya," said the dark figure in English overshadowed by a heavy Russian accent. "I am going to turn around slowly, and you will put down your gun."

The man turned around. As he did, his face finally came into view, and she instantly recognized him as Lieutenant General Budnikov.

Mishka blinked as a sudden black and white scene flashed in her mind. As if looking askew through a window into a room, she saw the image of her younger self sitting in a medical exam chair. She watched as a doctor who stood beside the chair injected a syringe of fluid into her right arm. The image also contained another person in the room. His facial image was obscured by a haze. He was much older, darker, and he spoke slowly in a monotone voice that echoed through the tilted room in her mind.

Keeping the gun on Budnikov, Mishka grabbed her forehead with her free hand and shook her head, trying to make the image leave her mind and voice to stop. She felt confused and dazed for a few seconds.

"Mishka Krasnaya, are you listening to me?"

Mishka's flashback ended when Budnikov spoke again, the words in the hazy room in her mind matching the words he spoke in the present room, making the haze finally dissipate and reveal the face of the man in her mind. It was Budnikov in the medical exam room.

Mishka shook her head but kept her stance. "Yes, I can hear you. What are you doing here?"

Like a dark wolf that had cornered his prey, Budnikov approached her cautiously. "I could ask you the same thing. Getting a little too friendly with the person you're supposed to be observing, perhaps? It's a little odd you being here without him, isn't it?"

"Don't play games with me. You people at the GRU know just as well as the FSB that Dimitiry raised my brother and me. It's why I was given this assignment. Now. What are you doing here?"

"Actually," Budnikov said with a smile, "I was looking for you. Sokolov sent me to give you the orders for your next mission."

"Why didn't Sokolov just send them the usual way?" Mishka asked, her gun still pointed at Budnikov and her stance still firm.

"Because I am the only one who can give them to you," Budnikov said, looking into Mishka's eyes. "Now, listen to my words, and listen to them very carefully, Lt. Mishka Krasnaya. *The shadows in the corner are not entirely our own.*"

The phrase that Budnikov uttered had a very profound effect on Mishka. The phrase, known in the spy community as a "trigger phrase," was very unique, for it had been subconsciously implanted deep into Mishka's memory. When the phrase was mentioned, it awoke a suppressed memory of secret instructions and behavioral adjustments induced by hypnotherapy professionals many years before during her training. Mishka was the absolutely perfect sleeper mole.

Her eyes blinked hard, and her head ached with a wave of a migraine that overwhelmed her calmness. She felt her heart rhythm begin to race, and she felt massive amounts of adrenaline that coursed through her veins.

What is happening to me? she asked herself as she fought hard against the unknown attack to take over her mind.

Mishka wavered for a brief second as she swayed back and forth fighting with herself in her mind. The images of her in an exam chair and being injected with some unknown fluid returned, and they caused her pain. Again, she saw Budnikov in her nightmarish vision, but there was also another person in the room.

In her quasi-dream, she fought back the haze that was enshrouding her view. Within her mind, she waved with her arms to push away the gray from the tilted image inside the room. She finally cleared the obtrusive obscurity, and she was able to discern that the other person in the room was her brother, Josuf. He, too, was being subjected to the same procedures as she.

Then, just as quickly as it had started, the symptoms began to fade. Mishka felt more confident and invigorated by some untapped energy from within. She felt led to listen to Budnikov's commands.

"The shadows in the corner are not entirely our own," Budnikov repeated.

"Yes, sir. I understand," Mishka said in a low voice with a soldier-like manner.

"Good, Mishka! Good! You were always more strong-willed than your brother."

She lowered her pistol, acknowledging Budnikov was in charge. He then explained her next mission.

"You are to follow the Santa Code protocol. You know the W72 is here. You will take it to Fontana Dam. There you will make the sacrifice for your country that you know within you will be the most important contribution to Mother Russia that you could ever make."

CHAPTER 22: WHAT DOES "*YAD*" MEAN?

Steve, Michael, and Elizabeth raced to the park area. As they got within sight of the park bench where Dimitiry Federov was slumped over, Michael programmed the CIA drone that had been keeping watch on their target to land back at the apartment's rooftop using its remote control.

Steve was the first to reach the old man and approached with caution. Malinky was howling and pulling on her master's arms, but she moved obligingly over to allow Steve to lift up Dimitiry's head. The old man rolled over onto his back yet was still on the bench with his legs slung over the side.

Elizabeth approached and took off her light blue sweater and formed it into a pillow for Dimitiry's head. Michael was last to follow suit. He stopped about ten yards away and called emergency services on his cellphone.

Steve knelt beside the old man who was struggling to breathe. "Sir? Sir, my name is Steve Cotter, and I want to help you. What is the matter with you?"

Dimitiry was dying, and with each of breath, his air intake grew fainter. In a labored motion with his right arm, he slowly pointed to his watch on his left wrist.

"*Yad!*" he whispered.

"Time?" asked Steve confusedly as he fumbled to look at the old man's watch.

"*Nyet,*" the old man responded in the negative, barely shaking his head.

"That's Russian," Elizabeth said and pulled out her cell phone. She opened up a translation app on her phone, her fingers flying across the touch screen. "Yad is... it's poison!"

Dimitiry nodded slightly and tried again to point to his watch, particularly the place where the watch strap fastened. One finger painfully pulled back a piece of the leather strap to expose a puncture wound that was hidden behind the strap. The hole was tiny, about the size of a vaccination injection.

Elizabeth bent down and looked where Dimitiry was pointing. She quickly undid the watch and placed it in his shirt pocket. Carefully, she inspected the area until she found the pinprick mark. "Steve, he's been poisoned. That's the puncture wound, see, right there."

"Ambulance and police are on their way," Michael announced as he joined them, putting his cellphone away in his pants' pocket.

The three Cotters watched helplessly as Dimitiry rested on the bench dying. Malinky, realizing the adults were good people trying to help, climbed upon Michael's shoulders and gave a small kiss on his left cheek.

"Budnikov...," Dimitiry whispered, his eyes rolling back into his head.

"Budnikov? Who is Budnikov?" Steve asked, gently shaking the old man's shoulder in an effort to keep him conscious. "Who is that?"

"Budnikov... Mishka... nyet...," Dimitiry mumbled as he barely lifted his hand before letting it drop again heavily onto his stomach.

"Mishka? Who are Budnikov and Mishka? Who are they?" Steve's voice rose in frustration as he gently shook the old man's shoulder. "Don't die on me, old man! Who are they?"

"Budnikov... Mishka... nyet... nyet...," Dimitiry whispered and closed his eyes.

"Who are they?" asked Steve, grasping his forehead and closing his eyes. After several moments, he looked up at Elizabeth and Michael. "I can't believe this happened while we were just sitting there watching!"

"Steve, your lady friend's name is Micah, right?" asked Michael.

Steve nodded and then looked back down to Dimitiry. He shook the old man's shoulder, jarring him enough so that he opened his eyes. With an urgency in his voice, he asked, "You mean Micah? When you say 'Mishka,' are you talking about Micah?"

"Nyet... nyet.... Mishka," whispered the old man before falling into unconsciousness.

Steve looked down at the still man lying before him on the park bench for a few moments then stood, turning to Elizabeth and Michael. "Guys, I have got to get to this man's home. There is very important information in that townhouse and possibly even something that the department was speculating might exist. Plus, Micah was on her way up there. She may be in trouble. Stay here with Federov until the ambulance gets here!"

Steve quickly turned and began to run towards the townhouse's location up the hill from the park.

"Wait, Steve! Wait for backup!" Michael shouted to his brother. "Call your bosses and report what has happened!"

Steve looked back over his shoulder as he continued to run in the direction of the townhouse. "I can't! I need to rescue the data in that townhouse and get it all done before any of the local authorities get involved! Stay with Federov! I need you to do that for me!"

Michael let out a frustrated breath and reached up to remove the monkey from his shoulder. Elizabeth placed her hand on Michael's arm, stopping him. He looked at his cousin to speak, but before he could, sirens filled the park as the emergency services arrived. Michael and Elizabeth waved to catch the attention of those vehicles to hurry them to where they were.

Steve bounded up the concrete steps, aided by pulling on the dark green iron handrail. Once on the top deck, he spotted Micah's white convertible in the adjoining parking spot. Steve's heart quickened as he realized that she could definitely be in danger. In his excited rush, he ran through a holly bush. Oblivious to the sharp barbs that shredded his bare arms, he proceeded onwards. The crimson scratches looked as if he owned an angry pair of cats that enjoyed stretching their sharp claws into flesh.

Steve made it to Dimitiry's door and banged heavily on the brass knocker. He didn't even realize that his scratches had bled down to his hands causing red stains on the shiny door knocker.

There was nothing but silence, so Steve hammered on the door again and rang the doorbell repeatedly.

"Open the door! Are you in there?" Steve shouted through the wooden door, but no one answered.

CHAPTER 23: A BANDAGE WON'T FIX THIS

Inside the den, Mishka looked at Budnikov. "We have company."

Budnikov walked casually to Dimitiry's desk and began to shuffle papers with one hand, his black hat still grasped in the other. "So it seems."

A feeling of conflict arose within Mishka as her love for her grandfather sparked a thought in her mind. "What will happen to Dimitiry now that I am to take control of the W72?"

"What does that matter? Federov was a means to an end. The radiation from the long-term maintenance of the W72 would have killed him eventually. You were what was important."

Mishka's eyes narrowed. "What do you mean?"

The banging on the door grew louder.

"I know you're in there!" Steve shouted from outside the townhouse. "Dimitiry Federov has been poisoned and is dying! Some man in a dark coat and hat did it, and you may be in danger!"

Mishka looked towards the door and then back at Budnikov. "What is he talking about? What does he mean Dimitiry was poisoned?"

Budnikov didn't even glance towards her. "I just told you. Federov was expendable. You weren't. He would have died from cancer from the radiation soon enough. I just put him out of his misery. Consider it a favor."

Mishka's legs began to shake. As she realized that Budnikov had killed her grandfather, she had felt the uncontrollable surge of honor pulling on her soul, an immense sense of righting a wrong to her family. That tremendous pull of duty and honor tied to her family was like the centrifugal forces when riding a merry-go-round as a child that had attempted to pull her off the ride—in the present case, her duty and honor tied to her work.

The pounding on the door continued as Budnikov noticed a handwritten note mixed in with the papers on the desk. He read the note silently: *"Poppi, I hope this little monkey brings you much joy and companionship! Your loving granddaughter, Mishka."*

Budnikov's eyes widened in disbelief, and his head spun towards Mishka. "Federov is your grandfather? I thought your name was Krasnaya?"

Mishka's icy stare pierced through Budnikov as the realization of his own mistake made the bile rise to the back of his throat, gagging him and making him cough and sputter. He grasped his black Hamburg style fedora with both of his hands, but he had already put his pistol away.

"Mishka, Mishka! *The shadows in the corners are not entirely our own!*"

The speed of Mishka raising the gun to aim and firing the bullet from her pistol caught Budnikov in mid-sentence. The impact of the 9mm bullet to his forehead was equivalent to 368 foot pounds to the square inch. His skull was violently thrown back as the kinetic energy of the round continued its trajectory. He dropped hard onto the floor. The hole in his head oozed a garnet red pool of blood that flowed out onto the carpet in the den. She walked over to his body and fired a second round into the dead man's chest.

The pounding on the door stopped.

As Budnikov's words fully registered in her mind, a wave of calm flowed over Mishka. Deep within her, something seemed to click into place.

She took a deep breath and carefully hid her pistol with one arm behind her as she turned and walked to the front door. She turned the lock and opened the front door to let in Steve. She stepped aside and pointed to the den as Steve quickly entered with his pistol drawn and in position to return fire. Mishka quietly closed the door behind Steve as he hurried over to the lifeless body, knelt down, and checked for a pulse. He exhaled loudly and rested on his heels as Mishka entered the room.

"Are you all right?" asked Steve as he stood and lowered his pistol.

"Yes." She stared blankly at the motionless body on the floor.

Steve walked over and stood beside her. "Are you sure that you are all right?"

"Yes, I just can't believe he poisoned my grandfather." A tear rolled silently down her cheek as she continued to stare blankly at Budnikov's body.

"Federov was your grandfather?" asked Steve as he placed his hand on her shoulder.

"Yes," replied Mishka, her voice devoid of emotion. She looked at him coldly. "What are you doing here?"

"I know you know me as Michael, but my name is actually Steve Cotter. I work for the CIA. I was assigned to watch Dimitiry Federov."

Mishka nodded. "I see."

"Who is this man? Why did he poison your grandfather?"

"His name was Lieutenant General Konstantin Budnikov of the GRU, and he was a complete pig. I am glad I shot him."

Steve's eyes widened slightly, and he gripped his gun tighter in his hand. "Are you Mishka?"

"Yes, I am." Mishka looked at Steve and raised her eyebrow. "Don't act so surprised that I didn't use my real name. Neither did you."

"I know you're involved with what Dimitiry was working on somehow. You're supposed to take his place on whatever his mission was, aren't you?"

"That was the plan," Mishka admitted. She looked down at Budnikov on the floor for a moment and then back at Steve. She smiled. "But it's all changed now. With Budnikov out of the picture, there's no reason for me to have to keep up this double life anymore."

"You want out?"

"I've wanted out for a long time, but I couldn't get out from under Budnikov. Now I'm free from him."

Steve relaxed a bit, loosening his grip on his gun. "I can help you. I want to help you."

"That's what I want, too. But, Steve, we've got to hurry. It won't take long for a scrubber team to show up here to get rid of any trace of what Dimitiry was working on. You'll need all that to help me get out of all this."

Steve nodded. "Let's gather what we can."

Steve walked over to the dark cherry wood desk, holstering his pistol. He pulled open a desk drawer and saw a picture lying on a stack of papers. The image was of Mishka, Dimitiry, and another man. He picked it up. "Who is the other man in this picture?"

"That is my brother Josuf. He is on a mission to destroy Jerusalem with a special bomb," Mishka said coldly behind Steve's back.

Steve froze in a split second. His life flashed before his eyes. From images of Michael, Elizabeth, the homemade *Wolf* submarine, England, and even his new job with the CIA, his brain was frantically sorting the information before his eyes. The papers, a dead Russian general on the floor, and a photograph of a terrorist about to destroy a city. He knew instantly that he was in real trouble, for he had already holstered his gun.

"I am sorry, Steve," Mishka said softly as she pulled the trigger on her pistol and shot Steve in the back of his head.

Steve's body leapt forward and hit the top of the desk, and then he slowly slumped backwards and onto the floor. His body lay motionless on the den floor, just several feet away from Budnikov.

Mishka stood there looking at Steve's body on the floor. She was emotionless as she quickly determined what to do next.

Mishka walked over and searched Budnikov's coat pocket for his pistol. Upon retrieving the gun, she wiped off her fingerprints and placed the pistol into the dead hand of Budnikov. Next, she repeated the same procedure with Steve's gun, also with the pistol in a dead hand. She posed the arm in such a way on each body to represent that they had shot each other.

CHAPTER 24: THERE ARE ALWAYSCREEPY THINGS IN THE BASEMENT

Knowing that basement would be the most logical place for her grandfather to store the weapon she was after, Mishka walked over to the basement door and tried to open it. The knob turned, but the heavy door remained firmly shut. The hinges for door were on the inside, so it prohibited anyone from prying the door off by removing the three hinge pins. She also observed eight flat bolt heads on the door that were almost unnoticeable. These bolt heads meant only one thing: her grandfather had bolted iron plates to the other side of the door. The heads were very flat, and using a chisel to pop off the heads would be to no avail.

Mishka quickly noticed the non-working thermostat on the wall next to the door. She lifted it to reveal the security keypad that was hidden underneath and knew her grandfather must have installed it to control the lock for the door. She also knew it was going to be a very hard nut to crack.

To add to the mix, Mishka was aware of FSB and GRU tactics of espionage. If an agent, such as Budnikov, hadn't reported in within a predetermined timeframe, meaning he was either captured or killed, a scrubber team would immediately descend to the target area and cleanse the area of any evidence that an operative had ever been there. All papers, computers, fingerprints, or pictures caught in the scrubber's net would be eliminated. Mishka knew that she would be expendable as well. Budnikov's seniority would probably only heighten the intensity of the scrubber's effectiveness. She had to work fast in order to keep moving forward with her mission.

Mishka already knew that she was going to be in trouble with headquarters if they found out that she had killed Budnikov. She hadn't intended to pull the trigger, but Budnikov's actions couldn't be excused. It was the first time that her loyalty to her family and her loyalty to her country had come into such a direct conflict. She had been pulled away from her conditioning long enough for her rage to allow her to kill Budnikov, but her loyalty to her country remained.

To Mishka, righting the wrong of her grandfather's death was justification in her mind for killing her superior, but if she could get Dimitiry's weapon, she could carry out the mission that Budnikov had been meant to oversee. Her loyalty to her country could still be preserved, something that her very essence depended upon. She knew that it was all up to her, and it would also serve as two factors in her redemption: honor for herself and honor for her grandfather.

Mishka wracked her brain and entered an eleven-digit sequence of numbers based on her family's birth dates into the keypad. The keypad flashed red, signaling the code was incorrect.

Feeling the weight of time ticking away, Mishka knew she had to think quickly. She closed her eyes and took a deep breath.

"Eleven numbers, letters, or words," she said aloud, opening her eyes. "How about *n-u-c-l-e-a-r-b-o-m-b?*"

She took out her phone and used the numbers matched to the letters to determine the code. She entered it. The keypad flashed red.

"*M-i-s-h-k-a-j-o-s-u-f.*"

Again, she determined the code, entered it, and the keypad flashed red. She even put Josuf's name in first and still got the same result.

It had been over fifteen minutes since Budnikov had been shot. If she took into account the time he had probably spent stalking and then approaching Dimitiry in the park, possibly over an hour had passed. An upper-level GRU officer serving in the field was to report six times during daylight hours. That would translate to reporting in every two hours, and, by Mishka's watch, that time was running out.

"*Der'mo!*" she cursed in Russian, slipping her phone in her pocket. She walked over to Dimitiry's desk to search for clues and stepped around Steve's lifeless body.

The picture that Steve had found in the drawer lay on the desk. It had been taken five years before on a semi-vacation for all three members of her family. They had met up with each other in Istanbul, Turkey, because it had been easy for all three to travel to without raising too many red flags. She remembered how passionate Josuf had been about his newly rediscovered Islamic faith. Though a bit overdramatic for her tastes, as well as Dimitiry's, they had been happy for Josuf and his focused pathway to Allah.

She paused and picked up the picture. It reminded her of the ferry ride they had taken to cross the Bosporus, also known as the Istanbul Straight. She remembered their day cruise and the orange and white striped smoke stacks of the Sehir Hatlari ferries, a favorite among travelers that had been in business for over 160 years.

Floating across the Bosporus, they had watched the sun set behind the beautiful *Hagia Sophia,* meaning "Holy Wisdom" in Greek. Once a magnificent Catholic church during the Byzantine period, it had been captured by the Ottomans and converted into a grand mosque when Constantinople had been sacked in 1453.

She put down the picture and rummaged through the open drawer where Steve had found it. Under a stack of papers was a hand-carved picture frame that contained an autographed picture of the late Syrian president, Hafez al-Ahini. She knew Dimitiry had received it as a gift for his scientific research on radiation therapy for cancer patients from a Syrian government official during his years serving President Hafez. Even though they were Syrian by birth, Dimitiry had served Russia for many years. She also knew Dimitiry believed that the current Syrian president, Bashar al-Ahini, Hafez's son, would destroy Syria.

Mishka, too, hated Syrian President Bashar. Not long before, Russian President Pelevin had wanted everything he could find on Syria. He had wanted to know the politics, religious elements, military capabilities, civil unrest, and even the media relations of the country. The goal had been to use that information and Bashar to create a ruthless civil war in Syria so that Russia could intervene in the name of peace and obtain Syria's only Mediterranean port, giving Russia's navy access to the warm and lucrative waters of the Mediterranean Sea.

She had been successful in her mission to uncover that information, but, perhaps, too successful. When she had discovered the records of detainees and subversive elements that had been arrested in Syria, she had uncovered that President Bashar had ordered the execution of her parents, something that she wasn't sure that even Dimitiry had known.

Mishka tossed the frame back into the desk, thoughts of her mission overtaking her thoughts of the past. She rummaged around the desk and found a scratch pad where Dimitiry had written her and her brother's names. She counted at least three different places where their two names had been written. He had also written the word "sunset" at least six times in a scratchy, bold print.

"Sunset... sunset.... What about the sunset?" She looked around the desk some more. "What does 'sunset' have to do with Josuf and me?"

The beautiful moment in time when the three of them had enjoyed that boat ride with the Hagia Sofia in the background, silhouetted by the sunset flashed in her mind.

"Sunset. Josuf and me. The boat ride! The Hagia Sophia—wait! That's eleven letters! Hagia Sophia is eleven letters!""

Mishka pulled out her cellphone quickly picked up a pencil from the desk. She wrote down the numbers that matched the letters of the name.

"4-2-4-4-2-7-6-7-4-4-2," she whispered. "Got it! It was indeed beautiful wisdom, Poppi."

She hurried to the basement door and entered the eleven numbers. The security keypad flashed green, and the basement door opened. Mishka smiled brightly and proceeded down the steps.

"This must be where Papa kept the bomb." Mishka whispered as to the extra detail he used to camouflage the door.

She quickly scanned the basement. Not seeing anything that grabbed her attention, she hurried around the sides of the room and quickly discovered the green metal door behind the chair stacked with boxes. She moved them out of the way and opened the door, revealing the secret door inside. She hurriedly entered the same numbers from the other alarm into the keypad on the door handle and was greeted with the familiar green light. She opened the door and slipped inside the cramped hidden room. Her training and knowledge of her grandfather's years of experience led her to believe that her grandfather would have set another alarm inside the room. She quickly scanned the room and found the button that bypassed the thermal scanner and pressed it.

Mishka turned her attention to the package she had spotted during her quick scan of the room. She instantly recognized the W72 bomb laying on the floor in the far corner by its dark green barrel with a harness to shoulder the weight. The bomb's canister was round like a beer keg and just as tall. It was an active weapon that had been in the United States inventory until 1979. Special Green Light teams would parachute in and place the W72 in strategic locations, such as the Fulda Gap in Germany during the Cold War.

Soviet—and current Russian—strategic commanders knew of the uniqueness of having the W72. Its existence and it being smuggled into the United States were a coup for the Russians. Dimitiry had never been recalled nor replaced, and he had faithfully awaited a "go code" from upper echelons to carry out his mission.

Budnikov wanted Mishka to attack the closest target—a target that no one would have guessed as a real danger—the Fontana Dam. He wanted her to make it look like a terrorist attack. She knew the mission must have been really important if he had flown there to personally guarantee its successful conclusion.

The loss of the Fontana Dam and the multiple hydro generators which created power would decimate the entire region, and it would also devastate the water supply with lethal amounts of radioactive fallout. With the valley below the dam filling up with radioactive water, the sudden swell would overwhelm the next TVA dam. That cycle would repeat itself like a string of dominoes until it reached the upper Tennessee and Mississippi rivers. The strategy was extremely simple: destroy the water and the power. Not killing millions upon millions of American citizens in the Southeast with a thermal nuclear device was also very appealing to the new Russian—and not Soviet—strategic thinking.

Mishka quickly gathered the W72, several electrical cords, and the battery charger with its fully charged replacement battery. She slipped out of the room, shut the doors, and laid her treasures on the arm chair. Following Budnikov's orders for her new mission, she pulled out her cellphone and pushed a speed dial button that she had programmed earlier to contact the Spetsnaz team who were waiting on standby. She wasn't sure if the Spetsnaz team had already been briefed as to the new target, and she couldn't chance a mistake of that magnitude. The go code, "Santa has a brown fur coat," was very thorough and followed a strict set of protocols. Mishka knew them all.

"Santa? Hello? Santa, can you hear me?" Mishka said in English.

"Ho ho ho, little girl, this is Santa. Merry Christmas!" responded a voice on the other end of the line.

"Santa, I need you to meet me at the waterfall."

There was a brief pause over the phone. Then a male voice responded. "Okay. Waterfall. What time?"

"Whenever you are open," Mishka answered and hung up the phone.

Mishka put her phone away and smiled. She knew that the phone conversation was probably being monitored by the CIA. She also knew that the one thing the eavesdroppers didn't know: the waterfall was the giant 50-story-high hydro-electric dam known as Fontana.

CHAPTER 25: HE TOUCHED ME

The paramedics began to work frantically as soon as they arrived. They hurriedly moved Dimitiry from the park bench to their gurney from the ambulance.

"He said he was poisoned at his wrist. Look there, where his watchband would be," Elizabeth said, her eyes brimmed with tears.

"Thank you, ma'am," one of the medics responded, looking up briefly as he worked to attach EKG probes to Dimitiry's chest.

Michael and Elizabeth stood aside to let the medics do their job to try to save Dimitiry's life. Michael looked up the hill towards where Dimitiry's townhouse was, wondering where Steve was and if he was okay. Elizabeth watched silently as the paramedics worked, her arms wrapped tightly around her torso. A hot, humid breeze whipped the loose hairs from her braid across her face, but she didn't notice. Michael glanced up at the little monkey on his shoulder, who was unusually still compared to what they had observed from the apartment, and then turned his attention to the paramedics.

As the medics began CPR, Elizabeth walked over to Michael for comfort, tears streaming down her face. Michael put his arm around his cousin and kissed her on top of her head. Malinky also showed a sweet sign of compassion as she placed a tiny black-haired paw on Elizabeth's head. For a brief second, Malinky's second hand reached for Elizabeth's head as if to perform the usual grooming of a fellow monkey, but the little monkey stopped her arm halfway and let out a quiet chirp that sounded very similar to a "no" in capuchin-speak.

As the medics continued CPR, Michael looked up the hill again. A dark, fast-moving storm cloud raced through the hazy August sky behind the hill, and the stifling wind that carried it rushed past. Michael felt a chill run up his spine despite the heat, as if the scene were all too familiar for comfort, and the urge to race up the hill after his brother swelled in his heart. He knew that

Steve was a trained CIA agent, but Michael couldn't shake the feeling that something was really wrong with their current situation. He knew he couldn't leave just yet, but he desperately wanted to.

"St. Gabriel, this is Fire House Unit Seven. Come in. Over," said one of the paramedics into his shoulder-mounted radio microphone, drawing Michael's attention back to the scene before him.

"Go ahead, Seven," a woman's voice responded.

"We are at the scene. Patient, Middle Eastern male, mid- to late-70s. Unresponsive. Vital signs are negative. We have no pulse, no EKG. We have no lung activity. Airway is clear." The medic glanced over his shoulder at Elizabeth and Michael and then quickly back to the patient in front of him.

Elizabeth looked up at Michael as the medic started to speak again.

"Citizens on the scene have reported possible poisoning. We see a puncture wound approximately one to two millimeters wide with light redness around entry hole. Our assessment: patient is Category 1 Foxtrot."

Michael wrapped his arm tighter around Elizabeth, and she looked back and forth between the medics and Michael. Her eyes were red as she looked up at her cousin. "What did he say, Michael?"

"Dimitiry is dead," Michael whispered to Elizabeth. "'Category 1' is regular EMS code for DOA. 'Foxtrot' is a state code meaning 'fatality.'"

Elizabeth embraced her cousin, laying her head against his chest. Michael held her and patted her back gently. He looked up the hill as a gust of hot wind rushed past them. As he watched the storm cloud pass, he noticed a solitary bird, black as night, circling in the sky below the cloud. He squeezed his eyes shut and shook his head, trying to shake off a familiar unsettling feeling. When he opened his eyes, the bird was flying away, disappearing into the distance.

A police officer and a detective, who had arrived at the park soon after the paramedics, began to take statements from all the witnesses, including Michael and Elizabeth. Elizabeth pulled herself together and stepped aside as Michael reported to the officers that they had seen a tall man in a dark coat approach Dimitiry when he was sitting on the bench. Once they had gathered his story and personal information, they moved on to question Elizabeth.

Michael tapped his foot anxiously as he waited for Elizabeth to answer all the officers' questions. He could not leave her there alone, nor could he immediately run off up the hill without arousing suspicion. He exhaled heavily as he waited, watching the paramedics zip Dimitiry in a long, black bag. As the paramedics loaded Dimitiry in the ambulance, Malinky made a sad chirp and climbed down from Michael's shoulder and proceeded to rest on his chest and give Michael a big hug.

After several more minutes of questioning, the police finished up with Elizabeth, and she walked over to Michael. He wrapped his arm around her shoulder and started to walk towards the staircase that led to Dimitiry's townhouse.

When she was sure no one was listening, Elizabeth whispered, "What do we do now?"

Michael looked up the hill, his heart filled with dread. "We need to get up this hill and find Steve. Let's go."

CHAPTER 26: THIS BELUGA TASTES FISHY

Moscow, Russia

The headquarters of strategic command for General Sokolov was a beehive of activity as final analysis reports came in over the third Beluga bomb that had been detonated. The third one had been the first time a super heavy artillery shell had been used to deliver the dispersal device that exploded over the target.

Instead of Chechen rebel towns, the latest target had been a small Kurdish town on the border, the very same Kurds that had been pestering Syrian president Bashar al-Ahini's men in Bashar's ruthless war against the rebels. The results had been the same, and, with the added security of Russian forces already in that region, it had been a boon for Sokolov. The Russian troops had established a secure zone around that target ahead of time that had prohibited Western media groups from reporting anything unusual.

Sokolov smiled as he laid down the most recent report on how well his device was working. He leaned back in his chair, relishing the success of his new weapon. He straightened and reached across his desk and pressed the intercom button that connected him with his aide. "Get me someone who knows what is happening with Budnikov."

"Yes, General. Right away," his aide responded on the other end.

Sokolov picked up the report and began to look over it again as he leaned back in his chair. After reviewing the documents for a few minutes, his smile became a chuckle of celebration.

There was a sharp knock on the door, and then the door opened. A young lieutenant stepped in the room and saluted.

"What is it?" Sokolov demanded, folding the report in his hands.

"You wanted to see me. About Budnikov, sir."

"Yes. What news do we have on Budnikov and his mission overseas?"

"We have not heard from him for some time, General Sokolov. If he does not report within the next five minutes, his absence would typically trigger a scrubber team to his target area. We plan to delay activation of the scrubber team out of respect for Budnikov's age and his unfamiliarity with the region, sir."

Sokolov threw the report on the desk. "You stupid idiot! You are not to deviate from the plan. You are not paid to think. Budnikov is more competent than you will ever be. If he hasn't already checked in, then something is wrong! Send in the team!"

The young lieutenant saluted and quickly backed towards the door. "Yes, General! Right away, General!"

Sokolov stood up and slammed his hand on his desk. "Hurry up before we are too late!"

CHAPTER 27: THEY EVEN LEFT
THE LIGHT ON FOR ME

Outside Jerusalem

It was shortly after midnight when Josuf entered the small village of al-Za'im, just east of Israel's new capital, Jerusalem, on foot. Local guides had escorted Josuf and his large locker box from the Jordanian city of Madaba. The escorts had known the ancient goat paths taken centuries before and timed their crossing with a herd of sheep headed west for better grassy mountain pastures. The shepherd and his young son of seven had easily been bribed, for their family had desperately needed the money. To a passing satellite or a drone with infrared sensors, the group of humans and sheep marching as one would have been almost indiscernible.

Josuf had spent two nights in a safe house in Madaba, a border town to the disputed West Bank of Israel. He had paid off the key members of Jordanian King Ahmad II's security forces. He had chosen that location because Israeli forces had honored Jordan's commitment to avoid harboring the Iranian-backed terrorist group Hamas and other terrorists since 1999. The safe house was close enough for Josuf to slip over the border and join Hamas forces in a small village called al-Za'im, which was east of Jerusalem, Israel's new capital.

Josuf had made inroads in communicating with Hamas' main leaders. Attempts with Fatah, the rival to Hamas, had all but failed due to ideology in dealing with Israel. He had also reunited with a Russian/Syrian college associate who was a tactical advisor to the regional Hamas leader. Josuf had convinced the leadership that he had acquired a small tactical nuclear device that only he could control.

His bold plan of attack sat well with the Hamas leaders. Josuf had also explained the significance of his mission, and how it would unite all the Palestinian territory under Israeli control in their desire to be free. Syria and Iran could finally fulfill the destiny they had so longed for. A Persian, not Arab, presence on the Mediterranean coast would mean a major shift in the political strength in the region. It would catch Israel off balance, which would result in a new and final jihad to clean out the Zionists.

Joseph's weapon appealed to the leaders of Hamas because it was able to invoke extreme damage but, according to Josuf, spare structures that weren't targeted. To Hamas and other religious fanatics, the sparing of the Dome of the Rock was paramount. The Dome of the Rock was once a temple, then a church, and eventually a Muslim mosque after the fall of Jerusalem in 1187 during the Crusades. The sacred place remained controversial as both the Judeo-Christian and Muslim faiths claimed ownership, and the Muslims believed that their great prophet Mohammed ascended to heaven from that location. The Jewish people also considered it a holy location and wanted to control it because they believed the Dome's location was the location of the Foundation Stone for Abraham when he had offered his son up to God for a sacrifice. It was also believed that the rock was the place where the Ark of the Covenant had been stationed in the temple.

Josuf had planned to launch his miniature nuclear rocket *Davy Crockett* during a heavy barrage by Hamas in the upcoming week on Friday. It would be the week of elections for the new prime minister for Israel, the same prime minister who had boasted that his Iron Dome of missile protection would not let a single enemy rocket hit Israel's sovereign property. The Israeli defense industry giant Rafael, who produced the vast array of missiles for the Iron Dome, had repeatedly asked the press not to overplay their capabilities. Josuf's attack would undermine the legitimacy of the prime minister's new government initiative known as the New Direction and his possible re-election.

Josuf was to stay at the home of Omar Hamdan and his wife, who were supporters of the Palestinian's claim to the area and also supporters of Hamas, the militant proxy for Iran. Their home was in one of the three territorial zones in the West Bank territory. The land was what the Israelis called Judea. Omar had always welcomed anyone who opposed Israel into his home. He had lost his father early in life when the senior Hamdan had been killed by an Israeli tank that had blasted their home during the War of Attrition from 1967 to 1970. Omar's intense hatred of any Israeli was his driving force from within.

Omar met Josuf at the door of his simple home and escorted him inside. Omar's wife had made a special Middle Eastern favorite just for Josuf: *tabbouleh*. It was a wonderful combination of chopped parsley, tomatoes, herbs, lemon juice, bulgur wheat, mint, onions, and olive oil. Tabbouleh had always been a symbol of friendship and welcome in Lebanese and Syrian cultures. As for Josuf, it reminded him of home and happier times. The woman sang softly in the background the praises of thanks that Josuf would soon free her people from the Israeli occupiers as he ate quietly.

Josuf thanked the kind woman and smiled. He remarked to everyone present that he was only doing the will of Allah and that he was no hero. He said his goodnights and again thanked the humble homeowners for letting him stay the night. It was almost one o'clock in the morning, and the air was cool and comfortable for a good night's rest.

Josuf closed the old wooden door to his room and shook his head. He whispered to himself, "These boring simpletons think I am doing this for Allah. I have other plans."

Josuf's personal cellphone rang. He pulled it from his pants pocket and smiled.

"Hello, my little Red Monkey," he said in English, knowing it was Mishka.

"Josuf, listen to me carefully. Poppi is dead. Budnikov killed him, so I killed Budnikov."

"Poppi is dead? By Budnikov?" Confusion overtook Josuf for a brief moment as tears welled in his eyes. As quickly as the surge of emotion had erupted from the news, it was quelled by something much stronger.

"Yes, but there is more. I, too, have my mission."

Josuf smiled. "Mishka, we can do this together. We will strike the blow that will cripple the imperialists and Zionists together. Where are you to strike?"

"It's the nearest target from the ones on Poppi's list. You?"

"It is the target I've prayed to Allah for now for many years."

"Josuf, I have to go. I've got to load up my car and get to my target. I love you," Mishka said as she hung up the phone.

"I love you, too, sister. We will make Poppi proud together."

CHAPTER 28: MY NIGHTMARE IS HERE, BUT I'M STILL AWAKE

North Carolina

Mishka ended her phone call with her brother and focused on the physical tasks ahead. The 50-pound W72 was a cumbersome load as Mishka trudged up the basement stairs, even with her heightened adrenaline levels and well-toned frame. The heavy bomb had been intended to be carried by a physically conditioned paratrooper of the 82nd Airborne Division. She exhaled deeply as she cleared the last step. She took the pack off and left it at the top of the stairs. She then proceeded back down to retrieve the rest of the equipment.

As she finished bringing up the remainder of the W72 parts, she glanced again at her watch. She winced at the time she was risking before the scrub team arrived to clean the entire townhouse of any incriminating evidence. Even the two bodies on the floor would be removed and dumped in a remote location, regardless of if it were a high-ranking Russian official or not.

Mishka took a quick look through the blinds on the window to see if she was in the clear to make it to her car. When satisfied that she could, she ran outside and moved her convertible to the front door of her grandfather's townhouse. A hot gust of air rushed past her, blowing her hair across her face as she popped the trunk of her convertible and retrieved her medical coat and put it on. Her FSB training had taught her that hiding in plain sight by looking like an important official was her best option to go unnoticed. It was a reverse psychology tactic that statistically worked 84 percent of the time, and Russians loved working the statistics.

Mishka left the trunk open and ran back into the townhouse to retrieve the weapon. As quickly as she could, she carried the heavy burden to the car. She knew that if she was only around this device for a brief time, she wouldn't

116

be at risk of too much radiation poisoning. Looking into the trunk, she quickly realized it wasn't going to fit, so she chose a different location. She placed the W72 on the front passenger seat and strapped it in with the seatbelt,

Mishka hurried back into the townhouse and moved the rest of the equipment to beside the door. She then went into the living room and gathered Dimitiry's orders and put them in with the equipment she had gathered. She then pushed a lamp off the foyer table and made a mess with other pieces of décor to stage the scene. Her strategy was to create the perception of a home invasion that had gone wrong. She then picked up the rest of the equipment and went out, leaving the front door just barely open. She hurried to the car, dumped the equipment in the trunk and closed it, and then climbed in and started the car.

As Mishka sped off through the parking lot, Michael and Elizabeth cleared the top of the concrete steps from the park below. Malinky, sitting on Elizabeth's shoulders, let out a large howl and pointed to Mishka as she drove off. The monkey was clearly disturbed at seeing Mishka driving away. Her reaction made both Michael and Elizabeth take notice of the dark-haired woman driving the convertible at great speed out of the parking lot.

"That looks like Micah's car… and Micah! LCD T312 license plate on a white Toyota convertible," Michael said out loud to Elizabeth.

"Got it!" Elizabeth said, rapidly typing the information into her phone as they hurried down the sidewalk.

"Something feels really wrong about this," Michael said, glancing at Elizabeth, who had stuffed her phone back in her pocket and was trying to comfort the screaming monkey on her shoulder. "If that was Micah, where's Steve? Why was she leaving in such a hurry?"

"I don't know, but I think you're right about something being wrong here. Look!" Elizabeth pointed towards the partially opened door of Dimitiry's townhouse.

Michael stopped and held his arm out, blocking Elizabeth from going any further. He quickly surveyed the scene, his military senses kicking in as he scanned the area. When he didn't see anything else out of the ordinary, he nodded to his cousin and lowered his arm.

The two approached the front door cautiously. Michael slowly pushed open the front door with one hand and peered inside, staying back from the door as much as possible. He noted the overturned lamp and scattered items in the hallway and stepped inside.

"Steve?" he called. Hearing nothing, he motioned for Elizabeth to follow.

Michael inched down the hall until he could see into the living room and spotted the body of the stranger in the dark overcoat first. He inched forward and saw Steve lying on the floor face down.

"Steve! No!" he yelled. Panic overtook Michael's many years of training, and he rushed into the living room toward his brother.

Elizabeth followed quickly but screamed immediately at the top of her lungs when she entered the room, scaring Malinky enough that she jumped from Elizabeth's shoulders to the ground.

Michael quickly knelt down and rolled his brother over. "Oh, my God, no! No, Steve, no!"

As he pulled his brother's lifeless body into his arms, the anguish and pain of the loss swept across Michael, burying him under a tidal wave of agony that threatened to drive the very breath from his body. He gasped for air as if he'd been struck in the chest by a truck and closed his eyes to try to stop the agonizing pain. Tears began to pour silently from his eyes, and his body shook with grief.

Elizabeth backed towards the entrance of the room, where she leaned against the wall, tears streaming down her face. Malinky scurried across the floor and climbed onto the desk beside Michael.

"Why? Why?" Michael cried, looking towards the ceiling. He clutched his brother's body to his chest. "Why did he have to die? Please, God, bring him back! Take me, not him! Oh, Heavenly Father, I beg you!"

Michael closed his eyes as his head collapsed against his chest. Everything they had been through together swam through his mind. Their childhood adventures. The wonderful memories at Lake Lanier. The adventures in England and solving the Vergers' Guild mystery. He remembered it all. Every bittersweet memory pulled him deeper and deeper beneath the crushing wave of sorrow.

Elizabeth remained quiet to let her cousin mourn in peace. Although the loss of her cousin was terrible, the pain of such a loss had been felt before when she had lost her father to cancer many years before.

Michael sobbed as he cradled his baby brother in his arms. A mild case of shock began to take over Michael's body. He'd felt that shock before when he had held his English friend David who had died in his arms back at the British firebase in Afghanistan.

"He's still warm," Michael said softly.

Elizabeth gathered her strength and walked over to the dark-coated stranger's body. She felt she had to do something, not because she was insensitive, but because she wanted answers about her cousin's murder. She observed that the man was lying on his back with his arm pointed toward Steve's direction. A pistol was in his hand.

The numbness that Michael felt eased his sobs, but the pain was still overwhelming. He closed his eyes and remained motionless, as if he were praying in silence. Behind his closed eyes, an all-too-familiar shadow began to creep up from behind him. It pushed its way through the tidal wave of pain and seemed to creep up his spine and across the top of his head. The giant black wings from his never-ending nightmare soared through his mind.

118

Elizabeth bent down, and after taking a deep breath to steady herself, reached into the man's coat pocket and retrieved some paper, a plane ticket to Moscow, and a passport. She then moved from the coat and picked up the pistol and noticed it was Russian. She also noted that the barrel was clean and without the residue of having been fired recently.

Inside Michael's mind, the raven wings swept towards the figure in the navy coat that now seemed to stand in front of him. As the wings beat forward, growing larger and larger and circling the figure in the distance, the figure turned towards Michael for the first time, and he could see its face. It was his baby brother.

Michael opened his eyes, but the shadowy raven from his dream seemed to linger in front of him, turning and staring at him with hollow black eyes before vanishing into the air. His nightmare had become a reality.

"Michael," Elizabeth said, standing and coming toward her cousin. "Michael, this is all wrong. I need your help. We have to find out why this happened to Steve."

Michael shook his head and took a deep breath. He looked down at his brother.

"I need your help, Michael." Elizabeth laid her hand on Michael's shoulder. "Steve needs you to do this for him. Do this for Steve, Michael. We need you."

Her words pulled Michael from his nightmare come to life. A surge of devotion and love came from somewhere deep inside, mixing with the hurt and pain and transforming into something stronger than Michael had ever felt. He gently lowered Steve onto the floor and wiped his face with his hand. "What did you find?"

Elizabeth breathed a sigh of relief and patted Michael's shoulder. "The dead man over there was shot in the front, but the angles are all wrong for them to have shot each other. Plus, his pistol hasn't been fired. I think this was staged to look like they shot each other."

Michael carefully picked up Steve's pistol and noticed the same thing that Elizabeth had stated. Neither of the men had shot their pistols, and yet both had been shot.

Michael, running on autopilot, retrieved the passport from Elizabeth and leafed through the small green book.

"Why is it green and not red like normally?" asked Elizabeth.

"It's a diplomatic passport. Passports have different colors which readily designate who you are and where you are from. We have blue, China has black, and countries in South America have brown. The CIA needs to know these things and what this guy's name is."

Elizabeth nodded.

"I need to contact Steve's boss and tell him Steve has been killed and give him our location."

Michael retrieved Steve's phone and punched the redial button. He remembered that the last call Steve had made was when he reported to MacAday that Dimitiry had collapsed on the park bench. He stood up and walked toward the hall as he began to talk to someone on the other end of the line.

While Michael was on the phone, Malinky chirped and pointed to something inside the desk drawer. Elizabeth came over to see what the little monkey was doing and why she was making such a racket. To her surprise, the monkey was pointing to a picture that lay on top of the scattered papers on the desk. Elizabeth picked it up. She recognized Dimitiry and Micah, but she was not sure who the other man in the picture was. She also noted the Hagia Sophia in the picture, as well as the beautiful sunset.

"The CIA people will be here in about 25 minutes," Michael reported as he hung up the phone and put it in his pants pocket. He walked toward Elizabeth. "They are sending in a Special Activities Division unit to secure this area. I am familiar with them and witnessed a few of their activities in Afghanistan. They want us to stay to answer questions. What do you have there?"

"It's a picture of Dimitiry and Micah with some guy." Elizabeth held out the picture to Michael, and he took it. "I know you're thinking what I'm thinking. If this was staged, and she's not here...."

Michael stared intently at the photo in his hand, his eyes focused on the face of the beautiful woman standing there in that beautiful sunset scene. Michael's hand began to tighten into a firm clench. From deep within his inner self, an immense hatred began to swell. He memorized that face as he internally swore that he would avenge his brother's death.

"Then it was her...." The words spit forth from Michael's drawn mouth like venom from a cobra. "And that was her in that convertible speeding away. We have to find her."

Elizabeth nodded as an idea struck her. "I'll check on *Is He a Bad Date* to find out what I can about her. I use it whenever I get asked out."

She pulled out her phone quickly and pulled up her web browser. She then typed in "www.is-he-a-bad-date.com." The site pulled up quickly, and she typed in the license plate number for the convertible that she had stored in the phone earlier. In less than a minute, the app revealed who the owner of the car was.

"Dr. Mishka Federov. That must be Micah's real name. She works at St. Gabriel Hospital in Asheville, North Carolina, as a radiologist instructor. She has an apartment on Stat Street just next to the hospital. She makes around $95,000 a year, and she has no priors."

"Now I'll find her," Michael whispered, looking down at the photo clenched in his fingers. "For Steve."

CHAPTER 29: A SPIDER CAN SET A NICE TABLE FOR HER GUEST WHEN SHE DINES

The flashing blue lights Mishka saw in her rearview mirror were an unwanted annoyance. Mishka tried to ignore the squad car following her and continued driving as if everything was normal. She did glance down to the dashboard, and she noticed that the speedometer was hovering around 78 mph. The police officer continued flashing his blue lights and then turned on the siren.

Mishka had to make a decision. If she sped up to evade the officer, he would use his radio and call for backup. If she pulled over, he might get suspicious of the large bag strapped in the seat beside her. The officer stayed well to the rear, so she couldn't use her special trick to make him crash like she had done to the trucker. The only option she really had was to pull over and use her guile to avoid any suspicion as to the large canister-shaped package in the passenger seat, so she pulled over onto the shoulder.

As she put the car in park, she glanced at the side mirror to get a better view of the officer in the car behind her. As he got out an approached her, she feigned fixing her hair in the rearview mirror so that she could watch him carefully.

"What seems to be the matter, officer?" she asked as she as he stopped beside her door, her right hand moving discreetly to her lap close to where her FSB pistol was hidden beside the driver seat.

Brushing her long dark hair behind her left ear with her fingers, she slowly turned her head to face him. Her green eyes peered seductively over the top of her designer sunglasses. She could see instantly by his reaction that he was stunned by her beauty. She could only imagine that his eyes grew wide with excitement as they remained hidden behind his very dark polarized sunglasses.

"License and registration, please. You were speeding, and that's not permitted in a 55 miles per hour zone." sputtered the officer as he desperately tried to regain his composure and initiative.

"I'm so sorry, but my grandfather just died. I was upset that my favorite Papa was gone."

"Uh, I am sorry for your loss, ma'am, but I still have to give you a ticket," he said as he retrieved his citation book from his back pocket. He looked around Mishka towards the passenger seat and noticed the military markings on the dark green nylon backpack. "May I ask what that is in your passenger seat?"

Mishka wasn't expecting that question, even though she knew it was sitting there like a red herring. She paused for a second and gathered her thoughts as to how fast she could pull out the pistol beside her seat and shoot the officer before he could return fire. The odds were against her since he could see everything in the car, so she changed her tactics.

"Oh, I'm a doctor at St. Gabriel's, and this is a double lung transplant that I'm transporting. We have a young girl who is waiting for these lungs. She's been on life support for almost three days. Could we hurry along, please?"

"Oh, I didn't know, ma'am!" The officer looked genuinely remorseful. "I tell you what, I'll let you go this time. Do you want me to escort you to the hospital?"

"Oh, no, that won't be necessary. Thank you, officer. Thank you. I'm sure the little girl will say 'thank you,' as well, just as soon as she gets these transplants into her."

The officer returned his citation book back into his pocket and readjusted his sunglasses. He then coughed back his emotions about the little girl and waved for Mishka to get moving.

"Whew!" Mishka whispered under her breath as she pulled away.

"Whew!" whispered the officer as his composure slowly returned.

CHAPTER 30: RENTAL CARS DON'T CARE WHAT LANGUAGE YOU SPEAK

Michael put his hand deep into the dead stranger's pocket carefully for fear of being stuck by the same lethal needle that had killed Dimitiry. As soon as he felt the car keys, he quickly pulled out his hand.

"Got 'em!" Michael stood up and looked at his cousin. He patted his own pocket with his free hand. "I also have the Russian's pistol. You stay here and see what you can get off Dimitiry's computer. It should be easy enough for you to hack if you need to, and there might be something important on there."

"Shouldn't you wait for the CIA folks?" asked Elizabeth as she sat down at the desk. "I really wish you would just stay here with me until they get here."

"I have to go after Mishka. I know she killed my brother… and this other man. She probably still has the pistol she used in these murders. If anything, I'm doing this for Steven. You stay here and let the authorities know what I'm doing and keep an eye on Steve."

Michael pulled out the Russian's gun and checked to be sure that it was loaded. He then slid it back into his pocket.

Elizabeth stared at him with a concerned look on her face. "You don't like guns. You said it yourself."

"Elizabeth, I don't have time to argue with you. I served two tours in Afghanistan with the US Army and was also attached to the British Royal Artillery. I think I know very well how to protect myself."

"Just be careful," she replied, shaking her head. She looked over at the little monkey as she jumped up and down on the desk instead of at Michael.

Michael turned without a word and left, closing the front door as he walked outside. He knew he had a very low probability of finding his brother's killer. At least he knew who she was, what she looked like, and where she worked.

Outside the townhouse, Michael walked up and down the parking lot pressing the unlock button on the Russian's key fob. After several clicks, the dead Russian's rental sedan lit up. It was a very large black Mercedes.

Michael walked briskly to it, climbed into the powerful German auto, and turned over the ignition. The car roared to life as he strapped on his seatbelt. The navigation system in the car came up first. He noticed a microphone icon on the right side of the steering wheel and pressed it.

"*Wo möchten Sie gehen?*" the Mercedes inquired in a German computer-generated voice, asking Michael a kind of "Where to?" question.

Michael quickly hit the menu option for the car and scrolled through the language selection for the car's navigation and other voice alerts.

"German… Spanish… Japanese… English! Yes!" Michael was intrigued that there was not a Russian language choice, so the dead Russian had probably had to use German for guidance. Michael quickly selected the English option and proceeded to scroll back to the navigation.

"What's your destination?" the car inquired.

"St. Gabriel Hospital!" Michael shouted loudly and slowly towards the dashboard as if the car's computer were hard of hearing.

The route guidance displayed on the navigation window, and the heads-up display highlighted his route.

"Okay, now we are cooking with gas!" Michael exclaimed.

"I am sorry. I do not know that command," announced the computer voice.

A puzzled look flashed on Michael's face as to why the car was still listening to him. Then he realized that in his eagerness to get on with the pursuit of his brother's killer he still had his finger on the microphone button on the steering wheel.

CHAPTER 31: EXCUSE ME, BUT YOU HAVE DROOL ON YOUR COLLAR

The blushing police officer watched as the white convertible sped away. He climbed back into his patrol car when a broadcast sounded on the radio. "PC 19, PC 19, do you copy?"

He closed the door on the vehicle to hear better. "Go ahead, dispatch."

"We have some more info on your 10-28," responded the dispatcher concerning his earlier request for a license and registration check.

"The car is registered to a 'Mishka Federov.' She is a doctor at St. Gabriel Hospital. She is a registered immigrant from Russia. She has a degree in radiology. She is a—"

"Wait a second! She is a doctor of radiology?" asked the officer as he stared directly ahead.

"That is correct."

His hands tightened into fists on the steering wheel with rage. "Dispatch, send out an alert. My 10-28 is not on a rescue mission with lung transplants. There is large military-looking barrel in the front seat that she claimed contained lungs. She might be a possible smuggler, thief, or even a terrorist. Inform Charlie ahead on the interstate that she's coming his way. PC 19, out."

The officer started up his car and turned on his lights as he maneuvered into traffic to intercept the spider who'd almost had him for dinner.

CHAPTER 32: CROSSWORD PUZZLES CAN KILL YOU IF YOU DON'T FINISH THEM

Elizabeth felt nervous and a bit frightened alone in the townhouse with Steve and the Russian's dead bodies. She glanced out the window to see if the CIA's SAD team had shown up. Seeing no sign of them, she decided to see if she could gather any information that might help them figure out what had happened. She sat the little monkey in her lap as she rummaged through the papers that were scattered across the desk.

She pondered over some of the handwritten notes that Dimitiry had scribbled. *Mishka-Josuf* was written over and over in pencil across a notepad. The photo of Dimitiry and the two others suggested that the woman named Mishka Federov and the young man were siblings and not lovers. There was a high probability that they were related to Dimitiry, so Elizabeth wondered if the man's name could be Josuf. That might make the names very important.

Being a student of computer science, she played with the letters in the names. There were six letters for "Mishka," and five letters for "Josuf." Elizabeth's brain was working on pure adrenaline as her anxiety increased.

She tried typing in the names on the keyboard to get in the computer. Each attempt ended in a failure. She tried the names backwards, and she even typed the names in all caps. Again, there was no success.

"Six and five. Could Dimitiry be 65? No, that can't be right. Eleven letters total. Damn! This is nuts. Why am I getting upset over numbers and letters?" whispered Elizabeth as she gave up trying to make sense of the names.

Elizabeth then proceeded to bring up Dimitiry's computer using the backdoor approach of going in as an administrator. Once there, she used the DOS start-up method and was able to get to the desktop screen of the computer by typing in a series of computer command codes that only computer repair technicians and DOS writers know about.

Once Elizabeth breached his computer, she began to explore. First, she opened his email account. She skimmed the first ten emails in the queue. She wasn't sure what any of it meant, so she decided to go through his files instead.

Her eyes scanned the file names for anything unusual. When she spotted a file with a name that matched the one on the passport of the dead man, Budnikov, she opened it. Her eyes grew wide as she read, and she knew she had to keep searching. Another file amongst the other hundred or so on the computer screen quickly grabbed her attention. The file had a simple name: Red Monkey.

Intrigued, Elizabeth opened the file, thinking it was all about the little furry friend sitting on her lap. Malinky was grooming herself and paid no attention to Elizabeth's work. Unfortunately, the file was password-protected and required and 11-digit code to open it. She could not breach it by a simple DOS rewrite.

"Eleven digits? How about good ol' *MishkaJosuf*? That's 11 digits, but what if it's a trap that deletes the file?"

Her first attempt failed at trying to break the code. Elizabeth grew frustrated, but she was relieved that the failure didn't delete file. She tried the standard reverse approach: *JosufMishka*. It, too, failed.

Elizabeth then remembered her computer science professors back at Georgia Tech and pondered what they would do in that situation.

"'Many people use pleasant memories of their past when creating passwords. Birthdays, anniversaries, first dates, and even first kisses are all very important. It's the tacit ones that trigger an easier recall for a password,'" Elizabeth whispered, quoting one of her professors' lectures.

She then proceeded to look around for a clue, anything that Dimitiry would have used as a memory recall catalyst. The desk was a total mess. Papers were strewn all about, but the picture of Dimitiry, Mishka, and the young man caught her eye.

She picked up the picture and examined it closely. The three were posing along a boat's railing. Elizabeth determined from the picture that it was a ferry boat because there were cars parked on either side of the people and the water behind them looked blurred as if the boat were in transit. Behind the people was a delightful sunset with the immense mosque called the Hagia Sophia in the distance.

"This must have been in Turkey. That's the Hagia Sophia."

Elizabeth blinked her eyes in excitement as she realized Dimitiry's passcode.

She quickly typed in the eleven letters: H-a-g-i-a-S-o-p-h-i-a. To her astonishment, the simple trick to find the password had worked, and the secret file opened in a new window on the desktop. It was written in Russian, so Elizabeth highlighted the Cyrillic letters and right clicked to translate.

"*Washington, D.C.; the city of Atlanta and the CDC; King's Bay Naval Base in St. Mary's, Georgia; Dobbins Air Force Base in Marietta, Georgia; Pensacola Naval Air Station, Florida; Fontana Dam near Asheville, North Carolina.*" Elizabeth read the list of places out loud.

She scrolled through page after page of maps, each matching one of the locations on the list. When the maps ended, there were diagrams of a W72 bomb with detailed instructions on how to operate and care for the nuclear weapon. Her right hand gripped the mouse firmly, and her left hand nervously stroked the little monkey in her lap. She scrolled to the last page in the document. There were only two mission codes.

"*Santa wears a brown fur coat: proceed with activation of W72,* or *Throw the hammer away: abort mission,*" she read out loud. "Oh, this can't be good!"

Elizabeth quickly pulled out her cellphone. Her hands shook nervously from the adrenaline that surged through her veins as she dialed Michael's number. Her nervousness even caused Malinky to notice that the red-haired human was worried about something. The little monkey reached out a brown paw and stroked Elizabeth's arm.

After three rings, Michael's answered the call.

"Michael, Steve was right! This Dimitiry was some sort of Russian spy. He was in charge of a nuclear bomb called a W72. He has maps and instructions on how to use this thing. His commanding officer was Lieutenant General Konstantin Budnikov—the name on the passport of the dead Russian! Michael are you listening to me? This is some really deep shit!"

Elizabeth paused long enough to take a breath and to wait for a response from her cousin.

"Okay. Now listen to me, Elizabeth. You show that to the CIA team when they get there. You tell them everything. Even the monkey—show them the monkey."

Elizabeth glanced out the window. A very big van with heavily tinted windows drove into the parking lot. Someone on the passenger side had a window down slightly and threw out a cigarette.

"Michael, does the CIA use rental vans? Because one just pulled up outside. Are they allowed to smoke? Michael, can you hear me? Hello? Hello?"

CHAPTER 33: DID YOU JUST HANG UP ON ME?

Michael sat in the black sedan which he had pulled to the side of the road to take his cousin's call, puzzled as to why the conversation had ended so abruptly. He glanced down at his phone and noticed that he had plenty of reception, so he knew it wasn't cut off because of lack of cell coverage. He quickly called Elizabeth back.

He held the phone to his ear and was dismayed that the call went straight to Elizabeth's voicemail. "Hey, cousin, we got cut off somehow. Call me back when you get this message, okay?"

A few minutes passed, and there still wasn't a response from Elizabeth. Michael repeated his attempt to call her. Instead of voicemail, Elizabeth's cellphone gave a different response.

"We're sorry, but the number you have dialed is not able to receive calls at this time," came the automated response from the phone service.

Michael began to sense something was wrong, but he couldn't figure out what it was or why. He looked into the rearview mirror and saw the reflection of his eyes staring right back at him. To Michael, this action was his unique way of consoling himself on urgent matters.

"She must be okay. The CIA van was there. They probably are talking at this very moment about Steve and the dead Russian."

Michael knew that things were getting out of control and that he needed some additional help. He closed his eyes and bowed his head gently forward.

"Dear God, please hear my prayer."

CHAPTER 34: YOU CAN'T COME INSIDE IF I LOCK THE DOOR, RIGHT?

Elizabeth stared at her phone. When her call with Michael had been cut off, all she had been able to hear was a very high-pitched static sound. She remembered how high frequencies from a powerful computer could cause interference in cellphone reception. Dimitiry's computer, however, wasn't that big. She felt uneasy, suspecting that something more sinister was afoot. Someone was jamming her phone.

She continued to peer at the van through the blinds facing the parking lot. The van's side doors sprung open, and eight large European-looking men exited the vehicle. Every man was smartly dressed in high fashion wear as if they were hot models for a sexy men's magazine. Yet, each man was also armed with a small carbine assault weapon.

Several of the men had backpacks filled with equipment—equipment that had but one purpose: to breach an entry and destroy everything inside. The men were headed towards the townhouse. Elizabeth quickly ran to the front door. She locked door and the dead bolt. There was also a foot dead bolt that Dimitiry had installed, so she pushed that bolt deep into the floor mount.

The men assembled in a human diamond formation with their weapons pointed in every direction as they went up the front steps to Dimitiry's home. The group moved as one. Their specialized training was clearly evident.

A front door opened three townhouses up the hill from the assault team. An elderly man dressed in his housecoat and slippers walked out with a small Yorkie on a red leash. He noticed the armed men and quickly pulled his dog back inside his home. The team's leader, Lieutenant Vadim Lenkov, clothed in a dark leather jacket and sporting a crew-cut, moved his chin in such a way as to signal two of his team to go to that door and scrub that townhouse.

The first man who reached elderly neighbor's door found it locked. The second man kicked the door in, and both men rushed inside. The sound of two muffled shots were heard from inside the home. A few seconds later, the men returned to their tactical formation before they attempted to breach Dimitiry's house.

The rest of the team was preparing explosive charges in key places on the front door of Dimitiry's townhouse and prepping a detonator. The demolition member looked back up towards the leader for permission to blow the door.

Lenkov looked at his watch as if he were timing the operation. He lowered his hand and readied himself for the blasting charges to go off. The loud noise that he heard, however, wasn't the sound of explosives blasting a door open, but the sound of a high-speed bullet smashing open his engineer's head before he could turn the detonator. The dead man slumped over towards the leader's feet. The blast charges never went off.

In a half second, another one of his men took a round to his head as well. The scrub team was being ambushed.

"Return fire!" ordered the FSB leader in Russian.

He and his men fired their carbines in the direction where the shots had come from. The suppressors on all their weapons made faint popping sounds that resembled CO_2-powered air guns firing pellets. Their aim was completely inaccurate and without any concern for anything or anybody in the way of the barrage of bullets. One round did find its target. A Central Intelligence Agency SAD operative fell from one of the trees inside the park. The battle had both sides exchanging fire with careless abandonment.

Elizabeth watched in horror through the front window blinds in the living room. She was appalled as the entire battle unfolded in front of her. She also knew she didn't have any option but to run from the living room and head deeper inside the house for cover. Malinky jumped onto her shoulder as she ran to the hallway. She tried the kitchen, but she saw a man's face in the window looking inside. He didn't see her, but she didn't want to be seen. There was a closet in the hallway, but she found it stuffed with junk, leaving very little room to get inside.

She tried the basement door next, but she found it locked. The monkey on her shoulder reached out and flipped up what looked like a regular household thermostat, exposing the keypad underneath. Elizabeth looked at the little monkey in surprise, and Malinky let out an excited chirp.

A small faint chime emanated from the keypad, drawing Elizabeth's attention. The illuminated green LCD panel display indicated that an eleven-digit code was needed before the door would open. She pulled on the locked door again in frustration.

Malinky chirped and reached out a small hand to touch the LCD screen. Elizabeth watched in wonder as Malinky touched the number four button on the keypad and made another chirp. She then withdrew her hand and patted her chest and let out another sound. That time, Malinky's sound was a higher pitched "*woo.*" She repeated the entire series of steps and touched the number two button, and she still made the same sounds.

Elizabeth recognized the pattern that Malinky was trying to make. The first two digits to the code were for something that had to do with an *H* and an *A*.

"*H* and an *A*? Is that the code, Malinky?"

Elizabeth recognized quickly that the *H* and the *A* were the same as the computer's passcode. Her best guess was the use of "Hagia Sophia" again for the keypad for the basement door.

"Yep, this works." She nodded towards Malinky as the door unlocked.

Malinky smiled back at Elizabeth, but she was suddenly startled by another volley of bullets being fired outside.

Elizabeth pulled hard on the handle, and the door opened. She stepped through the portal and closed it quickly behind her, causing it to lock from the inside.

Elizabeth quickly descended into the basement. She frantically looked over the entire place and let out a heavy sigh. Malinky leapt from her shoulder and onto the floor. The little monkey quickly ran to the far side of the room and hid behind the large chair stacked with boxes.

"It's okay, little girl," Elizabeth said as ran over to the chair and pushed it out of the way to find her little friend.

The little monkey jumped up and down and pointed to the green door on the wall. Curious after the other clues Malinky had shared with her, Elizabeth opened the green door, revealing the inner door. She quickly noticed the same type of lock that had been on the basement door. Remembering the eleven-digit code, she quickly solved the lock and opened the secret door.

Inside the small room, the concrete floor was covered in a brownish dust. Elizabeth noticed a round mark on the floor as if something large had been there for quite some time. An oddly shaped battery, similar in shape to a stackable potato chip can, was on its side, as if forgotten. The battery was painted olive drab and had military markings printed on the side in yellow. The two battery prongs at the top were clearly marked positive and negative respectfully.

An explosion upstairs caught Elizabeth's attention as the Russians blew the front door open. Gunshots and heavy footsteps could be heard upstairs as the battle continued. Muffled commands in Russian penetrated the walls. Elizabeth started to climb into the room, but the little monkey grabbed her shirt and screeched loudly as it pulled her back.

"What? You don't want me to go in there?"

Malinky pointed to the inside wall, and Elizabeth peeked inside as best she could without putting her head in the room. She could make out the outline of some sort of alarm system. She looked down at the little monkey.

"Oh! Thank you!"

Malinky flashed her a smile. Elizabeth shut both the doors and crouched down behind the large chair as footsteps continued to pound up and down the stairs and from room to room in the townhouse above. After what felt like ages, there was a brief pause in the shooting and yelling, giving Elizabeth hope that maybe the battle was over. She peeked above the arm of the chair. Suddenly, an explosion thundered through the basement as the Russians blew open the basement door at the top of the stairs with demolition charges.

Elizabeth ducked behind the chair as three Russians scrambled down the stairs through the smoke. A new barrage of pounding footsteps thundered above and a hail of bullets rang out. The three Russians rolled down the remaining stairs into a heap of men and sinew.

Lt. Lenkov, the commander of the scrubber team, lay at the bottom of the staircase. He knew the two men beside him were dead and that he was not far behind with the extensive bleeding he could see spewing from his shoulder with each beat of his heart. He was growing weaker as his heart struggled to maintain a steady flow of nutrient- and oxygen-filled blood to his brain. Knowing that he only had seconds left before he lost consciousness, Lenkov reached for a special transmitter he wore on his wrist. It had two buttons. The green button was for signaling that his team was successful, and the other button was red, indicating his team had failed their mission. He pressed the red button before he passed out from the mortal loss of blood.

"All right, we got 'em, boys. You two, check out the basement," ordered Baiser, the lead officer of the SAD response team. "The rest of you form a perimeter and secure this location. Call Langley: tell them we secured the target. All tangos are down. We are commencing a search of the area."

Elizabeth heard the man's voice and the two men coming down the stairs. She peeked around the arm of the chair. "I'm an American! I'm in here!"

The men aimed their weapons at Elizabeth's perfectly still head as they approached. Malinky remained hidden behind the chair and dared not make a sound.

"Come on out, miss," one of the men ordered, "but keep your hands where we can see them."

Slowly, Elizabeth raised her hands and inched out from behind the chair. The two men helped her to her feet and reported that she appeared unarmed. One of the SAD team members upstairs was a female officer, and she was ordered to come down and quickly frisk Elizabeth for weapons. When she was cleared, the lead officer came down.

"Alright, miss, you have got a lot of explaining to do," Baiser said, his voice stern and authoritative, "and you better start now."

Elizabeth let out a sigh of relief. The words gushed forth from her like Niagara Falls. "My name is Elizabeth Cotter. I was working on an assignment with my cousin, Steve Cotter. He worked with you guys, I think. He's been killed! Steve's brother, Michael—he was working on the assignment, too. Well, Michael and I got here too late. Steve was already dead. We think a woman who is somehow related to this Dimitiry fellow we were watching is the one who killed Steve."

Baiser nodded. "We identified Steve upstairs. Your story matches what your cousin Michael reported earlier."

"But there's more, sir," Elizabeth continued. "After Michael left, I was able to get into Dimitiry's computer. There were maps and destinations, and there were diagrams and instructions for using a nuclear weapon!"

"A nuclear weapon? You're sure?"

"Yes! It was called a W72!"

"Go check that out!" the lead officer commanded one his team, pointing upstairs, and a man ran quickly up the stairs. "Is there anything else?"

"Oh! There's this!"

Elizabeth turned around quickly and went over to the chair. She held out her arms, and Malinky scurried up to her shoulder. She turned to the officer.

Baiser looked at her in confusion. "A monkey?"

"Yes. She was Dimitiry's. She showed me how to get down here. She also showed me this...."

Elizabeth turned and stepped to the green door on the wall. She opened it and entered the passcode. When the inner door opened, she stepped back and showed it to the officer. "But she also showed me that I shouldn't go in. There's some sort of alarm inside, and I wasn't sure how to disarm it."

"Get a Geiger counter down here and someone to disarm that alarm! And get me what's on that computer!" Baiser ordered.

The SAD response team in the basement began the procedure of securing everything. Additional specialists had already arrived, and Elizabeth and Malinky were escorted upstairs as the secret room was disarmed and scanned for radioactivity.

As they reached the top of the stairs, Elizabeth looked into the living room. She shuddered as she watched a black body bag being zipped over Steve's face.

The lead officer guided Elizabeth to the front porch. As she sat down on the doorstep, she noticed two new vans had appeared in the parking lot, ready to receive the bodies of the fallen response team, the Russian scrubber team, Budnikov, and her dear cousin Steve. Three doors down, CIA members were moving in and out of the neighbor's house as well. Elizabeth cringed, knowing it could very well have been her that had been killed. Team members reported to the lead officer and continued to interview Elizabeth, writing down all the information that she had found.

Shaking his head, Baiser pulled out his cellphone. "Langley, we have a report that a woman named Mishka Federov has possibly obtained a nuclear device. We have evidence that a radioactive device was here. We also have several codes from Dimitiry Federov's computer of possible target locations. Closest possible target is Fontana Dam. Awaiting instructions. Please advise."

CHAPTER 35: WHY DIDN'T YOU CALL?

Moscow, Russia

Sokolov abhorred the absence of new information. It had been over an hour with no new report from the scrubber team, and he still had not heard from Budnikov. Knowing it was possible that they had both been intercepted by the Americans, he pondered his earlier decision to activate the go code "Santa has a brown fur coat." He began to think that, perhaps, he had made the wrong calculation.

The two agents Budnikov had chosen for the Santa portion of the Beluga Project had been trained using unusual methods and were supposed to be the best agents to ever serve Russia. He'd had Budnikov's assurance on that. But if Budnikov and the sweeper team had been intercepted by the Americans after the two agents had received their instructions from Budnikov, Sokolov knew that their assignments could jeopardize all his plans. If Russians were discovered in any kind of nefarious activity on U.S. soil right before an attack in both the United States and Israel, there was no way that Iran would receive the blame.

Sokolov ran his thin hand down his hawk-like face and exhaled deeply. His clenched his teeth together and began to pace.

"Sir?" his aide said hesitantly from the door of his office. "We received a message from the scrubber team."

"Thank God for some information," Sokolov whispered to himself. He turned to face his aide as he walked hurriedly to his desk. "Bring it to me!"

The aide quickly opened the door and brought the report to Sokolov as he sat down. The general took the report and waved the aide out of the room. His eyes sped across the page. He lay the paper on the desk and leaned back in his chair, digesting the bad news that Lenkov and his men had failed.

No additional information had been given. Only failure. The status of Budnikov and Lenkov's team were still unknown. They were either dead or intercepted.

The shrewd general quickly made his decision. The Santa mission had to be called off. There was too big a risk that the Americans knew of Russian activity within the country, and the Beluga Project was too important to risk any slip-ups.

Sokolov grabbed a pen and wrote down the new orders for Budnikov's agents: *Throw the hammer away.*

CHAPTER 36: THE PUPPET MASTER'S STRINGS HAVE BEEN CUT!

Outside Jerusalem

The satellite phone that Sokolov had given Josuf to use for Operation Beluga emitted a small beeping sound as a new message was received. Josuf sat up in the darkness of his tiny room and pulled the phone from his pocket. He activated the mechanism on the phone to unscramble the coded message from Moscow. It simply read: *Throw the hammer away.*

Josuf laughed softly to himself as he switched the phone off. "Moscow thinks it's that easy, huh? Well, it's not. I'm here. I'm all set to head to Jerusalem. And the only man who I am supposed to answer to is dead. I guess they're out of luck."

Josuf looked over to the footlocker that housed the weapon. He crawled over to the box on all fours then sat next to it with his legs crossed. Josuf then opened up the footlocker to stare at the Davy Crockett missile. He suddenly felt a rush of tremendous power well up inside him, and he knew he had fate in his favor.

Budnikov's orders and activation of his special training had come at the perfect time, just when a missile of mass destruction had been delivered right into his lap. If he hadn't agreed to take Sokolov's assignment with the Chechens, even that would not have happened. The irresistible chain of events that fell before him like dominoes only reinforced his belief that he was on the right path to historic change. He knew with every fiber of his being that he was the one to destroy Jerusalem.

Budnikov had chosen well when he had selected Josuf for his special program. Not only did Josuf have an education in radiology, but his singular dream was a free Syria—free from al-Ahini's dictatorship. Josuf wanted what every Syrian patriot wanted: a return of his Syria back to being a wonderful country filled with all types of art, history, and sciences. Russia wanted a port, and if Syria could flourish by having a maritime landlord, so much the better in his opinion.

Budnikov had known these things, and the skills and devotion to a cause that he had been able to implant within the young man's mind had all culminated in the single assignment that lay before Josuf: destroy Jerusalem. Budnikov had made sure that in his special training, Josuf equated Jerusalem's destruction with Syria's freedom.

Josuf began to get sleepy as wonderful thoughts of a free Syria and Jerusalem in ashes filled his head. Plus, the wonderful meal he had eaten earlier helped his body relax and prepare for a good rest. He soon dozed off.

CHAPTER 37: COME INTO MY PARLOR
SAID THE SPIDER

North Carolina

Mishka wasn't surprised when she noticed another set of flashing blue lights in her rearview mirror. Mishka pulled her convertible over and waited for the policeman to come near. She baited her trap by unbuttoning another button on her white blouse. A quick toss of her dark hair and the snare was ready to catch her hopeless prey.

Officer Charlie "Chucky" Stanton quickly climbed out of his patrol car and approached the convertible from behind. He had received the heads-up dispatch on the radio about a suspicious woman transporting a large container that supposedly had lung transplant organs inside. From people who placed a manikin in the passenger seat to make it appear that there was another human in the vehicle to qualify for the HOV lane, to college kids who hid their alcohol stash underneath the backseat during Spring Break marathons, Stanton had seen it all. He approached Mishka's side of the car and made eye contact with her.

Mishka's seductive eyes mesmerized Stanton in an instant. Stanton, stunned by her beauty, felt confident that he had the situation under control. Unfortunately, his gaze traveled down her blouse, and his concentration shifted to the last button fastening her shirt across her chest. He knew he was staring too much, for indeed he was truly beguiled. Mishka's eyes never strayed from her prey.

The officer didn't see her gun aiming at his face until she fired. Stanton took the round just underneath his right eye through his jaw, impacting the back of his skull. The bullet struck hard and was instantly lethal. Stanton swung backwards as the kinetic force of the bullet pulled him up and away.

He fell to the ground almost immediately with a hard thud.

Mishka slid the gun back beside her car seat and sped off. A few miles down the road, she realized that no one was following her. She checked her rear-view mirror once more to see that the coast was clear. A brief smile flashed on her beautiful face.

Within a few minutes, her satellite phone went off. She picked up the phone while she was driving. It wasn't a call; it was a coded message.

She noticed a side road to a subdivision up on the right, and she turned into the quiet neighborhood. At the top of a hill in the subdivision, past the open security gate, there was a small parking lot on the immediate left designated for the residents who wanted to use the swimming pool located near there. She quickly glanced around, and then she parked her car.

The satellite phone she held in her hand was Russian. Issued to FSB, GRU, and other agencies that needed uplinks to Moscow, the phone was also vital for diplomats. The Americans knew of these devices, but they did not know who had one. That was an advantage that Mishka enjoyed. She pressed a ten-digit code into the keypad.

Within a second, the encrypted code materialized and displayed in plain Cyrillic on the LCD screen: *Throw the hammer away.*

Mishka laughed and tossed the phone into her purse. "It's too late for that. Fate has the rudder now."

The old saying was from the battle of Stalingrad in World War II, when the ferry captains would carry supplies and soldiers over the treacherous Volga River, testing fate each time. Budnikov had sealed her fate with his words: *The shadows in the corner are not entirely our own.*

Mishka laid her head back against the headrest. She glanced over at the thermal nuclear device in the passenger seat of her car and exhaled deeply. She was tired, very tired. She was also dizzy and feeling very dehydrated. A small wave of nausea crept through her throat as she began to self-diagnose her symptoms. She realized that she was experiencing the beginning stages of radiation poisoning.

Her eyes were heavy, and as she fought to keep them open, she couldn't help but think that if she could only catch a quick nap, she would be refreshed for the very difficult challenge that lay ahead: destroying the Fontana Dam. The amber-illuminated dashboard of the car blinked in and out of view as her eyelids fluttered close and she fell asleep.

Mishka startled herself when she began to snore. She cursed and straightened herself upright in the seat. Then she noticed the dashboard's clock. She had been asleep for twenty minutes.

"Shit! I have to meet my team at the dam. I can decontaminate myself after I'm finished."

She started up the car and left the subdivision, heading north.

CHAPTER 38: IT'S HARD TO PLAY HIDE AND SEEK WITH YOU WHEN YOU AREN'T HIDING

Michael drove up to the employee parking lot of St. Gabriel's. There was not a guard house, but he did see a lot of security cameras covering the lot. It was getting late, and he turned on his headlights. He drove up and down the lanes looking for the white convertible that Mishka Federov had been driving. Michael started to tear up again as an immense hatred for her welled up inside him.

"Oh, Steve. Why her, why?"

After the fourth lane yielded no results, Michael turned to start the fifth. That was when he noticed a security guard come out of the hospital back entrance and approach him, waving his hand.

Michael stopped the car to allow the officer to catch up. He rolled down his window slightly as the slender, dark-haired man reached the car.

"Can I help you, sir?" the officer asked.

"Yes, sir. There is an employee of the hospital who drives a white convertible. She bumped my car in the grocery store parking lot, and then she drove off. I wanted to get her license plate to report her to the police.

"Well, I am sorry to hear that, but this is a private parking lot for the staff. I must ask you to leave. Please let the local police handle your incident. I won't allow you to track down someone here."

"Oh, good granny. Very well. Goodnight, officer."

The officer turned and went back through the door he had come out earlier. Michael rolled up the window and headed towards the exit, having lost almost all his initiative to catch up with Mishka. As he was about to leave, his cellphone rang. He noticed it was Elizabeth. He quickly pulled into a space and answered the phone, hoping for some good news to come about finally.

"Hey, Michael. It's me. How are you holding out? Have you tracked her down?"

"No, she's not here at the hospital. I have no clue how to find her."

"Your wife Debbie called me. She said she has tried to call you several times, and she's worried. Michael, I told her about Steve and our involvement. She started crying a lot. You need to call her, okay?"

"Thank you, Elizabeth. I'll call her just as soon as I can. Please call her back and tell her I will. Catching this woman is so important right now."

A quiet pause settled over the phone call as Elizabeth absorbed what Michael was and wasn't saying. "Listen, after our call broke off, I got attacked by some elite Russian unit—"

"You what?" Michael interjected. "Are you okay?"

"I'm okay. They tried to break in Dimitiry's house, but Steve's response team showed up and then there was a huge firefight. The team feels that Mishka has taken a nuclear bomb that was hidden in Federov's basement."

Elizabeth paused from talking for minute as she listened in on the CIA team reacting to some news.

"Michael, they just got a report over the radio that a law enforcement officer was shot in cold blood while writing a citation on the Scenic Highway The car was a white convertible!"

"That's her, Elizabeth! Was she going north or south on that highway?"

"North, I heard."

"Okay, then that's where I'm headed. North on Scenic highway. What's up that way?"

Elizabeth paused as she opened the map application on her phone while she put her cousin on speakerphone. She highlighted where the cursor showed her phone's current location. With two fingers, she expanded the map's view to a larger scale. She quickly followed the scenic highway northwards.

"Michael, it goes through a large, forested area. The only noticeable thing there is Fontana Dam. That was the closest target in the list of possibilities that they found here!"

Michael put the car in reverse and pulled out of the parking space. He maneuvered quickly towards the exit. By that time, Elizabeth's activities on her phone and talking out loud attracted attention. The CIA team lead approached her with concern.

"What about the Fontana Dam?" Baiser asked. "Do you have new information?"

Elizabeth nodded her head. "I'm on the phone with my cousin Michael. The woman who killed Steve was driving a white convertible, like the one that was just involved in that officer shooting. It's got to be her, and she's headed straight towards Fontana Dam, the closest possible target!"

Baiser turned to the agent beside him. "Contact the Nuclear Emergency

Response Team. Tell NEST we are *Oscar Mike* and to meet us at the Fontana Dam. Tell them this is mission critical. Okay, everybody, mount up! We are booking it to the dam. Let's go!"

"Oscar Mike?" asked Elizabeth.

"It means we are on the move. Okay, Miss, you have been very helpful. Tell your cousin we have this under control. He is not to approach her. Tell him to back off, now!"

Elizabeth turned off the speakerphone function and placed it next to her ear. "Michael?"

"Yeah, I heard. No way, Elizabeth. She killed Steve." Michael turned right out of the parking lot and headed north. "I'm already on my way. Don't try to stop me either."

"I'm won't, Michael. Please be careful. I can't lose you, too."

"I know."

"Oh, and, Michael?"

"Yeah."

"Make her pay for what she did to Steve, no matter the consequences."

CHAPTER 39: THE MOSSAD

Israel

In geosynchronous orbit above the Middle Eastern theater, flew a very large Israeli communications satellite. Launched in 2016, its reported mission was to provide reliable access to the Internet and cable services for paying subscribers throughout the country. The octagon-shaped jewelry box of gold and silver foil had two large black solar panels for wings. To some, it might have seemed like some flashy prehistoric bird, but it was indeed the proverbial "wolf in sheep's clothing."

The Ariel III, meaning the "Lioness of God," was built to look like a traditional communications satellite, but inside her hull was a vast array of hyper-sensitive long-range digital cameras, a bank of radiation sensors, infrared optics for heavy cloud penetration, Doppler radar for ballistic launches, and even one AN/SEQ 3 Laser Weapon System on permanent loan from the United States Navy. The laser system was primarily intended to defend the satellite if attacked, but due to current political status, the laser could be used for offensive purposes if needed. The entire satellite was powered by a micro nuclear reactor housed deep within the core of the vehicle.

Kitty, the colloquial nickname for the Ariel III, enjoyed the vast power of the reactor. It gave the electronic systems aboard Kitty a steady supply of power, and it could summon up 30 kilowatts for the laser to fry any enemy satellite that approached within a one-mile radius. Only one company, however, could afford to build or even launch such a weapon. That agency was not a telecom company, but the Mossad, Israel's version of the CIA, KGB, FSB, and MI6 all rolled into one.

The Mossad was the most feared, as well as most respected, intelligence gathering and covert operations agency in the world. It was their covert funding that helped launch the Ariel III. It was with such technology that terrorism and counterterrorism could be observed, reported, and dealt with in one complete step. The agency was totally separate from internal political policies of the country. The Mossad's main purpose was to prevent their country from being wiped off the face of the planet.

Colonel Abelson had the night's watch with Kitty. His team of technicians were known as the "A" Team. The *A* was for Abelson, but everyone involved liked the idea that they were the best team.

The colonel sipped a cup of steaming hot tea as he stood looking over some papers at his desk. Behind him, a young technician pushed his headphones back across his short, dark hair to rest on his neck and leaned back in his chair, still staring at the computer screen in front of him. He shook his head and then turned to his superior. "Excuse me, sir."

Abelson turned to look at the young man. "Yes."

"Sir, I have been going through some communications between America and Jordan. The receiver accepted a call in Jordan. We picked up a familiar name in this and another of the receiver's conversations: Red Monkey was mentioned twice."

Abelson put down his cup of tea and walked over to the tech's monitor. He put on an additional set of headphones and listened to the entire set of conversations. He had heard that name before.

"Run the call through the computer," Abelson ordered. "Let's get numbers, names, IDs, and location."

The tech nodded and became typing rapidly into the computer. Within moments, he nodded to the colonel. "Sir, Kitty has just acquired the location. It's in a small mountain village in al Za'im. This is the road. Here is the house."

Abelson gazed up at a larger viewing screen mounted on one of the walls in the security room. With real-time intelligence video, the officers viewed the house and landscape with absolute clarity from 23 miles above. It was night time, and the night vision cameras, with the assistance of infrared and computer capabilities, illuminated every crevice, every angle, and every approach to the house.

"Okay, I want surveillance on that house 24/7. Anybody who goes in or out. Even pets!"

The staff for Abelson went to work. The phone call from America did indeed get traced back to a western North Carolina location. It was on a personal cellphone, they also noted. The Mossad techs were able to interface with CIA and FBI intelligence computers to assess who the caller was. That information was received, and then the techs added the new information into the Mossad computer to search for other references and connections.

The "Red Monkey" phrase flagged again on their Internet search for the person who made the calls. They found the phrase in Russian during several older emails exchanged between the caller, Mishka Federov; the recipient, Josuf Federov; and a third party named Dimitiry Federov. That information led to further investigation of Dimitiry Federov.

"Col. Abelson, we have a *November Mike!*" shouted the young tech as he uncovered a much deeper secret about the Federovs.

The *November Mike* moniker was in military alphabet fashion to annunciate the letters *N* and *M*. For the Israeli Mossad teams, it meant only one terrifying threat: a nuclear mole.

A November Mike enemy behind or within the ranks was also known as a Fifth Columnist in days of old, referring to Napoleonic battles of long ago. An army commander back then would probably have been able to battle against several enemy columns that were assaulting from multiple avenues of attack. Four columns to fight against was the most any capable commander could handle, but it was the fifth column that came out of the blue that usually tipped the scales.

To some intelligence agencies, a mole was like a sleeping spider. The spider wouldn't move if provoked. It remained dormant and almost corpse-like for a very long time. Then, one day, something would trigger the spider's anger, and it would attack without warning. The result was always the same: the prey, caught in a deadly web, never saw it coming.

"Okay, pass this information, along with the rest of the stuff, to the CIA. Let them handle whatever threat Dimitiry and Mishka Federov might be," Abelson said as he patted the tech who discovered the new information on the shoulder. "We'll handle Josuf Federov."

Col. Abelson then picked up the phone and called his headquarters to let them know that an insertion team was needed to attack, capture, or eliminate the threat emanating from that house in Jordan. He relayed the coordinates and told them to hurry.

CHAPTER 40: THE TUNNEL, BUT WITHOUT THE OOH AND AAH

Outside Jerusalem

Josuf had been asleep for less than an hour when he was awakened by Omar. Rubbing his eyes, Josuf waved to him that he was up. Josuf dressed quickly and grabbed the foot locker box that housed the Davy Crockett missile and went to the kitchen of the little house.

"Here," Omar said, holding out a pita. "My wife made you some breakfast. Take this and a bottle of water. It is time to go."

Josuf took the pita in his free hand.

Omar nodded to a young, muscular man standing in the shadows of the room. "This is Ameer. He is my brother's son. I trust him. He is good and strong and can carry the heavy box for you."

Josuf lifted the pita towards his mouth. He glanced at the breakfast pita stuffed with scrambled eggs and stopped. "Oh, this has egg in it. Is it *halal?*"

"Yes, brother, I prayed over the eggs. Please remember my family as we do our best to help you in your mission. We would never have served you forbidden food," Omar, who was at least twenty years Josuf's senior, replied politely yet sternly.

"Forgive me, Omar. *Shukraan lakum.*" Josuf thanked him formally as he reached up with his right hand and touched his heart.

Omar responded by using his right hand with his fingers pointed downwards and making a motion as if sweeping away from his body. Josuf remembered that in many Middle Eastern cultures, that meant "Don't worry about it." Both Josuf and Omar then embraced each other as they said goodbye.

Ameer came over and took the weapon from Josuf. Josuf nodded and followed Ameer down a flight of stairs to an underground tunnel entrance. Josuf followed behind as they made their way through the tunnel and was amazed at how detailed the tunnel complex was constructed. It had electricity, circulation fans, rest areas to sit or take a nap, and even caches of water and food.

Josuf grabbed a bottle of water and two small loaves of pita bread wrapped in plastic wrap as he walked by them and stuffed them in his pockets. He thought he might need to use the food later.

"This is probably the most secret tunnel ever built to get closer to Jerusalem and its defensive border security," Ameer said, winded from the heavy case he was carrying.

"How deep are we?"

"About 7 to 10 meters in most areas. We had to go deep to avoid the Israeli ground sonar. Those bastards can also hear digging underground with their electronic sensors if we are too shallow. This tunnel has yet to be found. Also, with all the food and water, anyone could live down here for weeks."

Josuf quickly realized that the deep tunnel would be perfect for him to hide in after he launched the small nuke towards Jerusalem. The deep tunnel would protect him from the radioactive blast and fallout. Plus, as an added bonus, it would provide him an escape path afterwards.

When Ameer and Josuf approached the end of the tunnel, Josuf thanked the young man and sent him away to go home. Ameer protested the brush-off, but it was a common theme with all the others he had escorted.

Josuf pulled out his cellphone, and he found he had no service that deep underground. He pulled up an older encrypted email he had received using a social app called *LoveinME*, a website that allowed young singles in the Mediterranean to meet and socialize. The service used its own encryption firewall service to prevent stalkers and viewers who had not paid for the service. That worked very well for terrorists and other organized cells. Hamas used a pretty woman who would send the messages on the dating app since most of the recipients were male.

The attack was still on schedule. Josuf had been very careful not to let the local leaders learn of his rocket. Just the senior Hamas leaders had been informed and had approved his plan. The regular rocket attacks would confuse the Israeli Iron Dome defense grid. Josuf's rocket would be within the rest of the missiles but much lower to the ground. The Israeli anti-rocket defense would be aimed for the higher attacks.

"This is the day of a new Syria," Josuf said as he opened the Davy Crockett. A sinister smile spread across his face.

CHAPTER 41: THE RAINCLOUDS ABOVE HIDE THE SHADOWS BELOW

North Carolina

Michael knew that he had to catch the car he believed Mishka was driving. His powerful inner strength was on automatic. He could feel the flow of adrenalin coursing through his veins. To Michael, it gave him incredible focus to capture the person who had murdered his brother Steve. However, the adrenalin came with a heavy price, for it opened his mind to images that were terrifying in their realism to a man who was shrouded in painful grief.

A series of heavy clouds quickly formed overhead, forming a very dark and menacing ceiling of deep gray and black rolling wisps that entwined and circled above like serpents. Each band of cloud, which looked similar to a forming tornado funnel, made swooping gestures as if a giant monster with multiple arms was trying to scoop up Michael in his German sedan rental. The winds thrashed mightily against the massive cedars and pine trees that lined the highway, causing the car to sway back and forth.

To Michael, these images vaguely matched the repeating nightmare he had suffered through for months about the wintry storm in an open field. That dream had haunted his nights, foreshadowing Steve's death which, indeed, had come true.

The storm lurking above was different but still had the haunting touch that had spooked Michael on many occasions in the night. Instead of snow, it was a massive rain storm. Instead of an open cornfield filled with decaying stalks, it was a heavy forest of trees. The trees moved with their branches back and forth like giant green sentinels, warning Michael to turn back.

"Oh, Steve, are you trying to tell me something?"

He knew that when storms moved over a mountain valley area flanked by hills, it helped to funnel the storm into a more concentrated version of itself. The sudden downpour caught Michael off guard. The headlights in the car that Michael was driving were pathetic. They barely illuminated the road ahead as he drove. Mailboxes with their metal posts looked strangely like deer legs, causing Michael much grief in his driving abilities. Adding to his misery was a series of faint wisps of mist that flowed across the road. The ethereal clouds of mist, along with the torrential rain, wafted through the trees and over the road, forming shapes in Michael's imagination—from a cloud of white to shadows of a deer, a person, a group, and even a white car.

Michael jumped out of his muddled confusion as he realized that the image of a white car was actually real. A white convertible was, indeed, ahead of him and driving at a modest pace. The little white car was being buffeted by the heavy rain and winds as well. For a brief second, through the mist and rain, Michael thought he saw a brunette woman driving.

Michael picked up his cellphone and redialed Elizabeth's phone. While the phone was connecting, he noticed a road sign that indicated that the Fontana Dam was 16 miles ahead.

"Hello, Michael?" the voice said on the other end.

"Yeah, it's me. I'm behind Mishka, I think. We are on the scenic road headed north. The road sign says 16 miles to go. This storm has completely brought visibility to zero. Tell the CIA men what's happening. I can't talk more now. It's too dangerous."

Michael hung up the phone. He started sweating profusely. His heart exploded with adrenaline as the realization that he had luckily happened upon his brother's killer took hold. Michael crossed himself and thanked God for that stroke of luck.

His biggest concern was what he should do then. The CIA team might be too far back to catch up to him by car. He thought that a helicopter might work, perhaps, but it would have to have been in the vicinity to effectively fly to the dam and position a team of snipers or soldiers to stop her. With the heavy rain, it would be practically impossible.

With tears of frustration blurring his vision, he knew that he couldn't stop her. No one would be able to stop her. What made matters worse was a new road sign went by displaying that the dam was only six miles away, and it occurred to Michael that the white convertible seemed to have increased its speed.

"God, give me strength to stop this woman. Guide me on what to do."

Another two miles went by, and Michael felt something special in his heart. A new, invigorated sense of purpose and determination grew in his arms and chest. Completely focused on the wet road, he increased his speed to overtake the white car in front of him. The rental Mercedes had no problem accelerating, and Michael quickly found himself overtaking Mishka's car. The two cars were parallel as they sped down the two-lane highway.

Mishka wasn't prepared for someone to try to pass her on the lonely county road, especially with the rain as a factor in driving.

She increased her speed even more to avoid the strange car to her left. The wet highway played with Mishka's driving. The lighter white convertible did not have the same stability as the heavy German car. Ever mindful that she might be recognized and arrested, Mishka reached down the side of her car seat and retrieved her pistol. Readying her gun, she began to slow down to draw the flanking Mercedes up to be parallel with her convertible for the fatal shot.

"Come a little closer," Mishka whispered. "That's it. Closer. Closer...."

CHAPTER 42: THE DOORBELL WASN'T WORKING—MAY WE STILL COME IN?

Outside Jerusalem

The Mossad commandos moved quickly and silently to Omar's house in al Za'im. The commandos, using the call sign "Claw," were the ground element taking orders from the Mossad team based in Tel Aviv via Kitty. Lt. Asher Klein, the leader of the group, used the call sign of "Claw 1."

The team wore the latest night vision goggles. The Enhanced Night Vision Goggle-Binocular, or ENVG-B, offered each Israeli commando the ability to turn pitch black conditions into daylight viewing for their combat needs. A unique added feature for the Mossad soldiers was that the goggles were linked to Kitty above. Small viewing windows within the goggles gave each soldier the ability to see battlefield targets as either friend, in blue, or enemy, in red.

When the soldiers reached the home, Klein and four others quickly surrounded the doors in the front and to the rear. Four other commandos formed a security perimeter to keep people from coming in to help. They were also there to catch any scooters, slang for "escapees," from leaving.

From a distant rocky advantage point, an over-watch team of a sniper and two spotters surveyed the house and additional avenues of approach. The team had complete control of all communications for the unit. From satellite uplinks to battalion and platoon level frequencies, they were the real eyes and ears of the team. The sniper had a clear view of the valley below towards the city of Jerusalem. His sniper rifle was the advanced version of the new MRAD. It was a Barrett 768 model with an extended range of more than 2,000 yards.

The breach was performed with BDE, or Breach-Demo-Explosives, attached to the hinges and door lock. As expected, the door just fell out and away from the door sill. Two commandos rushed in and fanned to the left and right. The rest of the breaching team rushed inside and searched the small house for occupants and/or hotspots.

Omar and his wife quickly surrendered. Ameer was found hiding underneath his bed and was brought to the kitchen with the rest of the family. No one had any weapons, and the commandos quickly secured the home. Klein asked politely at first as to where the terrorist was.

"I do not know of any terrorist here. My house is open to all. You must be mistaken," Omar answered as he held his wife tightly around her waist.

"How about you, young man?" Klein asked, looking at Ameer. "You know why we are here. We traced a terrorist's cellphone transmissions to this home. Where is he hiding?"

Ameer stood stoically, almost defiantly, against the Israeli commando. His face distorted into an ugly sneer. The other commandos responded with angry tones and moved closer to Ameer. Two even showed signs that they wanted to hit the young man for his insolence.

The lieutenant snapped his fingers. "Stand down!"

The commandos moved backwards.

"Claw 1, we have two military-age males approaching the house from the east," whispered the sniper into his unit's radio transmitter. "They are approaching with weapons at the ready. I think they are on to us. One is armed with an AK-47, and we can't see the other's weapon clearly."

Each commando had an earpiece in and understood exactly what the sniper was asking permission for.

"Light is green. Light is green," answered Klein as he began to realize that his team was losing the initiative and the element of surprise.

In a split second, the sniper's rifle, muffled by a heavy suppressor, fired two rounds. The two targets were instantly dispatched. Two of the commandos that were surrounding the house came out of hiding and rushed out and grabbed the dead bodies and dragged them into the shadows.

"All right, that's enough of being polite," Klein said as he grabbed Ameer by the collar of his shirt and drew him inwards. A commando knife was produced and held at the young man's throat.

The room fell silent. Omar and his wife knew that the moment that they had always dreaded had arrived. The secret tunnel had always been their most valuable asset and the primary money maker for their household. Many had used the tunnel, and they had been paid for that use handsomely. The Hamdans were regarded as great supporters of the Hamas movement, and they were highly respected in the village. That night, they would either die as a family, lose their nephew Ameer, or give up the tunnel's secret entrance under the floor.

"Oh, please, please, no! Ameer is the only family we have left!" Mrs.

Hamdan shouted as she fell to her knees on the floor crying.

She wept uncontrollably as she pointed to the table against the wall that had some family pictures on it. A small rug was underneath the table.

"No! You stupid woman! Curse you for this!" screamed Ameer.

Two commandos quickly moved the small table out of the way, and a third pulled back the rug and discovered the small hatch in the floor. It had a recessed pull knob that he used to open the hatch. He aimed with his rifle into the opening. An attached flashlight to the muzzle of his gun illuminated the steps downwards.

Klein, pleased at the results of his battlefield interrogation tactic, released the young man's collar and pushed him towards his uncle and sobbing aunt. A commando at the doorway focused his weapon on the Hamdans as the officer radioed his commander and the other members of the unit that they were going into the tunnel.

CHAPTER 43: WE CALLED AND MADE RESERVATIONS

North Carolina

Elizabeth, Malinky, and the CIA team hurried in the van towards the dam through the pouring rain. They knew they were a long way off, but they still had to try to get there and assist in stopping the woman with the weapon.

A tech who had been listening to a radio communication via headset turned to the lead officer. "NEST has responded, sir. They are on their way by helicopter, but the conditions are extremely poor over the dam. Their ETA is 90 minutes to the dam—if the weather breaks."

"Shit! They'll never get there in time!" cursed Baiser.

The van occupants all got quiet as the news sank in that NEST would not get to the dam in time. The rain fell on top of the van in a heavy cadence, like a drummer playing a snare drum on a full double roll.

Elizabeth held Malinky tight and began to pray. The little capuchin monkey hugged Elizabeth around the head with her two furry arms. She chirped a bit so that she sounded like she was talking.

The CIA officers in the van began to chuckle quietly at Malinky's actions, but they soon got quiet when Elizabeth finished her prayer and crossed herself.

"Okay, listen up," Baiser announced. "Everyone, lock and load. We are going in, and we are going in hot. Yeah, we're running behind, and we have this shitty rain to give us trouble. But you never know what lies ahead. Get ready!"

He next used his phone and looked through its database for the dam they were speeding towards. He found an information number and dialed the Fontana Dam's main line.

"Fontana Dam engineering department. Collett speaking," answered a voice.

"Collett, this is Officer Baiser of the CIA. I have no time to explain who I am, but you must close the main gate to the road that crosses over the dam. Do not let any vehicles get across until I get there. There is a white convertible with a woman driving it. She is heavily armed and dangerous. This is a national emergency, Collett. Do not let her onto the dam! Understand?"

"Yes, sir. I was about to close the gates anyway, what with this heavy rain and all. The water level is rising very fast, and we have to release water soon or we will be in some deep trouble, if you know what I mean. I will close the gates and will not let her or anybody get across the dam. You can count on me. Nobody will get across."

"Excellent! We're on our way to you."

The man who had spoken with Baiser let out a laugh as he hung up the telephone. The work jacket he had stolen read *"Collett"* on the stitching outside, as well as on the identity badge that had a magnetic key for access to the bolted outer doors.

"We got company coming! Get ready!" he shouted to the rest of his team inside the control room deep inside the dam.

Spetsnaz Lieutenant Stalinko looked down to the metal floor at a middle-aged man who was the real Collett. The man's hands were bound with rope behind his back. There was a large piece of duct tape across his mouth.

"Thank you for helping us, Comrade Collett, and for closing off those flood gates. The rising river will swell to its maximum capacity before we unleash our little weapon. Don't worry. You won't feel a thing, but you will be entombed in here for all of eternity," Stalinko teased.

Collett mumbled in protest through the tape at the Russian Spetsnaz commando's teasing.

Earlier, the real Collett and his engineering team had been scheduled to refurbish some machinery deep within the dam's engineering area. Lyle Collett had been happy to let a tour group of four men claiming to be from the Ukraine accompany his team as they made their way through the dam's inner workings. Collett and his team of four assistants had shown the tourists some of the greatest engineering marvels of the TVA program, from the massive hydro-electric generators to the eight 20-ton metal and concrete flood gates that held back the Little Tennessee River. The tour group had been very polite and had taken many pictures, as with most tourists.

When the group had reached deep inside the interior of the dam near the control room, which was being shown as the last stop on the improvised tour, the tourists, as if on cue, had pulled out hidden automatic weapons and opened fire. The surprise salvo had slaughtered all of Collett's team. He had been spared only because the Russian commandos had needed an engineer alive to work the hydraulics for the massive flood gates.

One of the Spetsnaz men walked over to Collett as he struggled against his restraints on the floor and kicked him hard in his side, causing immense pain to the prisoner's ribs. The other commandos laughed at the cruelty. The commando then knocked Collett on the head with the stock of his gun, and the poor man collapsed on the floor.

"Okay, get out of those tourist clothes," Stalinko ordered as he quickly surveyed the scene. "Come on, move it. It's almost 200 feet to the base of the interior, and I need all of you to get to the bottom to see which of the flood gates we should use when we place the weapon. I have to go topside to look for the agent bringing the bomb."

The Spetsnaz team quickly changed clothes and then went down the stairs. The lower area was the base of the dam. The massive flood gates were closed tightly.

Once his men started to move to their stations, Lt. Stalinko made his way topside and went outside into the pouring rain. His newly acquired jacket had a zippered rain hood built into the collar, which he quickly deployed as he walked forward on the dam road towards the gates. He stood there in the rain, watching for an approaching car.

His job was to wait for Lt. Krasnaya to show up and then offer security as the bomb was taken inside the core of the dam. The detonation would destroy the dam, and the river, flooded by the torrential rain, would be unleashed. The immense flow of water would overwhelm the next dam, causing a domino effect. It was calculated that four of the six dams on the river would collapse that way.

The pouring rain beat down on Stalinko, but he paid it no mind. The grueling training he had endured to become part of a Spetsnaz team ensured that something as simple as bad weather would not deter him from his mission. He stood there stoically, the rain pouring off his coat like waterfalls in front of his eyes as a solitary car approached. When it wasn't driven by the agent he was waiting on, he casually waved the driver and his family through. He walked over to the edge of the dam and looked down at the raging river below and the mounting water against the dam wall. His gaze returned to the lonely stretch of road that led to the bridge as the headlights of an approaching car appeared around a curve in the road.

CHAPTER 44: THE AUTO RENTAL DOESN'T INCLUDE BULLET HOLES

Mishka's plan worked. Michael's Mercedes pulled forward as she slowed down. Michael gave one quick look to the right at Mishka as his car moved slightly past hers. He saw her determined face and knew it was her. He slowed a bit.

Mishka quickly surveyed the road ahead and then looked at him to her left. She waited until both cars were side by side, but the rain and wind made aiming more difficult. With the driver's window rolled down halfway, she fired the last three bullets in her gun until the gun slide locked in the open position, signifying that it was empty.

Michael was stunned as three bullets smashed into the heavy Mercedes vehicle. The first bullet smashed into the passenger side door then hit the side door electric motor that raised and lowered the passenger side window and was deflected away. The second round went through the passenger door and into the back rest of the front passenger seat. The bullet still had enough kinetic energy to continue toward the driver's door through the back of Michael's seat. He could feel the passing bullet behind his back within the seat until it exited and smashed into the driver's side door behind him.

It was the third bullet Mishka fired that threatened Michael the most. It smashed the glass in the passenger side window, travelled just past Michael's forehead by a few millimeters, and smashed his driver's side window into a million fragments of safety glass, creating a large opening for the rain to pelt his face and shoulders.

Michael jumped in his seat in response to the glass pieces showering his face. One shard in particular ricocheted off the side mirror and bounced back into Michael's left eye. The white part of his left eye, or cornea, was hit by the fragment. Its damage was to the left side of his pupil, and it caused him to recoil in pain.

Michael knew he was losing his advantage, and he did not know how many bullets were left in Mishka's gun. He was filled with immense anger and had to do something quickly, so he did what he had to do. He pulled the steering wheel to the right as far as it would turn.

"Take this! Yeah! You don't know what you started with me, Mishka!" Michael roared.

The heavy Mercedes collided with the left side of Mishka's lightweight convertible. The smaller car, overwhelmed by the intense weight of the German vehicle and the wet conditions of the highway, was sent out of control to the right as Mishka's efforts failed to correct her car from the collision. Michael continued his assault, intentionally ramming the car again, and forced the small white convertible off the road just as they approached a hard left-hand turn.

The last collision jolted the Mercedes hard enough that the pistol Michael had in the front passenger seat flew into the passenger door and down its side. Michael knew then that he was in a proverbial knife fight—but without a weapon. The speed and momentum of both autos dragged them to the right and onto the waterlogged grassy shoulder.

Both cars were locked together in a death spin that sent the vehicles gliding over the wet grass and into the tree line. Mishka's car hit the first tree and then flipped over sideways before landing upside down. Within a few seconds, the broken fuel tank emptied its contents onto the hot components of the broken undercarriage. The car soon erupted into flames, which proceeded to spread to the surrounding grass and shrubs.

Michael's car did not flip over, yet it impacted hard into a mighty oak tree that didn't budge. The car stopped dead in its tracks with its airbags fully inflated.

The intense rain showers which had hampered Michael throughout the chase began to subside. Almost as quickly as the storm began, it stopped altogether.

Michael was temporarily knocked out, but he came to minutes later when he smelled the acrid smoke of the burning wreckage of Mishka's car.

"This is Mercedes Care. We've noticed that your car has been involved in a crash, and the airbags have been deployed. My name is John. Are you okay?" came the innocent and naïve voice of a roadside assistant over the car's speakers.

"I'm hurt, John, but I'm okay," Michael said, trying to gather his senses. Responding to an unknown, faceless voice in the car was very surreal to Michael.

He reached up to hold his left eye with his palm. The pressure he applied with his hand felt good

"Okay, sir. I have dispatched the local authorities to your location. They will be with you soon. How are you holding up?"

"I just smashed the car into a known terrorist. She has a nuclear bomb in her car and has just crashed next to me. Please hurry! We all are in grave danger!" Michael shouted.

"They'll be there soon, sir."

John, the Mercedes Care assistant, switched off his intercom to Michael's car. In his frustration, he took off his headset in his cubicle at the headquarters in Atlanta, Georgia. He took a long swig of his diet cherry soda over crushed ice and stared glumly at the framed picture of his ex-girlfriend who had just dumped him the day before. Earlier, he had pondered whether or not to come into work because of his pain and sorrow. He always felt that he was making a difference in the world helping good people with car care, lost directions, the occasional fender bender, and even one driver who had been in labor as she had driven her own Mercedes to the hospital. John was there to assist all his clients. It was his ex-girlfriend who didn't appreciate his talents.

"This fool thinks I was born yesterday. Humph! He's got a long way to go if he thinks this will speed up those rescue folks." John shook his head and looked across the aisle at the woman sitting in the gray fabric cubicle across from him. "Hey, Veronica! Wait until you hear the playback tapes on this crazy mother!"

CHAPTER 45: OKAY, MR. MOLE, WHERE ARE YOU?

Outside Jerusalem

Lt. Asher Klein received the approval to send part of his team into the tunnel at great speed to catch up with the terrorist known as Josuf Federov.

"Overwatch," said Klein into his radio, "you're in charge of topside. If you can't get hold of me because of this tunnel, I need you to take command."

"You got it, boss," the sniper responded through the radio.

Klein readied his weapon and switched the channel for his radio transmission. "Hello, Kitty? This is Claw 1. We are entering the tunnel."

He switched the radio back to his unit's frequency. "Perimeter guard, split into two squads. First squad, you will be inside the house to watch the Hamdans. I want a radioman at the entrance of the tunnel so that he can possibly transmit signals down here underground. Second squad, you maintain outside security with the help of Overwatch. Nobody gets in or out."

Within moments, two men appeared in the doorway of the home. One took over guarding the three family members, and the other hurried to the tunnel entrance. He nodded to Klein, indicating he was ready.

Klein nodded and looked at the four men who would be entering the tunnel with him. "Let's go!"

The team quickly descended the steps.

The tunnel was indeed immense. The string of LED lights and circulation fans impressed Klein and his men as to the complexity of detail.

The point man for the lieutenant's group was a very young Israeli. Private Steinman was only five foot five in stature, but his heart was as mighty as a cedar tree. He was very agile and fast and led as point man with his service pistol at the ready.

His .45 Colt semi-automatic pistol was equipped with a heavy suppressor. When teased about his using an antique weapon that got its start during the First World War with the American Expeditionary Force in France, he only had to remember the gun's original purpose. It was a pistol to fire in close combat. It had tremendous knockdown power, and it only took one hit from that weapon to put a man down.

Steinman only had one direction: to scout ahead west towards Jerusalem. Steinman and Klein knew they were already behind when they heard the air raid sirens in the distance.

"Sir," the sniper on the hill said into his radio, "we have air raid sirens going off topside. Claw 1, do you read me? Claw 1?"

Overwatch knew then and there that he was out of radio contact with his boss.

CHAPTER 46: IS IT A TOTAL IF THE AIRBAGS DIDN'T DEPLOY?

North Carolina

Michael crawled out from the wreckage of the destroyed Mercedes. The radiator fluid seeped out onto the hot motor and made a horrible hissing sound. To Michael, the hissing sound was like a great dragon drawing its last breath after being slain.

He looked over to the white convertible. It was totally engulfed in flames. Pieces of the automobile were strewn over the grass and pine straw from the trees. Michael moved towards the mangled car. The driver and passenger seats had been ejected from the car and damaged severely, but there was no sign of the woman or the bomb.

Still stinging from the eye injury, he looked around wearily as to his condition and location. He noticed a road sign at the road's edge indicating that they had crashed a mile from the dam's entrance.

"I'm glad the rain has stopped," Michael said to himself.

He pulled out his cellphone to call his wife and also Elizabeth, but he found that he had no reception. He looked over to the burning white convertible again. The woman was nowhere to be found. Puzzled as to the whereabouts of the woman, he started to walk towards her car to see if he could find her. He took about seven steps, and then the burning car's gas tank exploded in a huge fireball.

The explosion caught Michael off guard so much that he was blown backwards by the intense blast and heat. He shook his head and then watched as flames leaped through the tree canopy above the flaming car. He got to his feet as quickly as he could and ran towards the road, slipping and sliding on the soft, slick ground. He knew he had to flag someone down to alert the authorities about the missing woman, the bomb, and the fire, but no one was in sight. He glanced at the road sign.

"One mile to the dam. I guess I don't have a choice." He looked back at the smoldering convertible and then the crushed rental car. "So long, Mercedes. John says hello, by the way."

Michael turned north and started walking.

CHAPTER 47: PICKING UP STRANGERS ADDS EXCITEMENT, RIGHT?

The van that carried the CIA response team and Elizabeth came around the corner only to see the tragic accident. One car was on fire and the other car was wrapped around a tree. As they rounded the curve and slowed down, Elizabeth spotted Michael walking along the side of the road about 150 yards from the accident. She let out a sigh of relief and pointed him out to the driver, who continued towards him. As they neared him, the van slowed down, and one of the men rolled down a window for Elizabeth.

"Hey, stranger," she teased, "need a lift?"

Michael shook his head. "Didn't your mother tell you never to pick up hitchhikers? It could be really dangerous to your safety and wellbeing."

The van stopped and the side door opened. Elizabeth smiled at her cousin. "Yeah, I got that covered. Oh, boys, care to show our hitchhiker how to behave?"

As if on cue, each of the CIA operatives raised his or her automatic weapon. The woman officer even put a combat knife in her teeth and gave Michael a wild-eyed look as if she were possessed.

Michael started to laugh, as did everyone in the van. The highs and lows of the day spilt over with everyone's emotions so raw. A soft hush fell over everyone as the laughter died down and the heavy weight of the day's events settled over the group. Malinky let out a chirp that sounded like a stretched out "Oh," breaking the awkward silence.

"You're right, Malinky!" Elizabeth said, chuckling. "Let's get going."

Michael climbed into the back of the van and sat on top of a duffle bag filled with boxes and pipes.

"We need to double back to the scene of the wreck and try to get that fire under control," the team lead, Baiser, announced. "We also need to secure the W72 and the body of the woman driving the car."

Michael squirmed. It was uncomfortable trying to stay steady on the lumpy bag as the van driver maneuvered a three-point turn, and he worried that he might damage something in the heavy green canvas bag. "Hey, am I okay to sit here?"

"Yeah, you're good," Baiser answered. "It's just our demo explosives and breaching tools."

Michael's eyes widened. "The explosives?"

"Yeah, you know, stuff that goes *boom*!" Baiser looked at Michael with a stern look. "Whatever you do, don't fart. If you have to, just let us know, and we will pull over. The methane you'd release would set off a blasting cap, which might blow the whole shebang."

"Wait, what?" Michael asked as he quickly tried to stand up and bumped his head on the van ceiling.

"He's just shitting you, dude," the female officer said as she joined the other agents in a hearty laugh. "Stay loose."

Michael and Elizabeth looked at each other and both rolled their eyes at being the punching bag for the practical joke.

It took only a couple minutes to arrive at the scene. The fire surrounding the car had actually dissipated somewhat since the fuel had pretty much burned off, and the moisture in the trees had controlled the fire in the canopy.

The team, as well as Michael and Elizabeth, climbed out of the van. The soft wet ground from the heavy rain was the perfect condition for mud. The operatives readied their weapons and formed a perimeter while Baiser moved towards the white convertible that was more charred than white.

He held his weapon at the ready as he moved around the car to view the inside of the vehicle. The entire interior of the car was burned black. The car's dashboard, steering wheel, and even cup holders were cinders and ash. The place where the seats had been was a smoldering cavern. Baiser looked around the ejected seats that had been reduced to a smoldering heap and moved on to the surrounding area. After several minutes of searching, he walked towards Elizabeth and Michael. He stopped in front of them.

Baiser shook his head. "No dead person and no bomb.,"

"What? That can't be! She was in the car when it burst into flames!" Michael shouted.

Baiser looked at him with a serious expression. "Did you see her in the wreck when it caught fire?"

"No, I was knocked out for a moment, but I saw the flames and figured she was burning, too."

Elizabeth touched her cousin on the arm, drawing his attention. "Michael, is it possible that this was not the woman who killed Steve? Could she have been an innocent victim involved in the crash?"

"No! It was her!" Michael shook his head and jerked his arm away from

Elizabeth. He looked back and forth from her to Baiser. "She shot at me with her pistol! My eye was hit by flying glass because of one of her bullets. Look inside the Mercedes! You'll find bullet holes, for Pete's sake!"

Baiser nodded and then walked back to the scorched convertible. He walked around to the trunk of the car and examined it. "I need a crow bar, someone."

One of the agents near the van retrieved a crowbar and brought it to Baiser, who manipulated the tool and popped open the trunk. Inside he found a cindered lab coat and a melted identification badge for the radiology department at St. Gabriel Hospital. He turned to Michael and Elizabeth. "It was her!"

Elizabeth looked at Michael. "Sorry."

Michael nodded. "Me, too."

"All right, listen up!" Baiser commanded as he walked towards Michael and Elizabeth waving his arm to gather his team. "There's a woman on the run, and she is hauling the W72 somewhere in these woods. Pair up and spread out. We need to oblique our search pattern in the direction of the dam, that way. We need to find her and find her quick."

CHAPTER 48: I SLEPT WITH THE GOPHERS LAST NIGHT

Outside Jerusalem

Josuf was completely unaware that at the other end of the tunnel, where Ameer and the Hamdans lived, an Israeli commando team was moving towards him. He felt very safe and secure in the deep recesses of the tunnel. He knew that he was about to create one of the worst disasters in history.

"My training has finally reached its ultimate purpose. Russia's assignment for me will help create a free Syria. My Syria! With Allah's help, I shall be rewarded in paradise for the bold actions that I do today," he thought to himself.

Josuf looked over the last few pages of the old paper schematic for the Davy Crockett missile that had been written back in the early 70s. He had been studying how the weapon was assembled and prepared, as well as how to arm the warhead. Satisfied that he was ready to begin, he started the assembly of the missile. The tripod was easy enough to set up; it had brackets that helped it fold up easily.

Josuf then took out the missile. The nuclear warhead was the shape of an American football. The nose of the bomb was aerodynamic. The body of the rocket was shaped like a very large can of store-bought cooked vegetables. The tube was five feet long and was filled with a solid rocket propellant. The fins that were in the bottom of the foot locker were simple, snap on wings that he attached easily.

He then quickly went to make a final examination of the tunnel exit. It was covered by a wooden frame of canvas and chicken wire that had dried grass tied to it. The framework was light enough to slide away so that Josuf could climb out quickly, set the rocket on the tripod launcher, activate the warhead to arm it, and then press the fire button. He would then jump back into the tunnel and race to the center where he could be protected from the blast.

"Jerusalem has seen its last sunrise," Josuf whispered with a smirk.

He returned to the rocket and gathered the entire rocket, tripod and all, and moved it to the steps that led up to the fake ground entrance. He firmly grabbed a wooden piece of the frame and waited for the sound of the other rockets that the Hamas group were to fire as his cover. That would be his signal to jump out and launch the missile.

A few minutes later, Josuf heard what he was waiting for. The rocket barrage had begun. Air raid sirens wailed their calling for all to seek shelter from the incoming rockets. He slid the fake ground cover away from the entrance to the tunnel. Confidently, he crept out with the rocket and tripod.

Everything was going according to Josuf's plan until his cellphone vibrated in his pocket. He pulled it out, looked at the screen, and pressed the button to answer the phone. "Hello?"

"Josuf, I've been badly hurt," Mishka responded on the other end of the line, "but I am still on target. I was able to contact my Spetsnaz team earlier, and they found me. I am making my strike against the hydro-electric dam. The package is being taken down the steps inside the dam now. Goodbye, my brother. Our mission is upon us."

"Goodbye, my Red Monkey." He gently pushed the button to hang up his phone and then slid it back into his pocket. He took a deep breath and turned his attention back to the rocket.

CHAPTER 49: IF YOU KNEW KITTY LIKE I KNOW KITTY

Israel

In the Mossad headquarters, Abelson and his staff witnessed the rocket barrage near Jerusalem via a live video feed from Kitty up in space. He watched the effectiveness of the Iron Dome missile defense system shooting down the missiles with precision.

Techs were busy counting the number of rockets and their launch positions for a response strike from the Israeli Air Force. The rocket exhaust trails also aided the techs in finding the enemy locations.

The immense cost of the surveillance satellite was justified within the very first minutes of the attack. Still, Kitty's sensors had another wonderful surprise for the Mossad team.

The infrared sensor that was designed for spotting rocket launches picked up heat signatures as well. Like the eight eyes of a large household spider, the spy satellite Kitty had eight different powerful "eyes" aimed directly at Israel.

"Heat bloom! I got a heat bloom, sir," a tech in the room shouted as he pointed up to the wall where a large LCD screen was mounted. "Southeast of the Jerusalem perimeter, about a thousand yards. It's in the middle of a desolate field. It's like someone took a cover off a running hot tub in the middle of that pasture. The coordinates are coming up on the monitor now."

Abelson switched his attention to the new information about the mysterious heat bloom. It appeared to be a six-square-foot heat source that was somewhat fainter than the hot exhaust of a rocket launch. "Communications, signal Claw that they have a new threat to their right about a thousand meters out from their position."

He then pointed to the satellite guidance officer who was waiting for any

171

new orders. "Pitch Kitty five degrees left to focus more with her onboard sensors on this new heat bloom."

In the cold vacuum of space, the large satellite received the signal from the Mossad headquarters and ignited a guidance booster that slightly tilted the Ariel III on its axis. Focused on Jerusalem proper, one of the hypersensitive lenses zoomed in to see if someone really did have a hot tub in the desert.

The tech operating the camera lens that was observing the heat bloom rotated his joy stick to sharpen the digital camera's focus. He moved his fingers delicately as he homed in on his target. His efforts were soon rewarded as the image of a man and a long, slender object near a square hole in the ground appeared on the screen.

"I got a visual!" he shouted.

"Colonel, we have another cellphone transmission!" shouted another tech in the control room. "The computer picked up the words 'Red Monkey' again in a cell phone conversation."

"Location of the sources?" Abelson asked.

"The state of North Carolina in the United States and Jerusalem," the tech answered.

"Okay, now display the coordinates for the phone call in Jerusalem on the monitor that's showing the square heat bloom. A hot tub?" Abelson shook his head. "Really, guys, your imaginations are going nuts, or I need to go out more. If my hunch is correct, the locations will be the same."

Exactly as Abelson had predicted, the golden yellow reticle of a targeting compass moved slowly across the LCD screen on the wall. It gradually glided towards the center and settled directly on top of the glowing heat source.

"Got 'em! Okay! Notify Claw," Abelson ordered. "Get them to take out that threat immediately. Hurry, dammit!"

CHAPTER 50: WHEN THE DAM DOOR WON'T OPEN

North Carolina

Mishka's body was running on pure adrenaline as she pressed the button to end the call to her brother Josuf and slid the phone into her pocket. The special training she had endured in Russia for such moments was finally paying off. Her clothes were tattered, wet, and stained with blood and mud. Her left kneecap was cut wide open and had bled profusely when she had been thrown from the car earlier. One of Stalinko's men had quickly patched her up to stop the bleeding with butterfly stitches. With renewed strength, Mishka readied herself for the next phase.

She looked at the giant water release gates of Fontana Dam. Standing silently like massive round concrete and steel doors, they were the main flood gates for the dam when it would normally release water. She had been informed that Stalinko's men, who currently controlled the dam, had stopped the scheduled water releases to increase the water level and pressure against the dam wall.

She had completed the first part of her mission—to get the bomb to the dam. The final part of her job was to arm and activate the W72.

Stalinko stood guard near the entrance to the dam. As Mishka turned to follow the other man to the lower levels of the dam, the headlights of a large white van caught her attention. She paused from going in long enough to see if Stalinko could handle the approaching vehicle. He waved to the van to flag it down as he walked towards it.

Inside the van, Baiser tapped his man that was sitting in the front passenger seat next to him to get ready for trouble. Michael, Elizabeth, and the rest of the CIA response team in the van tensed when they heard the man up front pull back on his automatic weapon, chambering a round.

Baiser slowed the van down as the operative in the passenger seat rolled his window down to talk to the man who had flagged them down. The man was wearing a typical Tennessee Valley Authority blue denim jacket with the name "Collett" embroidered on the pocket.

"Evening, folks," Stalinko said in his best impression of a good old boy from the mountains. "We need you folks to keep moving along in that van of yours. We are doing some maintenance on the dam road, and no one can stop and park right now."

Elizabeth quietly reached down and squeezed Michael's leg hard. Michael glanced at her, and she nodded toward the entrance door to the dam. Michael turned to look where she had indicated.

"Say, your name's Collett. Didn't I tell you to stop all traffic? Does this road lead back to the Federov townhouse?" Baiser asked sarcastically.

Stalinko knew at that very moment that his cover was blown. He quickly reached for his pistol behind his back under the jacket.

Two suppressed shots fired into Stalinko's chest. He never was able to pull out his gun as he fell backwards onto the road.

The gunfire did not phase Michael as his eyes locked on the woman standing at the door of the dam. "That's her! There she is! Hurry!"

Baiser punched the gas petal and sped the van towards the dam's top rails that led to the entrance door.

Mishka cursed and quickly slammed the metal door and locked it before running down the steps inside.

The CIA team readied their weapons and burst from the van as soon as it screeched to a stop. Baiser was the first to reach the door.

"Dammit, the bitch locked the door!" He turned quickly. "Michael, get our demo bag out from the back. You know, the one you were sitting on!"

The team formed a security perimeter as demolition charges were placed on the metal door. Baiser and the team sheltered themselves from the blast. When Baiser confirmed everyone was ready, he signaled for the charges to be detonated.

CHAPTER 51: DOES CALL BLOCK
WORK IN RUSSIA?

Moscow, Russia

Sokolov, with his elbows on his desk and his hands cradling his head, stared blankly at the two pieces of new information that had been placed on his desk by his aide just a short time before. Both reports were extremely bad news for him, and he knew he either had to hide the reports from Moscow or fix them immediately. Sadly, he knew all too well how a centralized hierarchy of government worked, which meant redundancy. With redundancy, everyone important got the same memos unless it was a matter of national security.

The first report was about his own Operation Beluga, his dream of creating the most secret of weapons that could eliminate the entire population of a city without detection. His agent Josuf and his team of scientists had reported firsthand the operational success on the test cities they had practiced on.

The report he was looking at, however, showed where his very own Budnikov had signed over all the plans of Beluga to Moscow's senior military leaders. In an attempt to gain glory for himself, Budnikov had reported that the weapon was operational and ready for mass deployment.

Such a betrayal dismayed the already depressed Sokolov, for he had wanted the radioactive fallout weapon to be his most successful and shining achievement. He knew deep in his heart that he would have received Russia's highest of honors for the development of such a weapon. With the senior military staff aware of the secret weapon's capabilities, they would each add their own initiative plans to any attack using Beluga.

Sokolov stood up slowly from his desk and stood at attention. He quietly fantasized that he was standing in front of a large audience. He could feel the imaginary pull on his military service dress tunic as the medal was being inserted into the cloth and was filled with an overwhelming sense of pride.

As quickly as the fantasy had materialized in his mind, the dream faded away as reality took over. Reluctantly, Sokolov had to accept that the Hero of the Russian Federation honor would not be pinned to his breast pocket by President Pelevin.

The next report he had to ponder was even more depressing. The report was simple and definitive and cut deeply into Sokolov's core. It read: *General Budnikov and the scrubber team have been eliminated.* Nine words that smashed any remaining pride and any hope for Sokolov and his future as a strategic commander.

"Yesli ty v ottsovskikh sapogakh kakashish', ty poydesh' na fermu," Sokolov whispered the old saying that petrified any general. The old saying had been popular during the days of the Soviet Union when generals had failed to achieve their objectives. Roughly, it meant, "If you poop in your father's shoes, you go to the farm."

For Sokolov, it meant only one thing—a hard labor camp in Siberia for the rest of his life. A life where he would be beaten, cold, and hungry, wishing for an early death.

The buzz of the intercom pulled Sokolov away from his worries. He pressed the button. "Yes?"

"General," his aide said hesitantly, "President Pelevin is on the line. He wishes to know your findings on Operation Beluga."

Sokolov slowly picked up the receiver on his telephone and then he cleared his throat.

"Everything is going according to plan, sir," Sokolov lied. "Several of my best operatives are in their final stages of Operation Beluga. General Budnikov is making sure everything is done correctly. I can assure you the conquest of the Syrian port can commence very soon."

"Then why am I holding a report in my hand that your General Budnikov is in the CIA's morgue, along with an entire scrubber team? Explain yourself immediately, General Sokolov!" demanded President Pelevin on the other end of the phone call.

Sokolov was petrified. He started sweating profusely and quickly looked up to the ceiling in his office as if to acquire some inspirational message as to a response. Sadly, nothing materialized, and he remained uncomfortably quiet.

"Well? Not a word? You have nothing to say, Sokolov? Not a sound?" Pelevin screamed over the phone.

Sokolov couldn't emit a single word. He began to cough and choke on the persistent phlegm in his throat. Still holding the phone close to his ear, he could hear his own labored breaths.

"Stop breathing into the phone, Sokolov! I am sending a detachment of the FSB to your headquarters. You are to remain there and surrender your command immediately!"

Sokolov slowly and quietly put down the phone. He felt strange inside. He grew suddenly tired and wanted to sit down, but he seemed to have lost control of his legs. His left arm started to shake violently, as well as his hand. He tried to grab his desk to help stabilize himself, but his hand wasn't strong enough to stop his falling. The chair flew out from behind the desk and smashed into the wall as Sokolov hit the floor hard.

The general's speech was slurred as he desperately tried to call out for help. The only result was that he gasped for breath. His eyes began to bulge in fear as his air passageway was compromised by his throat's constant inflammation. He took one half-breath and then fell into unconsciousness.

The incredible meteoric rise of General Sokolov and his glorious radioactive rockets faded like a star being burnt away in an atmosphere of failure.

CHAPTER 52: IT'S NOT WHACK-A-MOLE—IT'S BETTER

Outside Jerusalem

The Mossad sniper moved to his left and readjusted his gun's bipod. His spotters had to remain focused on the Hamdan's house and the team that was inside the tunnel. Several attempts were made to communicate to Klein and his men in the tunnel but to no avail. Even the radioman at the tunnel entrance couldn't raise Klein.

Overwatch contacted headquarters. "I've got eyes on the new target."

"You are authorized to take out the target," came the cold reply in the sniper's earpiece.

"May God give me strength to protect our people," the sniper whispered to himself as he readied for the shot.

He knew that he needed incredible luck if he was to hit the terrorist. He performed his ritual of three breaths and holding his last breath before he made his shot. For him, the pressure of an entire nation rested on his shoulders. A beautiful city and a nation with its incredible wealth of historical riches—everything was in his hands. He squeezed the trigger.

The bullet propelled towards the terrorist's chest. The impact would shatter the terrorist's ribs and spine as the velocity would shred his internal organs and pull them out through his back. The terrorist would be dead by the time he hit the ground.

The sniper watched through his scope, waiting the long seconds for the moment of impact. He was excited that he had gotten off a clean shot, but then he froze in shock. The bullet missed the chest, and it smashed into the terrorist's right shoulder. The massive impact completely ripped off the man's right arm with such force that the shirt sleeve remained intact on the severed limb as it hit the dirt.

Overwatch reloaded his rifle for a second shot. The bolt action rifle ejected the spent shell casing, and a new brass round moved from the magazine into the chamber. He reacquired his target, but the time it took to reload and fire was just not fast enough. The man had disappeared into the tunnel.

Inside the tunnel, Josuf screamed in agony from his entire arm being shot away. He was losing a lot of blood, but his determination to finish his mission warred with the pain, calling him back into harm's way to finish arming the Day Crockett missile. He knew he needed to get back out there to push the firing pin that activated the rocket's motor.

The soft sand and dirt floor in the tunnel soaked up Josuf's blood as he staggered back and forth staring towards the opening. He put his remaining hand over the bloody stump where his arm had once been. His vision was getting worse, and he was feeling weaker by the second.

The unbreakable control of his training overpowered the pain. Josuf gathered his remaining strength to make a last dash outside. He knew the sniper was waiting for him behind the long-range scope and gun. He knew he was going to die, but the programming within his mind was too deep and too strong.

Josuf started up the steps to the tunnel entrance, but then he felt a warm hand cup over his forehead and pull him backwards. To Josuf, for a split second, he thought he was back when he was a young boy in Syria and that his mother was holding him in her arms. As suddenly as the thought crossed his mind, it ended in a horrible reality of pain as Lt. Klein's sharp blade slit his throat from left to right.

Lt. Klein released Josuf, and the dead body collapsed onto the dirt floor.

Private Steinman unfolded the unit's radio set antenna. He poked the steel rod through the tunnel entrance and broadcasted a signal that they had eliminated the terrorist.

The sniper, relieved that he had not ruined the operation with a bad shot, let out a sigh of relief and radioed back that they were clear to exit the tunnel.

Klein sprinted up the steps and captured the rocket and its tripod. The other team members formed a perimeter around him as he disarmed the missile. Using his explosives training, Klein unscrewed the warhead from the rocket and disarmed the firing system, making the rocket useless.

The relieved lieutenant looked up at Steinman and the other men on his team. "I think it's time for a drink, men. Let's wrap this up and go home."

CHAPTER 53: THE BOTTOM FLOOR HAS SPECIALS

North Carolina

"Soldier, stay here and shoot anyone who comes through that door!" Mishka commanded the only Spetsnaz soldier who hadn't gone all the way downstairs yet.

Mishka, well inside the dam, headed for the stairs to go down to the bottom. She knew that the rest of the men had found an ideal spot to detonate the W72. It would be only a matter of minutes before she would start the firing sequence to arm the bomb, so she continued the long journey down to the bottom of the dam.

"The Americans are outside! We have to hurry!" she shouted towards the three men who were huddled around the bomb.

The blast on the dam's security door was indeed spectacular and deafening. The placement of the explosives blasted the four corners of the door, which caused it to be blown off the doorframe.

The Spetsnaz soldier who was guarding the door on the inside was stunned by the blast but quickly recovered. He opened up with a salvo of bullets towards the entrance. Three rounds impacted and killed the first CIA operative as he breached the opening.

The second CIA operative fired his weapon and dispatched the Russian. When he was satisfied that the Russian was indeed dead, the CIA officer pulled his deceased colleague from the doorway. He then motioned for the others to enter.

Quickly, the team went through, as well as Michael and Elizabeth, who had Malinky in her arms. As the Americans got their bearings, they soon noticed a bewildering labyrinth of stairwells going downward in many directions. Michael was the first to notice that each stairwell had a sign nearby with directions indicating where the stairs led to.

"This way to the control room!" he shouted as he pushed forward through the group and proceeded down that particular set of stairs.

The rest of the men and Elizabeth followed suit. The four flights of metal steps Michael and the group took downward were in groups of 12 followed by a landing then a 90-degree turn to the left followed by another 12 steps.

Deep within the middle section of the dam was a box-like control room. The 22-foot square room was supported by iron railings and support cables. The important structure resembled something like a brain with its multiple wires and pipes that intersected the room from multiple locations. Another series of stairs descended the far side of the control room and led to the bottom floor of the dam.

When Michael and the team entered the control room, they noticed someone on the floor. His hands had been tied behind his back, and he was struggling to sit up.

"Hey, are you okay?" Elizabeth asked, running over to help the man. He nodded and she pulled the duct tape from his mouth, causing him to grimace. "What's your name?"

"Collett. My name is Collett. I'm okay, I guess. I'm the engineer in charge of this plant," he said as his hands were untied.

Collett rubbed his neck from the stiffness that had developed while he was tied up. He looked down at his dead team members with a quiet reverence.

"These were my friends. We worked together for over 10 years inside this dam. Now they're dead. Why? Why did those men kill them?"

Malinky turned around on Elizabeth's shoulder to look down for herself. She let out a small, sad chirp of sorrow for the older gentleman as she glanced around her new surroundings. The little monkey suddenly stood straight up when she saw something down below. With one hand holding on to Elizabeth's red hair, Malinky started pointing through the control room's window and screaming.

Alerted by the monkey's commotion, Michael and the CIA crew rushed to look where Malinky was pointing.

"There she is!" Michael said quickly. "She's trapped!"

Baiser's team readied their weapons.

"Don't shoot inside the dam!" Collett warned as he noticed the firepower displayed by the CIA team. He pointed towards the window they were looking out. "There are hydraulic pipes down there that move the flood gates. If they get damaged, we can't release the water that's probably at dangerous levels by now."

Malinky jumped from Elizabeth's shoulder and landed on the control room floor. She scurried through an open door at the other end of the room and proceeded all the way down the other flights of metal steps to the bottom of the dam.

181

As the little monkey bounded down the last flight of stairs, a hail of bullets aimed at her showered the control room. Michael, Elizabeth, and the team ducked down to the metal floor, and Collett threw his hands over his head and flattened himself on the floor with them. One of Baiser's men was hit in the calf by a stray bullet.

"Whatever they are doing down there, we can't stop them if they keep us at bay up here!" Michael shouted through the din.

Malinky made it to the bottom of the dam unharmed and ran towards Mishka. Surprised to see her grandfather's pet running towards her, Mishka stretched out her arms to welcome the small friend.

"Hello, Malinky! What on Earth are you doing here?" Mishka asked as the little monkey was busy looking at all of the activity near the bomb.

Malinky immediately noticed the shiny golden arming key that dangled teasingly in front of her eyes on the W72. Her little brain could not fight the impulse that she felt inside. The last time she had held that key had been with her master Dimitiry. She had to get her key—it was her key—and so she jumped. She leapt from Mishka's arms to the concrete floor and then bounded in an upward jump to pull the key out of its socket.

Mishka watched in amazement as the monkey grabbed the very thing that she needed to arm the bomb. The monkey, grasping the key tightly, glanced around and then scurried to the stairs and up them.

"Come back here! I'll shoot you, dammit!" Mishka screamed.

Mishka picked up a nearby weapon and unleashed a flurry of bullets at Malinky as she ran up the stairs. Each bullet seemed to inch closer to the little thief as she ran.

"Shit!" Mishka cursed. She looked at one of the men standing by the bomb. "Go up there and get that monkey! If I don't have that key, I'll have to arm the bomb manually."

The soldier began climbing the stairs, but Malinky reached the control room before he had made it up the first flight of stairs. The monkey jumped into Elizabeth's arms and held out her prize with glee— the gold nuclear arming key that she had coveted since the first time she had seen it in Dimitiry's basement.

"Can someone tell me where they are?" asked the old engineer, still crouched on the floor.

Michael crept to the window and looked down below.

"They're hiding in one of the giant round holes. Gate Number Two." Something on the stairs caught Michael's eye. "One of them is coming up the stairs! He must be after that key!"

He was the closest person to the door connected to the steps the Russian was using. He motioned for one of the CIA men to give him a rifle.

As the Russian topped the stairs, he saw Michael aiming at him with a gun. The soldier fired his weapon first towards Michael. Michael expertly rolled out of the way.

Elizabeth screamed in horror as the bullet ricocheted dangerously throughout the control room. Michael was second in firing his weapon. The shot hit the Russian dead center and killed him instantly.

"We're good!" Michael shouted. He peaked out the door and saw Mishka join two other men huddled around the bomb. "We've got to come up with a plan to stop them. It may be possible for them to rewire the bomb and start it without that key!"

Baiser and his team whispered among themselves about possible maneuvers to get below and thwart the terrorists. Michael scurried over to where Elizabeth and Collett were. He looked around the room and then to Collett. "Is there a way to seal off that room?"

The CIA team grew silent as Collett shook his head. "No. That's where the water comes through when the flood gates are opened, and there has to be adequate space to allow for the different water levels."

Michael smiled. "You can control those gates from here, can't you?"

Collett smiled back in understanding. He shuffled on his knees to the control panel. With the press of a button, yellow lights flashed throughout the structure and loud klaxons rang out.

At the base of the dam, Mishka's fingers worked furiously to finish rewiring the W72. She let out a cackle of triumph as the bomb's firing rods began to heat up. "The rewiring worked! We got this. A few more seconds and I can press the F key to fire!"

In the control room, Collett pressed and held the buttons for Flood Gates One, Two, and Three to open. Despite the danger involved in his decision, he conducted a manual override to keep the exhaust flood gates from opening.

The sound of metal bending and concrete cracking echoed through the dam as tons of water flooded the interior. Collett was well aware that his dangerous actions were exerting tremendous stress on the dam's superstructure. There was a moment when it felt that the dam was breaking apart.

In an instant, over half a million gallons of water shot inside the chasm with incredible force. The strength of each of the three gates produced the same amount of thrust that the Saturn 5 rocket engines had produced on the *Apollo* missions to the moon.

Mishka's men were the first to get swept up. In a split second, the two men were there then gone. Mishka grabbed the W72 and hugged the barrel like a life preserver. Her hand that had been above the keypad quickly depressed the F key to detonate the bomb, but nothing happened. She clicked again on the key, and, again, nothing happened. As the rushing water overpowered her, she realized all too late that she was pushing the D key by mistake.

Her body was lifted, rolled, and shoved in multiple directions with incredible force, and the bomb was ripped from her grasp as the concrete shredded her hand away. Mishka felt her legs break under the stress. Her head smacked hard against the concrete floor, and then her lifeless body slammed into the concrete and steel doors of the dam

Mishka, her men, and the bomb were completely torn apart by the incredible tidal wave of rushing water as if they were in a giant blender. There were no arms, legs, bodies, or any semblance of who or what they were originally. Their entire destruction took only a few seconds, and the tremendous flow of water wiped the entire basement floor clean.

Satisfied that the dam's energy had done its duty, Collett released the override and opened the exit gates to allow the dam to operate normally. He then opened the other five gates to reduce the water pressure against the dam's interior walls. With the push of a few buttons, Collett had created the world's largest toilet.

The four melon-sized cylindrical nodes that were the main reactive agents inside the bomb were all that was left of the barrel-like W72. Each metallic ball was shrouded in titanium and lead-lined. The spheres just rolled along with the current like giant prehistoric fish eggs and were later found by the authorities several hundred yards downstream.

Michael, Elizabeth, and the rest of the team all cheered as they watched the massive water flow through the dam. They knew that Mishka, her men, and the bomb were destroyed. Malinky, with her key in one hand, jumped from Elizabeth's shoulder and landed on Mr. Collett's shoulder.

"Hey, little fella." Collett chuckled. "My name is Lyle. What's your name?"

Malinky then gave him a big hug and smiled before jumping onto Baiser's shoulder. The CIA officer just laughed and shrugged his shoulders as the monkey clambered all about him. He didn't realize that Malinky had secretly reached into his tactical vest and stolen a candy bar she had noticed earlier until the little monkey waved the candy bar and screeched.

"Hey, you little thief. That's mine!" Baiser shouted as he reached for the treat.

Malinky jumped again and landed on top of Collett and handed the older man the candy bar that she had just stolen. Collett opened the candy bar and broke two pieces off the bar. He popped one in his mouth and then he handed the other piece to his new little friend. Malinky produced a large cheesy smile as she ate the piece whole.

"She earned it," Collett said with a smile and chuckle. He held the candy out to Michael. "We all did!"

Everyone soon laughed as the immense tension of their experience began to melt away.

Michael shook his head, and Collett handed the candy bar back to Baiser. Michal came over to Collett and held out a hand. Collett shook his hand as he looked into Michael's eyes the way a loving father would have looked at his son if the young man had completed a great accomplishment. Michael suddenly felt a strong bond with Lyle Collett, as he was missing his father, Mike Cotter, at that very moment. To Michael, their connection felt right in his heart.

"Good job, son. I am very proud of you," the engineer said aloud as he continued to shake Michael's hand.

EPILOGUE: A MEETING WITH A CARDINAL

The little Episcopal church in Barnesville, Georgia, filled up quickly for Steve's afternoon funeral. The church's rector, Charlotte Jackson, stood at the front of the church and greeted all who attended. She wore her black cassock with a very ornate stole. Michael, Debbie, Elizabeth, and Sonya Cotter waited patiently in the priest's office while the church filled. The clock on the office wall displayed ten minutes before three.

"Mom, are you okay? How are you holding up?" asked Michael, noticing his mother's ashen face.

"I have some gum," offered his wife Debbie.

"Do you want some water?" Elizabeth added.

"I'm fine," Sonya replied as she reached over with both hands to Michael and Elizabeth. "It is so strange right now. I buried my husband, and now I am burying my son. It's not supposed to be this way."

Michael pulled his mother into his arms and gave her a big hug. Elizabeth and Debbie joined them. The family's embrace momentarily warded off the oppressive gloom that hovered around them.

After a minute or two, they all sat down to wait in silence. Sonya was wearing the same black dress that she had worn for her late husband Mike's funeral. Michael wore a black suit with a tie, and Debbie and Elizabeth had bought black dresses from the local department store.

Right before the clock struck three, they were escorted by the funeral home attendants to their reserved pew in the front next to Steve's casket.

The brown metallic casket was closed for the service out of respect for Sonya. It was positioned sideways in front of the altar rail. The service began with the procession of the Cross. A mysterious guest verger led the procession, followed by several acolytes, the choir, and then finally Rector Jackson bringing up the rear.

During the service, Michael was asked to say a few words about his brother. The silent verger, with his beautiful wooden mace that he had brought from England, escorted Michael to the lectern.

Michael looked out at the room full of friends and family. He gathered his strength and began.

"My brother Steve was my very best friend. We laughed and played together every day growing up. Wherever I went, Steve was always by my side. He loved to build things with me. We even built a homemade submarine up on Lake Lanier. Some of you here today remember how much trouble we got in. We didn't mind. We saved the city of Atlanta—at least that's what some officials said."

A smile flashed on Michael's face at the memory. He looked at his mother. She was wiping a tear from her cheek, but a smile was on her face. Encouraged, Michael continued.

"Steve loved his country. After college, he could have taken a job with any high-tech company, but that was not in Steve's plan. While I was serving in the army, Steve joined the CIA. His talent in electronics moved him quickly in the ranks. He was happy. He was smart. He loved his country. My Steve...."

Standing behind the lectern, Michael started to cry. The crying then became uncontrollable. His hands held the podium with such intensity that his knuckles turned white. He had been in a quiet state of shock since his brother's death. As he was giving the eulogy, the reality of Steve's passing began to hit home, and it hit hard. The nightmare of a black raven taking Steve away flashed in his mind as he faced the congregation. Michael froze in place. He couldn't move or speak anymore. Debbie, Elizabeth, and Sonya both bawled as well.

The verger quietly and respectfully stepped up to the lectern and reached out and touched Michael's arm. He was a frail gentleman with gray hair. He wore the traditional verger ensemble: the black cassock with an Anglican cincture and a loose, sleeveless robe, known as a chimere, made of gray cloth with black velvet edges. An embroidered Verger's Guild badge was attached to the chimere, which completed his attire.

"May I say something about your brother while you gather yourself?" the elderly man whispered.

Michael nodded and stepped down from the lectern. He walked back to the pew and sat between his wife and his mother. Debbie put her arm around him, and Elizabeth reached across Debbie and patted his knee.

"My name is Donaldson," the old verger started. His English accent caught everyone's attention. "Several years ago, this young man we honor today...."

He stopped briefly to clear his throat and continued speaking as one of his hands gestured towards the casket.

"This brave young man, his brother Michael, and their cousin Elizabeth saved our beloved Canterbury Cathedral in Canterbury, Kent. They foiled the villainous plot of ne'er-do-wells to steal the bones of our King Henry VIII. This young man, Steve, stopped one of the thieves by holding him at bay long enough for Elizabeth to knock the bad guy out cold. Steve is an unsung hero to us all. My predecessor, Phillips, who was in charge of the reliquary in the crypts of Canterbury, swore these three Americans into our Verger's Guild. He believed in their courage, and he believed that their hearts were true."

The elderly man looked directly at Michael and Elizabeth. "Phillips made you swear the three words 'protect,' 'save,' and 'serve.' Isn't that right, you two?"

Michael had regained his composure by then and reached over and held Elizabeth's hand. They both nodded acknowledgement to Donaldson.

The verger then stepped down from the lectern and approached the family. He quietly and reverently bowed and shook each of their hands. He then walked a few steps to the casket. He placed one of his hands on the top part the coffin and held a small velvet box in the other.

"As a representative of my guild, I hereby posthumously award Steven Cotter knighthood into the Verger's Guild." He turned and faced the congregation. "Would the congregation please stand?"

The people in the church looked at one another, for they were not sure what to do. Rector Jackson stood up from her chair and raised both her arms to gesture for the people to stand.

Donaldson turned back to the casket. He pulled a lacquered medal with a cross and two maces from the velvet box and laid it on top of the casket. "In accordance with your vow, Steven Cotter, you have faithfully executed your charge. You are hereby a valuable Knight of the Silent Guard."

The gray-haired verger then made a slow and solemn bow towards Steve. Someone in the church started to clap. Soon others followed suit, and then the entire church erupted in a wonderful applause.

The choir began the last hymn, *Oh God, Our Help in Ages Past*, as Donaldson formed the procession to go up the aisle and through the front door.

After the service, everyone gathered out front. Donaldson shook Michael and Elizabeth's hands, thanking them again. He then presented the decorated box that had held Steve's cross to Michael and Steve's mother. Sonya thanked him for the lovely words and for honoring her son. Then, as mysteriously as he had appeared, Donaldson slipped away and took the next flight back to England.

Later that afternoon, the clouds were heavy and dark over the cemetery in Barnesville. It had rained for three days, but the showers had held off long enough for Steve's funeral and burial. As the service ended, a light rain had begun to fall again. The funeral home's massive tent sheltered the gravesite from the rain.

All the visitors, including several of Steve's colleagues from the CIA and the church members, had already driven away. Elizabeth had asked a girlfriend to watch over Malinky back at the house. Other than the four immediate family members, only the two grave diggers remained, patiently waiting in their old municipal truck some distance away.

Michael, Debbie, Sonya, and Elizabeth stood in silence next to the grave, staring blankly at Steve's casket down inside the dark hole. Handfuls of dirt that had earlier been clumped in people's hands as they had said their goodbyes lightly coated the top of the brown metallic coffin. The burial vault had yet to be sealed.

Steve was being laid to rest next to his father's side. Mike Cotter's marble gravestone read *"Loving husband, loving father, and he loved his God."* There was an empty spot where Sonya would someday be buried on the other side.

"We need to go, Michael. Your mom is getting tired," Debbie whispered in his ear as she gently squeezed his arm.

Michael did not move.

The four stood quietly for a few more minutes until a red cardinal flew by them and landed on a branch in a tree nearby. Michael slowly walked over to the tree where the red bird was perched. Debbie was not far off, and Elizabeth and Sonya moved to the spot where the grave diggers had temporarily placed Steve's headstone.

"I'll miss you, Steve," Michael said as he looked up to the cardinal.

Elizabeth walked over to Michael. She looked up at the bird and then to her cousin. A smile spread across her face. "Steve's headstone says, '*He earned it.*'"

Michael smiled at her, and Elizabeth walked back over to Sonya and Debbie and put her arm around her aunt. Michael looked from them to the beautiful red bird in the tree.

"You sure did, brother. You sure did," he said, just as the bird flew away.

THE RED MONKEY

THE RED MONKEY

Made in the USA
Columbia, SC
12 April 2021

36016190R00124